EXPEDITION
Darwin IV - 2358

B.
PLANUM HUDSON
PROMUNTURIUM W
ANUM
THEAS
PROMUNTURIUM W
MARE AMOEBICUS
PLANITIA BOREA
VALLIS BERING
FOSSAE de CORONADO
MONS STEFANSSON
CHASMA de SALLE
LACUS MAUCH
VALLIS
PRZEWALSKI
LACUS de ANDRADE
LACUS HEARNE
LABYRIN
PRINCE
MONS LEWIS
GRIMSHAW
CHURCH
MONS CLARK
MONS CORTES
FUGUM ERIKSON
LABYRINTHUS
THOMPSON
MONS MARQUETTE
MONS PIZARRO
MONS WALLACE
MONS JOLIET
MONS
SPRUCE
MONS BATES
MONS AUDUBON
LACUS MCCARTHY
PATERA
von HUMBOLDT
LACUS de SOTO
LACUS HOLLANDER
MONS
MONS FAWCETT
MONS de la CONDAMINE
PATERA ORELLANA
PROMUNTURIUM
MAGELLAN
LACUS de CHAMPLAIN
PLANITIA AUSTRALI
LACUS MCMURDO
LACUS WILKES
CHASMA GUNNBJORN
PROMUNTURIUM
SHACKELTON
CREVASSE AMUNDSEN
CREVASSE SCOTT

GLACIER BOREALIS
CREVASSE PEARY
CHASMA ROSS
CHASMA NANSEN
CHASMA BARENTS
LACUS FROBISHER
LACUS PALMER
LACUS HERBERT
LACUS PARRY
FOSSAE PHILBY
FOSSAE TEMUJIN
LACUS BISSON
LACUS HEDIN
FOSSAE DOUGHTY
SHINGEN
LACUS HANSEN
CHASMA PRESTER JO
MONS de GOES
MONS LEE
MONS LIVINGSTONE
MONS BELZONI
ONTES AEQUINOCTIALIS
SINUS COLUMBUS
MONS STANLEY
MONS LAING
NS PAULINOS
MONS ALEXANDER
MONS ST BRENDAN
BURIAN
MONS SPEKE
MONS CAILLIE
MONS YOSHITOSHI
MONS BURTON
MONS SPAULDIN
MONS BISCOE
MONS de QUIROS
MONS DRAKE
MONS de TORRES
MONS HOUTMAN
VALLIS BAR
MONS FLINDERS
LAC PA
LACUS TASMAN
VALLIS BURCKHARDT
LACUS van RIEBEECK
CHASMA COOK
LACUS de GAMA
CHASMA MAGNIFIC
CHASMA d'Urville
PROMUNTURIUM BYRD
GLACIER AUSTRALIS
0   500   1000   1500
1 CENT. = APPROX. 500 KM

GRAND EXPLORATOR YS, YMA DISCOVERER OF DARWIN IV

EXPEDITION

BEING AN ACCOUNT IN WORDS AND ARTWORK
OF THE A.D. 2358 VOYAGE TO DARWIN IV

WAYNE DOUGLAS BARLOWE

Published by Echo Point Books & Media
Brattleboro, Vermont
www.EchoPointBooks.com

Expedition
ISBN: 978-1-63561-951-5 (casebound)
          978-1-63561-952-2 (paperback)

Cover design by Kaitlyn Whitaker

Cover images, by the author: *Front Cover* "Daggerwrist"
                              Back Cover "Gyrosprinter" (main),
                              "Sac-back" (inset top), "Emperor Sea
                              Strider" (inset center), "Bladderhorn"
                              (inset bottom)

Preceding page: Diverse species gather in relative peace at
Darwin IV's rare dryland waterholes. A pair of Brain-balls—
huge, colonial earth-bound floaters—approach in the distance.

CONTENTS

The Yma faster-than-light satellite image that launched the first expedition of Darwin IV in 2355.

hen I was a small child many years ago, my great-grandfather would take me on his knee and tell me wonderful tales of places and creatures long gone. His were not the usual tales of knights and dragons or fairy kingdoms. No, his were stories his own great-grandfather had told him, vivid tales of the creatures that once roamed freely all over our globe.

He would tell of great herds of graceful Giraffes, Antelopes and Zebras that would cover a plain from horizon to horizon; of titanic fish-like Whales that swam the ocean depths battling huge multi-armed Squid; of majestic Elephants that cared for each other with tenderness and intelligence; and of hundreds of other animals. I was engrossed and my child's mind would play with these images long after the stories were done. But beyond the telling of the tales, my great-grandfather was always teaching me, for he would always end his stories sadly, by reminding me that the creatures he had described no longer existed in the wild and that they would never return. His teaching had its effect, for as I grew from a carefree boy into a serious man, realizing along the way that I was committed to art and natural history, I also became bitter at the indifference, cruelty and selfishness that caused the mass extinction of almost an entire planet's animal population.

What would have happened to Earth if its flagrant abuse had continued? No one can say, for, as we all know, over a hundred years ago a benevolent, starfaring people came to our aid. Whether it was out of love for all life or simply a clinical desire to mend something broken, the Yma took our seared world in hand and began to teach us how to repair it.

Today Earth is very far from being healed. True, the Yma have worked wonders—as a result of the Yma/Human Accord of 2231, following the last Rainforest War, we no longer manage our world—but, because of the extent of the damage, the improvements in our ravaged ecology and climate are very gradual. And the results of our centuries of short-sightedness are striking. Hosts of chemically-mutated insects, larger and more aggressive than their natural forebears, crawl and fly through our toxic cities. These children of the poisoned night are the legacy of toxic waste, defoliants and acid rain. As for terrestrial vertebrates, nothing larger than the Norway rat (which is quite abundant) exists outside the few pitiful zoos that still survive. The oceans, thought of in the distant past as a limitless resource, and more recently as an open sewer, are virtual garbage and chemical broths, contaminated and nearly lifeless. The skies, too, are empty and gray. With this degree of global devastation, it is with only small comfort that humanity walks, alongside the almost-parental Yma, through its blighted and ill-tended garden.

With the discovery of the Darwin binary system and its six planets, a sense of hope arose in the breasts of those anachronisms, like myself, who were lovers of Nature. The Yma sent an unmanned probe to that distant system and began planning for a bi-species expedition under their guidance and auspices—an opportunity for humanity to both enlighten and re-educate itself. They assembled a broad-based team of explorers, scientists, technicians and surveyors for a three-year odyssey. I was chosen to participate as wildlife artist on the strength of my paintings and drawings of extinct Earth fauna. I was to provide a "more subjective and atmospheric impression of Darwin IV and its lifeforms" than the Expedition's host of conventional holographers and photographers. I leapt at this amazing opportunity, as did many more renowned personages, such as Sir Hideyoshi Gunn of the Titan Expedition, Drs. Otillia Steadman and Cayley McCarthy of the Olympus Mons Ascent, and Professor Hsien Cho of the ill-fated Great Red Spot Descent.

The Yma carefully screened us to determine our feelings regarding solitude and our ability to leave Darwin IV exactly as we found it. We would be solitary observers, wandering above the surface of the planet in small one-man hovering capsules, like airborne seeds on the wind. The Yma devised a network of artificially intelligent microsatellites that would spread above Darwin IV, keeping all lone explorers in constant touch with three huge orbiting motherships. These vessels, known as Orbitstars, would serve as expedition headquarters, repair and maintenance shops as well as research facilities.

reparations for the Expedition began in 2355. The Yma parked their Orbitstar designated for human occupancy (nicknamed "Starfish" by Terrans) in orbit and proceeded to Darwin in the two remaining ships. One year later, after supplies and equipment were loaded, we left Earth orbit and began our nineteen-month journey at conventional speed to the edge of the Solar System. My fellow Expedition members and I were tucked into our sleep-pods. Once past Pluto our Yma pilots engaged the main drive, and in the blink of an eye we traversed the 6.5 light years to the Darwin system. We attained orbit above Darwin IV on January 6, 2358.

From an altitude of roughly 39,000 kilometers we had a splendid view of the planet we had come to explore. With an equatorial diameter of 6,563 km, Darwin IV is somewhat smaller than Earth. Its predominant color is dusky ochre, relieved by a sparse mottling of red and two crisply defined polar caps. The fourth planet and its two small moons circle the F-class binary at a distance of two AUs, taking two Earth years for one complete revolution. These two stars, quite different in size, are so close together as to frequently give the impression of a single star; this proximity almost completely eliminates the odd daylight optical effects that occur with a more pronounced double-star. The Darwinian day lasts for 26.7 hours.

Great open grasslands, which many in our party believe to be ancient seabeds, are home to the overwhelming majority of Darwin IV's fauna. Many species have evolved into giants, a phenomenon believed to be a result of the planet's relatively low gravity (.6 of Earth) and the oxygen-rich atmosphere.

The plains support a wide assortment of fauna ranging in size from small ground-burrowing scavengers, through the browsing tripedaliens and the predatory bipedalien liquivores, to the immense air-sifters, each delicately situated in its ecological niche.

Darwin IV's largest and most famous lifeform belongs to another biome, the Amoebic Sea. This bizarre and misnamed region is blanketed by a gelatinous, ten-meter-deep organism covering almost five percent of the planet's surface; it is, in fact, the largest single colony animal known. The Amoebic Sea is home to the huge Emperor Sea Strider, the enormous, implausible organism seen stalking across an unnaturally smooth plain in the Yma probe's most celebrated sequence of transmitted images. Possibly because of the shock absorption and weight distribution qualities of the jelly-like "sea," the Sea Striders have attained truly behemoth proportions. No known creature rivals them in size.

Darwin IV's montane region almost completely encircles the globe along the equator. While not impassable, the mountains present many problems for the planet's huge migratory herds. Storms and fogs claim thousands of individuals each year as they traverse the difficult and often icy mountain passes.

As there are no oceans or seas on Darwin IV, the polar caps are the largest concentrations of water, in the form of ancient ice. These glaciers recede and advance with the seasons; as with Mars, the southern cap grows larger than its northern counterpart due to the prolonged southern winter.

Evidence in the form of countless fossilized tree stumps scattered throughout the plains had led our chief botanist, Dr. Dorothea Kay, to postulate that Darwin IV was once a far warmer and more humid planet. At present the pocket-forests account for only about five percent of Darwin IV's surface vegetation; even so, they pre-

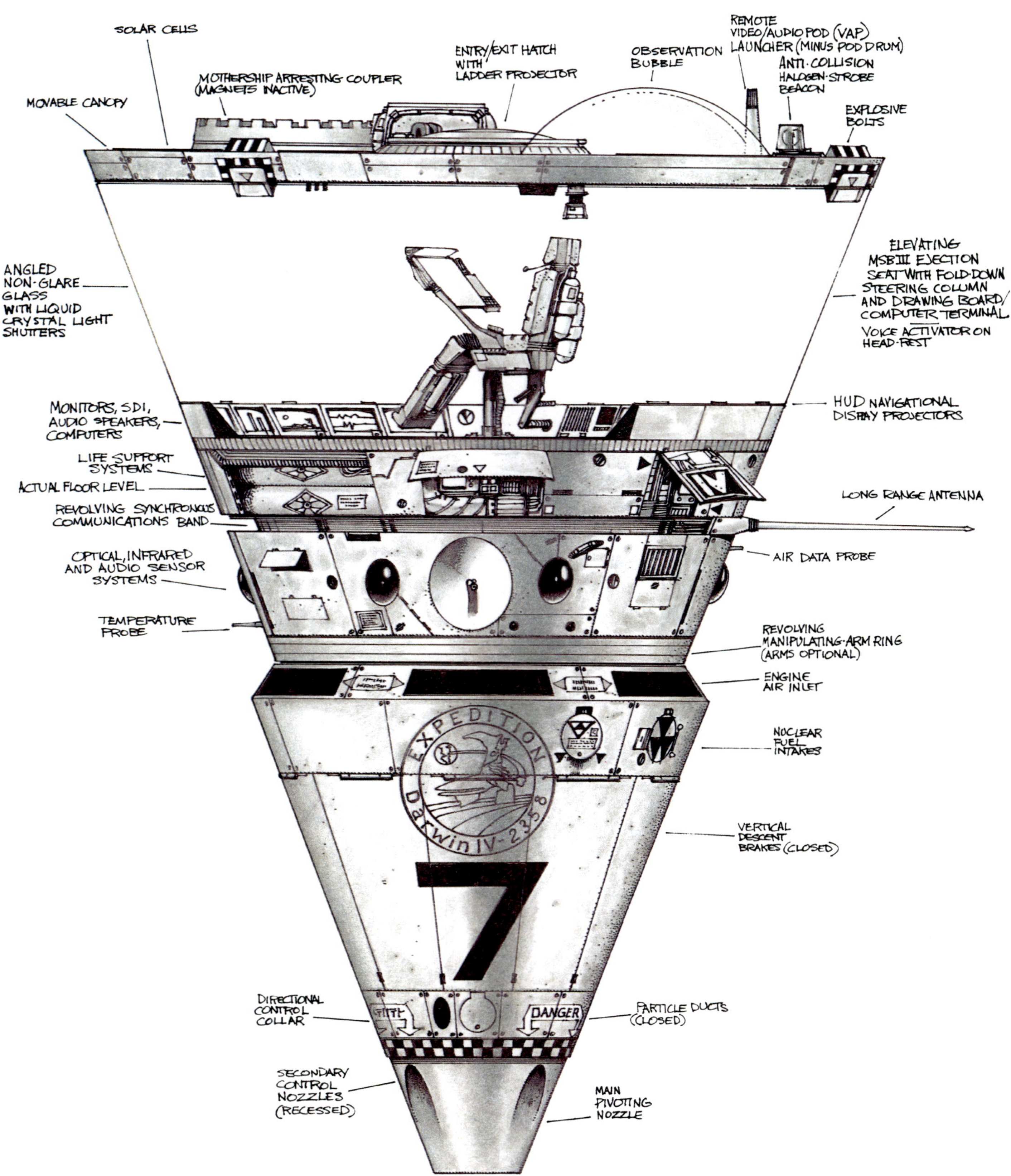

SOLAR CELLS
MOVABLE CANOPY
MOTHERSHIP ARRESTING COUPLER (MAGNETS INACTIVE)
ENTRY/EXIT HATCH WITH LADDER PROJECTOR
OBSERVATION BUBBLE
REMOTE VIDEO/AUDIO POD (VAP) LAUNCHER (MINUS POD DRUM)
ANTI-COLLISION HALOGEN-STROBE BEACON
EXPLOSIVE BOLTS
ANGLED NON-GLARE GLASS WITH LIQUID CRYSTAL LIGHT SHUTTERS
ELEVATING MSB III EJECTION SEAT WITH FOLD-DOWN STEERING COLUMN AND DRAWING BOARD/COMPUTER TERMINAL
VOICE ACTIVATOR ON HEAD-REST
MONITORS, S.D.I., AUDIO SPEAKERS, COMPUTERS
HUD NAVIGATIONAL DISPLAY PROJECTORS
LIFE SUPPORT SYSTEMS
ACTUAL FLOOR LEVEL
REVOLVING SYNCHRONOUS COMMUNICATIONS BAND
LONG RANGE ANTENNA
OPTICAL, INFRARED AND AUDIO SENSOR SYSTEMS
AIR DATA PROBE
TEMPERATURE PROBE
REVOLVING MANIPULATING-ARM RING (ARMS OPTIONAL)
ENGINE AIR INLET
EXPEDITION
Darwin IV - 2358
NUCLEAR FUEL INTAKES
7
VERTICAL DESCENT BRAKES (CLOSED)
DIRECTIONAL CONTROL COLLAR
DANGER
PARTICLE DUCTS (CLOSED)
SECONDARY CONTROL NOZZLES (RECESSED)
MAIN PIVOTING NOZZLE

ORBITSTAR LOCKS INTO GEOSYCHRONOUS ORBIT UPON ARRIVAL AT DARWIN IV. COMMUNICATIONS SATELLITES AND FUEL PODS ARE LAUNCHED.

Mk. IVA OBSPODS ARE DEPLOYED. CERAMIC PROTECTIVE SHEATHS CAP MAIN NOZZLES AS HOVERCONES ENTER UPPER ATMOSPHERE. ENTRY TAKES UP TO 24 HOURS

CERAMIC SHEATH IS BLOWN AWAY AS SLOW DESCENT IS CHECKED.

VERTICAL DESCENT BRAKES OPEN AS DESIRED ALTITUDE IS ACHIEVED. EXPLORATION BEGINS.

sented the Expedition with its greatest challenge to exploration. Giant plaque-bark trees, with their massive trunks and twisted boughs surrounded by dense underbrush, made penetrating the forests via hovercone impossible. We had to content ourselves with following the occasional stream a few hundred meters into the woods, or more often, simply circling and probing with our instruments.

Due to its near-flawless performance, a few words about the Yma's marvelous vehicle, in which I spent so much time, seem appropriate. The Mark IVA Obspod (observation pod) hovercone was developed some twenty years ago by Yma engineers with human pilots in mind, with sensors that would augment and heighten human senses. With a weekly reprovisioning and refueling, I traveled across Darwin IV in splendid climate-controlled comfort and in constant touch with the Orbitstar. As I sat in my Universal MSB-III seat, I had every control and monitor at my fingertips. And as I peered through the 360-degree glass canopy, I could see and hear things no ordinary human could. A deluge of images and information would play across the liquid-crystal-augmented glass, showing me navigational information as well as

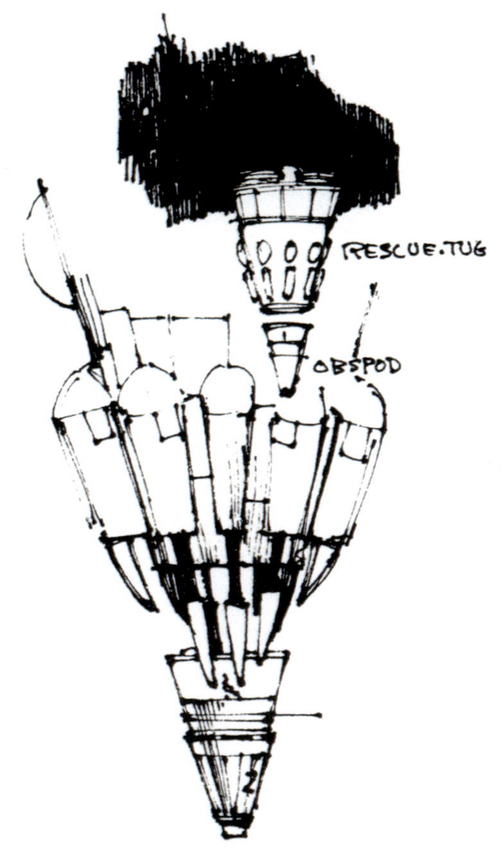

EXTENSIBLE GRIPPERS OF RESCUE-POD GRASP CRIPPLED OBSPOD AND DRAW IT UP WHERE IT IS CLAMPED IN PLACE. PILOT CLIMBS UP INTO RESCUE-POD VIA OVERHEAD MAIN HATCH.

infrared and magnified images. The audio system, in addition to providing Mozart for my quiet times, could amplify ultrasonics or filter out extraneous sounds. Beyond the hovercone's capabilities, I was equipped with a battery of remote flying Video/Audio Pods (VAPs), with which I could explore in four different directions simultaneously. In all, it is hard for me to imagine a sturdier, more versatile craft than the ceramalloy and titanium Obspod.

Darwin's vegetation varies to a lesser extent than Earth's did before it was blighted by man's pollution. Succulents are by far the dominant class of plant life. The plains, arid as they are, are blanketed with thick tube-grass, a stalky pencil-thin succulent that grows astonishingly fast. This tube-grass and its cousins, fodderball weed and bladder reed, are the forage of the herbivorous plains-dwellers, providing a ready source of necessary moisture. In a sense the succulent-rich savannahs are the closest Darwin IV comes to true oceans, for the quantity of water trapped in the plants is vast.

Only when approaching the mountains or forests do the succulents give way to other plant forms. Impenetrable underbrush, composed of sticklebush, whisperbrush and grenade vine, with its explosive pollen sacs, begins to dominate the landscape. These in turn give way to towering plaque-barks, the lords of the plant kingdom on Darwin IV and the principal tree of the planet's limited forest lands.

The sub-polar region's flora is limited by the demanding environment. Low, ground-dwelling, lichen-like plants cover the almost frozen soil in a gray-green mantle that is broken by spidery, blue whipweed and the tiny flowering polardots. This is a biome in which the mechanisms of nature are at their most fragile.

In addition to the ground plants, Darwin possesses seemingly limitless quantities of tiny air plants, the aerophytes that make up the primary

One of the Expedition's Orbitstars was especially fitted out for human comfort and safety. This was characteristic of the sensitivity and consideration shown by our benefactors, the Yma.

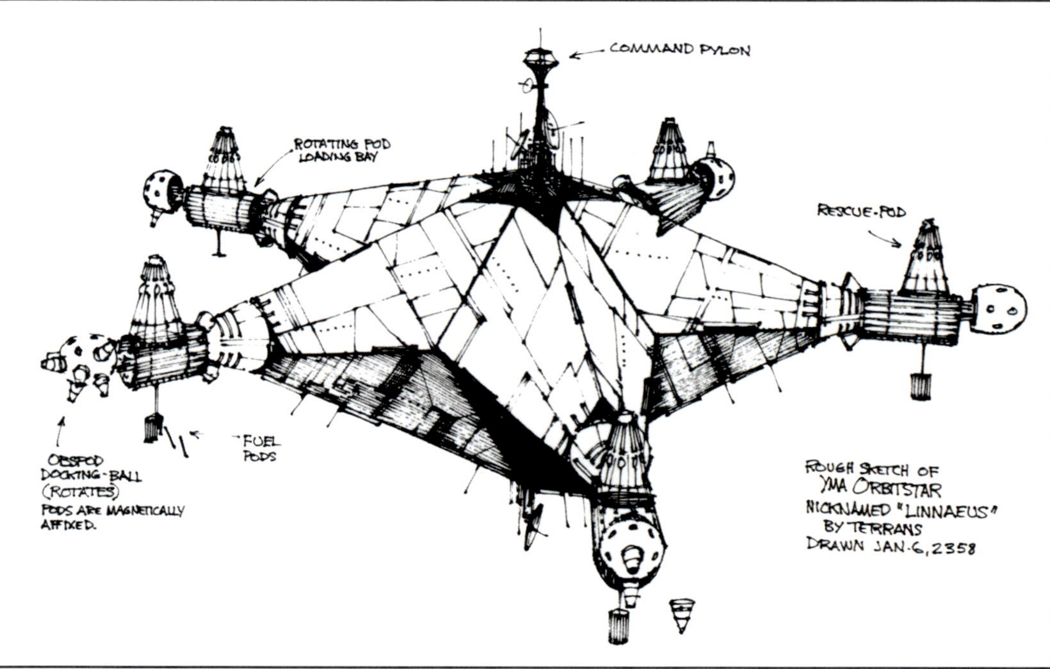

diet of the herbivorous air-sifters. Along with their animal counterparts, the abundant and varied microflyers, these aerophytes can, at times, darken the sky with their numbers.

Darwinian vertebrate morphology is quite different from its terrestrial counterpart. Most of Darwin IV's larger inhabitants fall into one of five classes: floaters and flyers (no real locomotive limbs to speak of); monopedaliens (one powerful saltatorial, ricochetal limb); bipedaliens (two-legged cursors); tripedaliens (three-legged cursors); and quadrupedaliens. Cursors are agile ground-runners, whereas saltators are hoppers. In some cases, such as most of the air-sifters, the rear limb has become a passive skid to support greater weight. Mass is usually supported by a hollow, thin-walled bone structure similar to that of the birds of Earth's past. This lighter structure predominates among Darwin's larger fauna and allows large predators to maneuver and run quickly; some Raybacks, for example, have been clocked at almost fifty kph and the fastest of Darwin IV's animals, the Gyrosprinter, frequently tops ninety kph!

Food-gathering and ingestion are, especially for predators, radically different from old Earth carnivora. Liquivores, which secrete digestive juices into their victims (alive or dead) abound. Absent are powerful, fang-lined jaws; in their place are a wide array of scalpel-sharp extensible tongues, each designed, as if by some master armorer, to pierce a particular skin or bony armor. With blinding speed these lethal tongues, guided by hyperdeveloped accelerator muscles, can pass completely through a medium-sized animal, injecting paralyzing digestive fluids on impact. Actual feeding, with broken-down body fluids being siphoned through the tongue, often begins even while the prey is still living.

One of the most obvious and significant points of departure from Earth's ancient fauna is the planet-wide lack of true eyes. Optical sensory organs are absent, having been supplanted, through eons of evolutionary selection, by a bat-

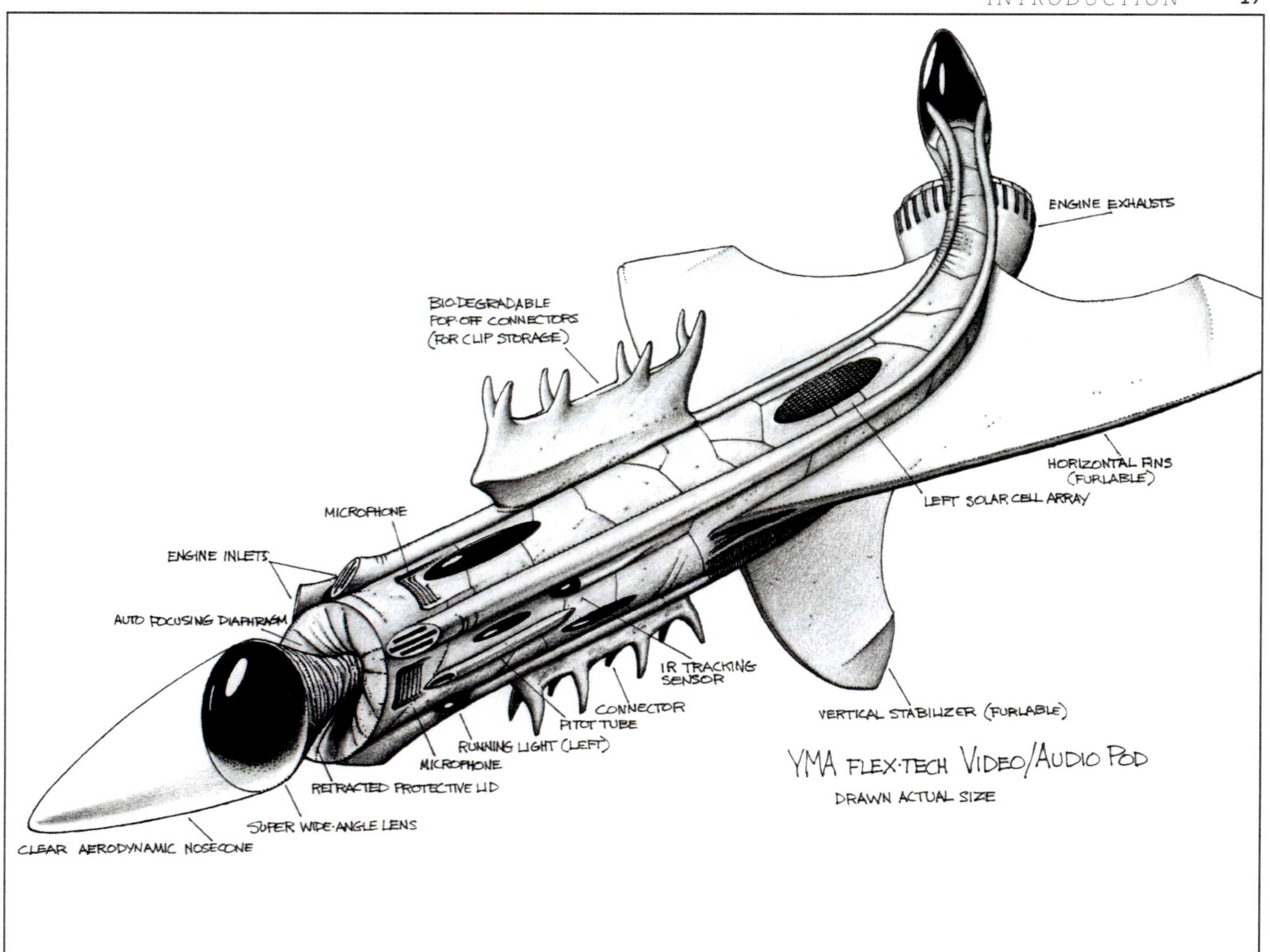

tery of sonar and infrared faculties. These senses are, in most cases, complemented by a sophisticated lateral line system of sensitive, subcutaneous pressure receptors which, in conjunction with numerous, tiny infrared receptor pits, gauge both the surroundings and the proximity of other creatures. In addition to this somewhat difficult to discern receptor system, Darwin IV's creatures possess biolights, heat-radiating bioluminous spots that appear quite vivid to infrared sensors. These light arrays (which probably aid in herd-member or enemy identification) are especially important during courtship, when subtle color shifts and the dramatic overall brightening we call "flaring" occur in the mating pair's biolights.

This mating beacon can attract mates from as far away as ten km.

To the creatures of Darwin IV, temperature, not visible light, is the sole means of determining the difference between night and day. As a result, the concepts of light and dark are meaningless, and activity is predicated on relative temperature variations. Temperature regulation through metabolic activity and insulating layers of fat has eliminated the need for fur in Darwin IV's temperate climate; indeed it is doubtful whether any denizen of Darwin IV ever had fur, as the sonar and heat transmitters and receptors must remain uncovered.

Sonar projectors exist in all of Darwin

IV's inhabitants. Though they vary in size and form, the basic structure is the same from species to species. A large frontal cavity filled with dense fluid serves to focus the ultrasonic *pings* produced by a complex larynx-like organ. Because of the high frequency of the sonar and its concomitant short range, Darwin IV's creatures are forced to *ping* in a steady stream, making the planet a rather noisy place to one able to perceive the signals. We humans are not so equipped natur- ally, but the amplifiers in our hovercones can "hear" the sounds of the creatures around us.

These highly developed senses endow their bearers with a very precise and complex view of their world. It is the Expedition's best guess that animals who had developed these sen- sory organs proved too formidable for those creatures with rudimentary optical abilities struggling for life and dominance in Darwin IV's thick, primordial mists. Now the mists are gone — but so are the optically-sighted animals.

With notable exceptions (such as the Sac-backs), most higher organisms are her- maphroditic, and mating can lead to impregnation of both partners. The participants' genitalia are always identical: a long suspended tube hanging horizontally behind. During mating, these fleshy tubes unroll about halfway and clasp each other. Fine grooves or channels carry the sperm/egg mixture back and forth, mingling it for as long as ten minutes, depending on the species. Cou- pling is achieved in a dorsally aligned attitude, which, it has been suggested, allows for mutual defense. My colleagues and I saw many matings continue while the participants fought off attackers.

Darwin's higher lifeforms are not mam- malian. Though they are for the most part warm- blooded, they do not nurse their young. Young

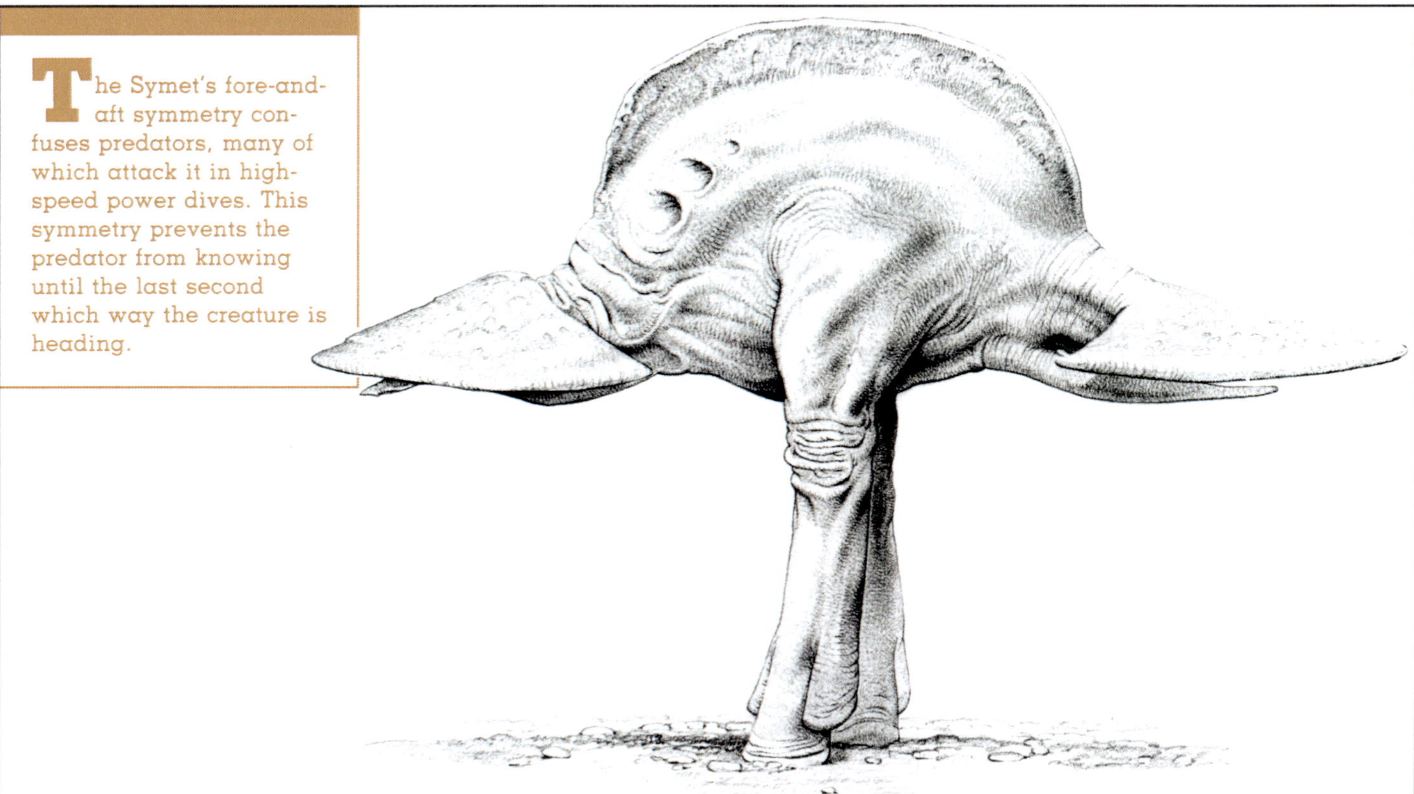

can be born alive, as with the Daggerwrist and Sac-back, or can hatch from eggs laid underground, as with the Grove-back and Keeled Slider. Great variation exists as to the amount of care and attention young receive immediately after birth. Generally, the egg-born young are precocial—that is, able to fend for themselves—and live-born young are altricial, or in need of care. Exceptions to this rule exist, such as the nurturing Keeled Sliders whose egg-born, altricial young are in the parent's tow for about two years and need much attention. Strange crossovers also exist, as in the case of the Emperor and Lesser Sea Striders. The eggs of these huge creatures are dropped onto the "sea's" undulating surface, where they remain until they hatch. Upon emerging from the eggs, the nymphs must find their way back to their parents until they are fully independent.

Certainly the most remarkable of Darwin IV's assortment of wildlife is the floaters. They constantly evoked a sense of otherworldliness in us all, Yma and human alike. These magnificent beasts—huge, finned, and covered with breathing float-bladders—dot the sky in great sailing herds, gliding lazily through the warm breezy air. Manufacturing hydrogen from water vapor in the atmosphere, through some form of organic electrolysis, the floaters drift ceaselessly, descending to the surface only to hunt. At night I often watched their beautiful arrays of biolights drifting silently overhead. They are bizarre, placid creatures of poetry, graceful and ethereal.

The Expedition's visit to Darwin IV lasted about three Earth years. During that time I traveled continually, covering a considerable amount of territory; but by no means do I feel that the planet yielded more than a fraction of its secrets. Our supplies depleted, we left Darwin IV on March 24, 2361.

Absorbed in our own very personal recollections, we watched from the windows of the Orbitstar as the small, ochre world diminished to a point of light. On many levels our expedition

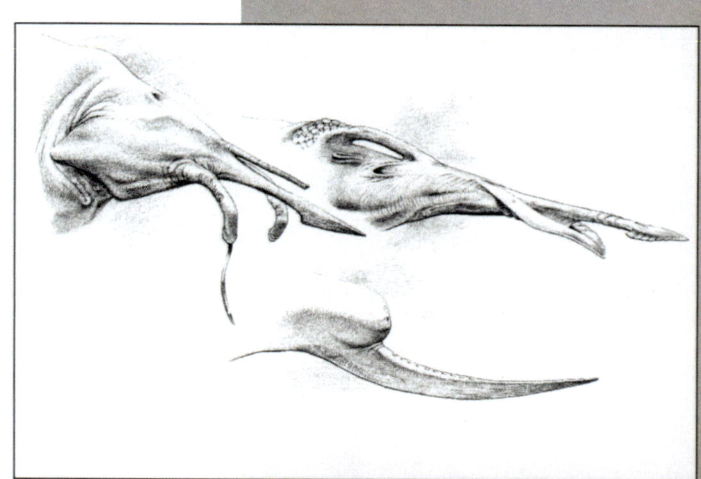

had been successful in achieving its goals, not the least of which had been to leave Darwin IV exactly as we had found it: wild, beautiful and untouched. Since our departure the entire Darwinian system has been off-limits and is patrolled continuously by Yma robot drones.

Five years have passed since our return to Earth. Since then I have been hard at work in my studio which, lined with sketches and mementos, has become a veritable shrine to Darwin IV and its creatures. Outside, a defiled planet is trying to cleanse itself while I, in my sanctuary, have tried to select those images that might best depict another, healthier world. The Yma are considering a second, possibly larger Expedition, and it is my hope to help advance that goal. It is toward that end that I dedicate these field studies and paintings, limited to the larger and more dramatic Darwinian fauna; in the hope that they might give you, the reader, the sense that you traveled with me on our voyage to Darwin IV. And might wish to join us in the future . . .

Wayne D. Barlowe
New York City, 2367

PLATE I. Thornbacks grazing in shadow of steeple-gourds.

THE
GRASSLANDS
AND PLAINS

RAYBACK AND GYROSPRINTER

On January 11, 2358, the First Darwinian Expedition began launching its 180 hovercones toward the planet's surface. We had all agreed that we should begin our explorations in what appeared to be the most easily navigated part of the planet, the grassy savannahs or plains.

After a textbook descent to the Planitia Borealis, I impatiently ran through my regimen of systems checks and links to the Orbitstar. As I awaited final clearance I gazed out at the world around me. It was a beautiful afternoon; the rich, blue sky was dotted with feathery cirrus clouds, and a gentle breeze riffled through the rubbery, brownish grass that extended as far as the eye could see. I was hovering about thirty meters

PLATE II. *"This was the most bizarre creature I had ever laid eyes upon."*

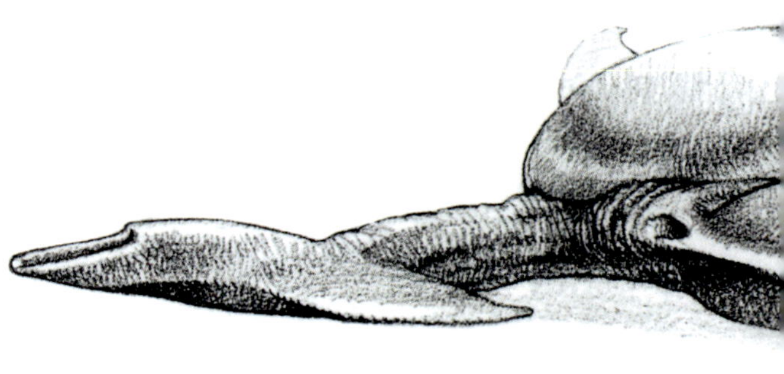

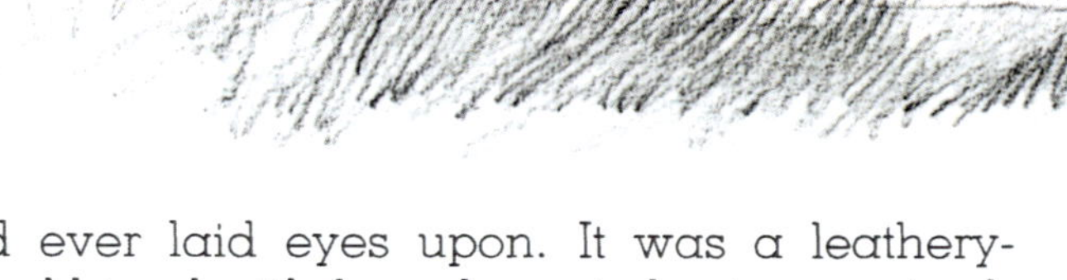

above the ground, nervously playing with my navigational controls when my clearance came through. With that final go-ahead I tentatively punched in a random course on the navigational computer and sat back as I began to move forward smoothly over the prairie.

Nothing in the hovercone flight simulator could have prepared me for the elation I felt as I traveled that first day. Indeed, this elation lasted to varying degrees throughout most of my stay, but it was never again at quite the euphoric pitch of that day. I was captivated by the sheer miracle of movement over a new world.

Nearly an hour passed as I crossed about sixty kilometers of waving grass and drier flatlands. In the distance, a dark line indicated the outlying foothills of rougher terrain, a small chain of low mesas. I set these as my first goal and had covered another ten kilometers when I spotted my first Darwinian inhabitant.

It was what we came to call a Rayback; and it was, as I came upon it, squatting close to the ground. As I drew to within fifty meters, the creature got to its feet and began to walk in the direction of the hills toward which I was heading. I was ecstatic. This was the most bizarre creature

I had ever laid eyes upon. It was a leathery-skinned biped with four elongated spines protruding from its broad back. Most intriguingly, it did not appear to have any eyes on its triangular head. How did it perceive its surroundings?

And clearly, perceive them it did. As I incautiously drew closer, the Rayback quickened its pace to a fast trot, leaping over broad ravines and pushing through the thick grass with ease. I dropped back, and instead of slowing the creature stopped short. While following the Rayback I had imprudently dropped to about five meters above ground level, and without warning the creature wheeled and ran straight at me. I reached for the console and pushed a wrong key, which brought me face to face with the enraged animal. In a panic, I found and pressed the right key; instantly, I was gaining altitude. The Rayback, knocked off its feet by my 'cone's nozzle-wash, lay sprawling in the grass. How had this eyeless creature sensed my presence? In moments it was a small, dark, angry dot in a sea of grass eighty meters below.

I checked my ascent and, slightly chagrined, dropped back to about ten meters. I thought this would be a height acceptable to my ill-tempered Darwinian companion, but it was

not. Once again it charged, and once again I brought my 'cone up. We repeated this maneuver a number of times until my altitude was acceptable. We settled on thirty-one meters.

This first encounter was to prove unusual. By far the majority of Darwin IV's lifeforms were totally unaware of (or unimpressed by) our presence and went about their daily routines uninterrupted. In the future, however, I would be more careful.

As I resumed my observations of the Rayback I noticed a new determination in its gait, and I wondered what could have caught its attention—and how. In a moment of revelation I turned on my interior speakers, which were connected to the 'cone's external mikes, and was immediately greeted by a barrage of high-pitched *pings*, which were obviously coming from the Rayback.

It was using sonar!

By now it had brought its speed up to a formidable forty-five kph and was covering the terrain with great leaps. From my greater altitude, I could barely make out a small shape some four-hundred meters off, running through the tall grass. When it broke out of the grass onto a flat stretch of ground, its speed increased and I was sure the pursuing Rayback would not be able to catch up. I was right.

The pursuit, accompanied by incessant sonar *pings*, covered almost five kilometers, with both animals careening in wide turns and bounding over rocks and depressions. Even though I clocked the Rayback at forty-eight kph, its

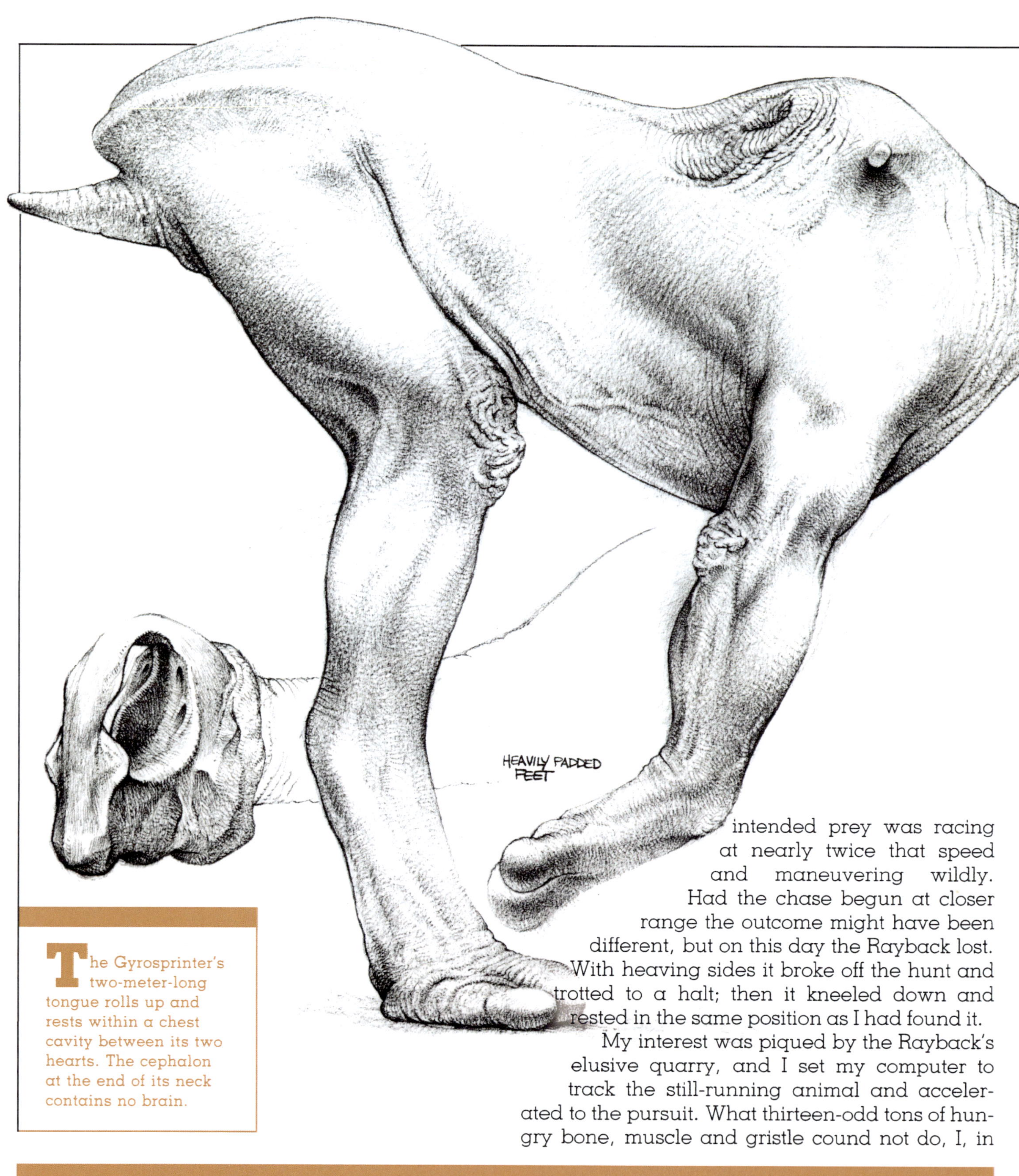

The Gyrosprinter's two-meter-long tongue rolls up and rests within a chest cavity between its two hearts. The cephalon at the end of its neck contains no brain.

intended prey was racing at nearly twice that speed and maneuvering wildly. Had the chase begun at closer range the outcome might have been different, but on this day the Rayback lost. With heaving sides it broke off the hunt and trotted to a halt; then it kneeled down and rested in the same position as I had found it.

My interest was piqued by the Rayback's elusive quarry, and I set my computer to track the still-running animal and accelerated to the pursuit. What thirteen-odd tons of hungry bone, muscle and gristle cound not do, I, in

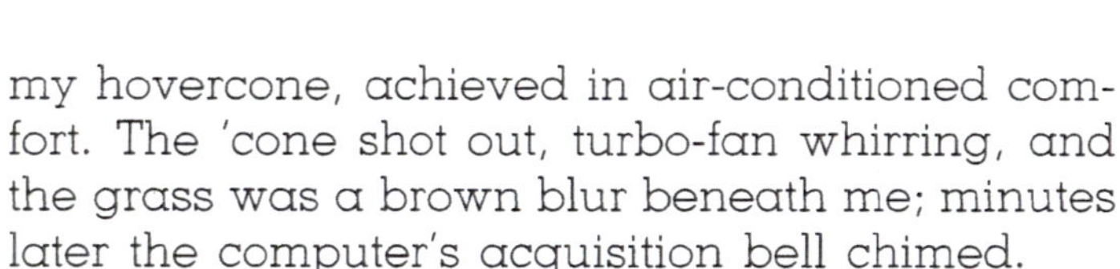

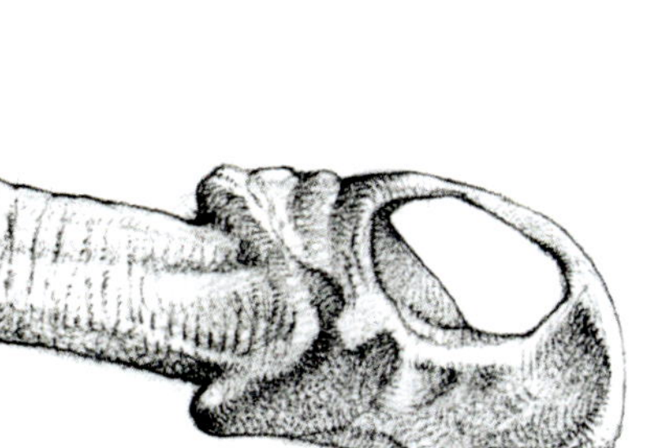

my hovercone, achieved in air-conditioned comfort. The 'cone shot out, turbo-fan whirring, and the grass was a brown blur beneath me; minutes later the computer's acquisition bell chimed.

I slowed down to match speed as I caught up to the running animal. It was every bit as large and as strange-looking as the Rayback had been. Tiny biolights glowed on its hairless body. Two large nostrils gaped on its back. A disproportionately small head bobbed ever so slightly on the end of a long, sinewy neck. It had two muscular legs which were jointed as if, perhaps eons ago, there had been four.

The creature moved with an almost rubbery ease as its legs rhythmically flexed and extended. This impression of fluidity was enhanced by the flexibility of the animal's body; its stretching spine seemed, at times, to almost detach itself from its internal shoulder and hip joints, further lengthening its stride to what I estimated was an unbelievable fifteen meters. It seemed obvious that the animal was built for speed.

It had one other very odd feature. Situated above and behind its neck were a pair of post-like organs that remained absolutely horizontal regardless of their owner's position relative to the ground. I deduced that they were organs of balance, a vital necessity for a biped with such a leg arrangement. They were so striking that I took the liberty of naming this animal, the

second I had encountered on Darwin IV, the Gyrosprinter.

It charged along, oblivious to my proximity, intent on putting as much distance between itself and the Rayback as possible. I spent a quarter of an hour following the Gyrosprinter across the plains, until, finally, it slowed and, like the Rayback, dropped down to rest in the grass. I "parked," brought out my pad and treasured antique pencils, and began sketching. The Gyrosprinter was a most willing subject, hardly moving for the better part of an hour. After finishing a few studies of the animal, I decided to leave it in peace and relocate the luckless predator it had left behind.

I found the Rayback wandering not far from where I had left it. My heart went out to it in a moment of anthropomorphism, for I felt that it looked dejected. It was walking along a dry riverbed, *pinging* occasionally in what I took to be a half-hearted manner. I could not have been more mistaken. Suddenly I saw the object of its interest. The predator was stalking yet another Gyrosprinter, which I had failed to notice concealed in the high grass. Now sympathizing with the prey, I felt a sudden urge to alert the Gyrosprinter to the danger that stalked it. But I caught myself. I was not on this planet to interfere with its workings.

The kill took place with blinding speed. The Rayback leaped forward and, too late, the Gyrosprinter reacted. There followed a short one-hundred-meter race which ended with the Rayback using its short, knife-like proboscis to slice a huge, crippling wound into the side of its prey. The Gyrosprinter, now trailing its entrails, collapsed in a cloud of dust. The triumphant Rayback trotted up to it and hunkered down to feed. Because of my angle, I could not see how this was accomplished, but I later learned that the liquivore had inserted its tongue deep within its victim.

Persistance had paid off for the hungry Rayback, and I was later to appreciate the fact that it was rare for a Darwinian predator to go through a night of hunting without at least one kill. I myself felt well-nourished artistically as I sketched the feast.

Thus ended my first day on Darwin IV.

PLATE III. *"It seemed obvious that the animal was built for speed."*

PLATE IV. The ubiquitous Prairie-ram.

The powerful, liquivorous Prairie-ram is one of the more ubiquitous predators of the Planitia Borealis. Death for the Prairie-rams' victims is always by thoracic impalement, a method which affords the hungry killer quick ingress for feeding. These creatures are so strong that many have been observed, heads imbedded in gory viscera, carrying their impaled prey across the plains for kilometers.

A strange sidebar to the Prairie-ram's killing technique was the eloquent pair of skeletons I came across one evening. The predator's cephalon was still buried in the rib-cage of its prey, locked in between the ribs and vertebrae of an internal puzzle that it could not solve and would ponder for eternity.

PLATE V. "It looked to me as lethal and as threatening as any predator I had seen on Darwin IV."

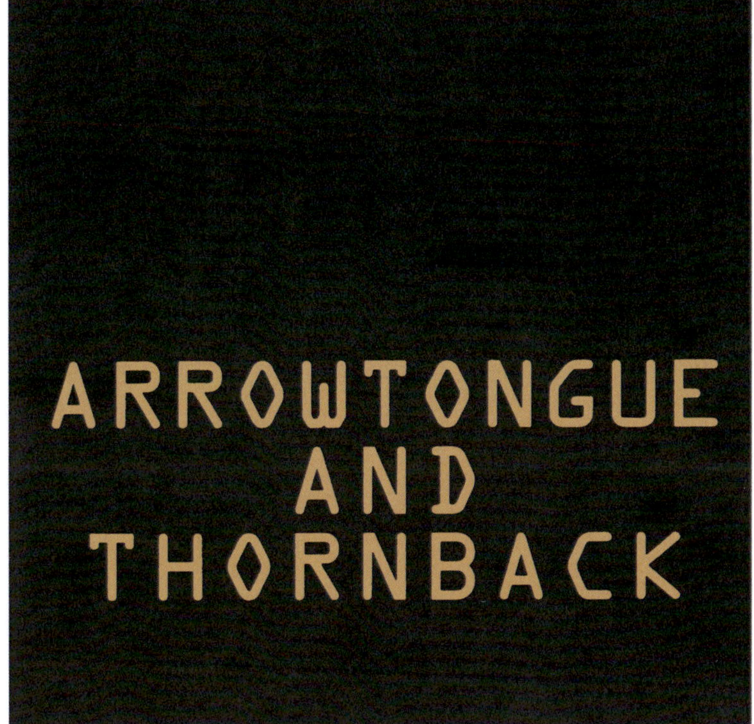

ARROWTONGUE AND THORNBACK

Late one fall afternoon I "parked" my cone above a stretch of dried-up riverbed in Chasma de Salle that twisted in ghostly oxbows across the plains. Hovering at twenty meters above the rocky ground, I quietly reflected on the sudden loneliness that I had, that day, begun to feel. As I watched the pale blue sky deepen to a pink-tinged azure, all that I wished was that my wife and child could be with me to share in the beauty of the moment.

Below me, the shadows of the plant-topped hillocks lengthened and blended into one another as the light faded and the luminosity of the scattered flora increased. Soon the world around me was bathed in a wash of evening blue. The herds in the distance seemed a twinkling, tattered carpet of pink and blue lights, while in my immediate vicinity, brilliant Rainbow Jetdarters flashed through the foliage in small, scavenging schools. These sights, indeed beautiful, awakened in me an aching need to share them with those I loved. Even the sounds from outside depressed me. From my speakers I could hear the breeze sighing in what seemed a most doleful way, heightening my sense of aloneness.

It was odd, considering the number of creatures browsing around me, that I could feel as isolated as I did. There were at least two major herds, each composed of about a hundred individuals *pinging* and eating not more than six hundred meters from where I hovered. Five small pods of triped-alien Thornbacks had broken away from the main herds. They meandered around the dusty ravines, searching, I supposed, for the round, rolling succulents that made up their usual forage. These common plants of the plains, which our botanist named fodderball weeds, are small spheres formed of thin, water-rich branches emanating from a central axle. Their lightweight construction puts them at the mercy of almost every breeze, which carries them great distances across the ground. I have even seen fodderballs airborne, though they were traveling neither very far nor very high.

A few kilometers to the west, a colony of electrophytes opened up with a flickering display of miniature lightning bolts. This in turn triggered neighboring stands of the red, stalky plants to sympathetically fire their charges, which created a vivid chain reaction across the horizon. These plants are endowed with the unique ability to protect themselves with strong electrical discharges, often of sufficient intensity to kill small animals. Amidst this dazzling light display, I noticed a small cloud of dust rising into the air. Almost simultaneously I heard the warning *pings* of some unseen Thornbacks and I quickly realized their danger. Within that shifting cloud of dust, I could barely distinguish a large, dark creature stalking purposefully along the rocky riverbed, obviously the source of the electrophytes' agitation.

A moment later, a pod of eight frantic Thornbacks burst into view, racing at full gallop through the maze of the riverbed, kicking up a roiling cloud of dust. In attendance was a school of Jetdarters, the small flyers opportunistically sensing an imminent kill. As the Thornbacks reached a rockier portion of the riverbed, the dust subsided and I had a better look at their pursuer.

It stood about eight meters tall and

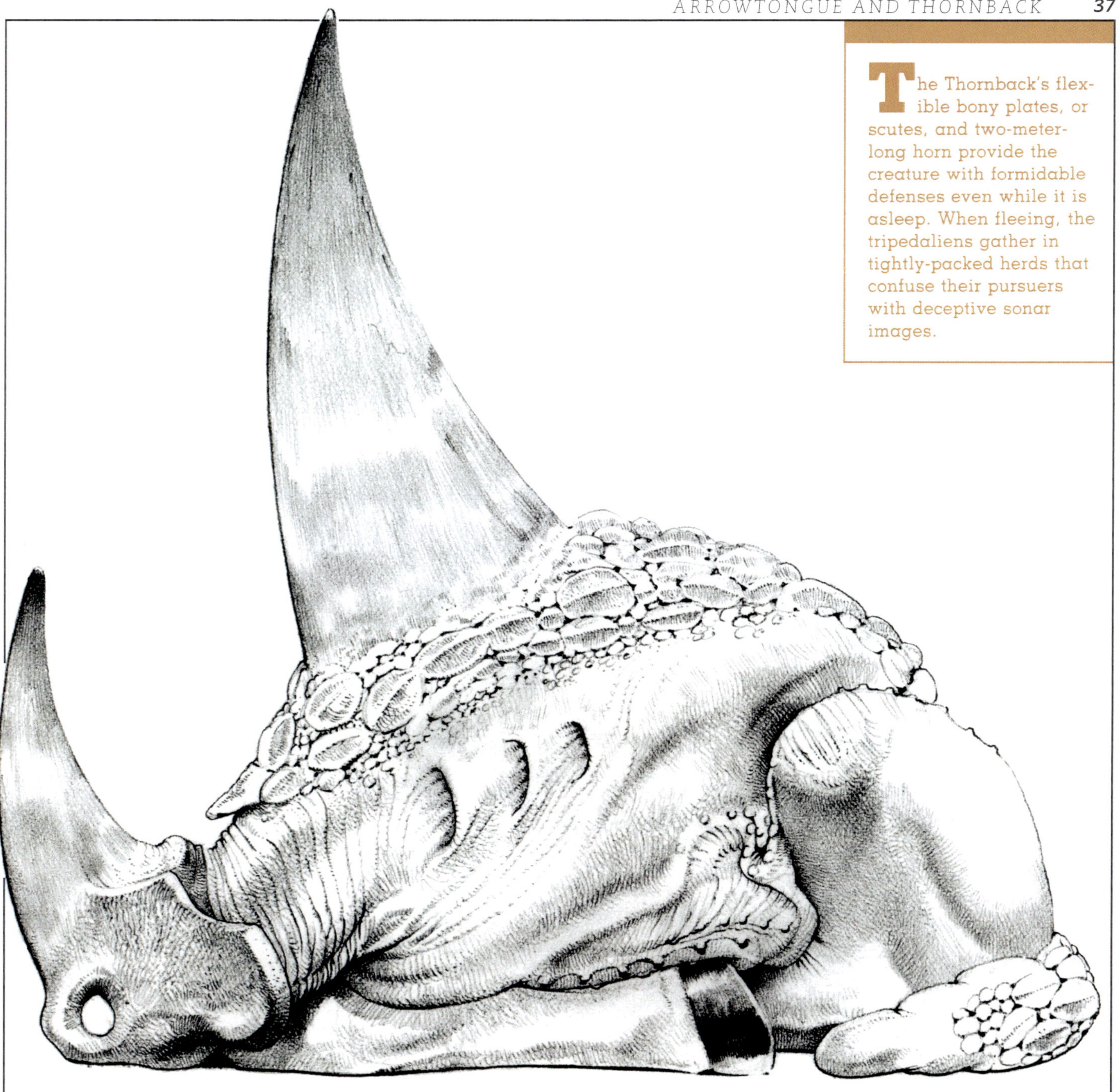

looked to me as lethal and as threatening as any predator I had seen on Darwin IV. Its black-hided body was muscular and tight, and was surmounted by a large, pointed head which continuously swung back and forth in a meter-wide arc. With each swing it emitted a pair of shrill, grating *pings* that I knew were targeting the fleeing Thornbacks. Darting from its bony head was a red arrow-tipped tongue, serrated and glistening with saliva. I named the animal an Arrowtongue. As it ran toward me I thanked the stars above that I was not its quarry.

PLATE VI. "A pod of eight Thornbacks burst into view."

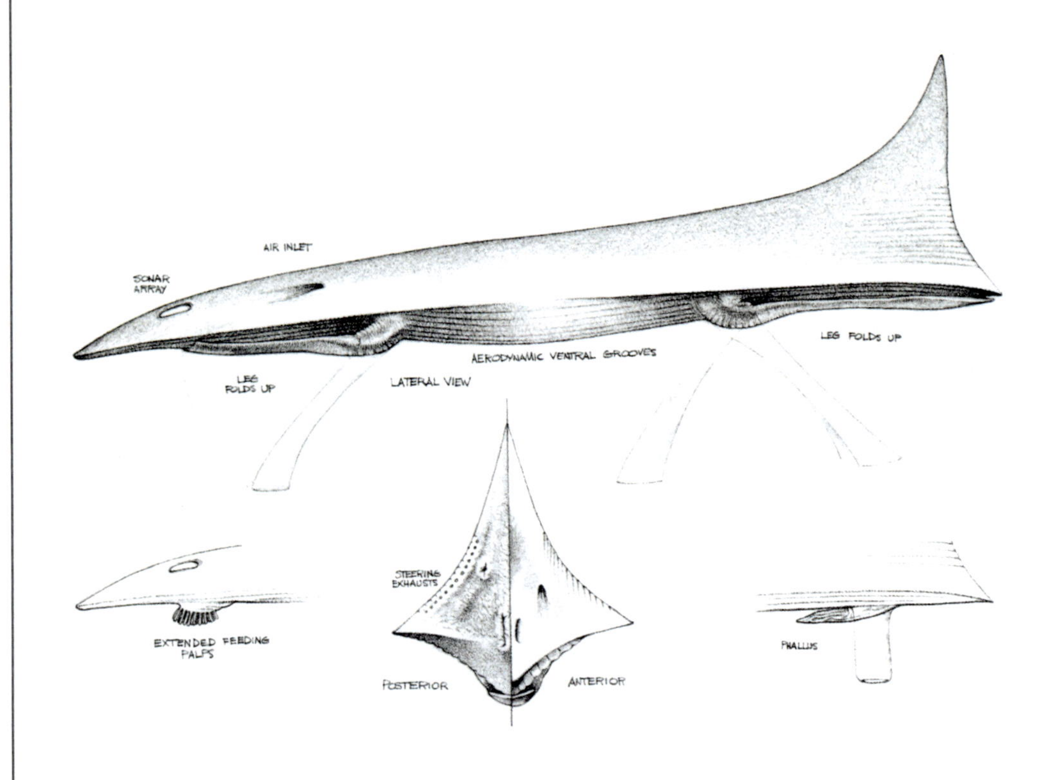

The Jetdarter retracts and folds its legs into aerodynamic trim for flight. Powered by the biological equivalent of a ramjet engine (with a bone-and-gristle turbine), this swift flyer sometimes reaches speeds of up to one-hundred-fifty kph.

The Thornbacks were getting closer. Their clattering hooves seemed to barely touch the rocky riverbed. I could see the animals' dorsal nostrils puckering and flaring as their foamy breath moistened their armored backs. They ran as one, instinctively knowing that security lay in their joined efforts. Running in a mass with only their horned backs exposed, they provided their pursuer with a confusing sonar image. Without a single target to focus upon, the hunter could only follow its prey and hope for a killing opportunity.

The Arrowtongue did not have long to wait, however. As the pod of Thornbacks passed below me, one of them lost its footing on the loose rocks, colliding with a second and sending them both down. The Arrowtongue, for all its bulk, was enormously quick and was upon them before the stunned tripedaliens could regain their feet. Its long tongue lashed out and speared one Thornback through the dorsal nostril with such ferocity as to send a geyser of dark blood a meter into the air. The tripedalien collapsed with a gurgling sigh as its killer quickly retracted its tongue, turned, and with a flick of its head, knocked the second beast sprawling.

Again the red blur of the predator's tongue found its mark; and this time, without withdrawing the organ, it crouched down and began to feed. Powerful muscles rippled on the Arrowtongue's sides and throat as it sent powerful digestive juices into the Thornback's chest cavity, and then withdrew the liquified contents. Over the next half hour this process was repeated several times until the juices had completely cleaned the organs out of the dead animal's body. Apparently the Arrowtongue's diet consisted of only the broken down viscera of its victims, for it left the Thornback's carcass intact for the scavengers.

Powerful accelerator muscles extend the Arrowtongue's eight-meter-long killing- and feeding-organ with lightning speed and deadly accuracy. Like most predators on Darwin IV, this creature is a liquivore, injecting digestive juices that liquify the viscera of its kill, which are then sucked dry.

While the liquivore had been eviscerating one animal, a dozen or more Jetdarters had been feeding on the other, leaving bloody tracks across its back. When the Arrowtongue turned to the second Thornback, they took flight.

Thick black blood was still bubbling from the Thornback's gaping nostril-wound, and it was here that the Arrowtongue again inserted its tongue. After another half hour, its belly distended, the glutted creature rose somewhat unsteadily and slowly strode off about twenty meters, then lay down and rested. It had been a successful hunt and the fortunate Arrowtongue could now sleep through the night.

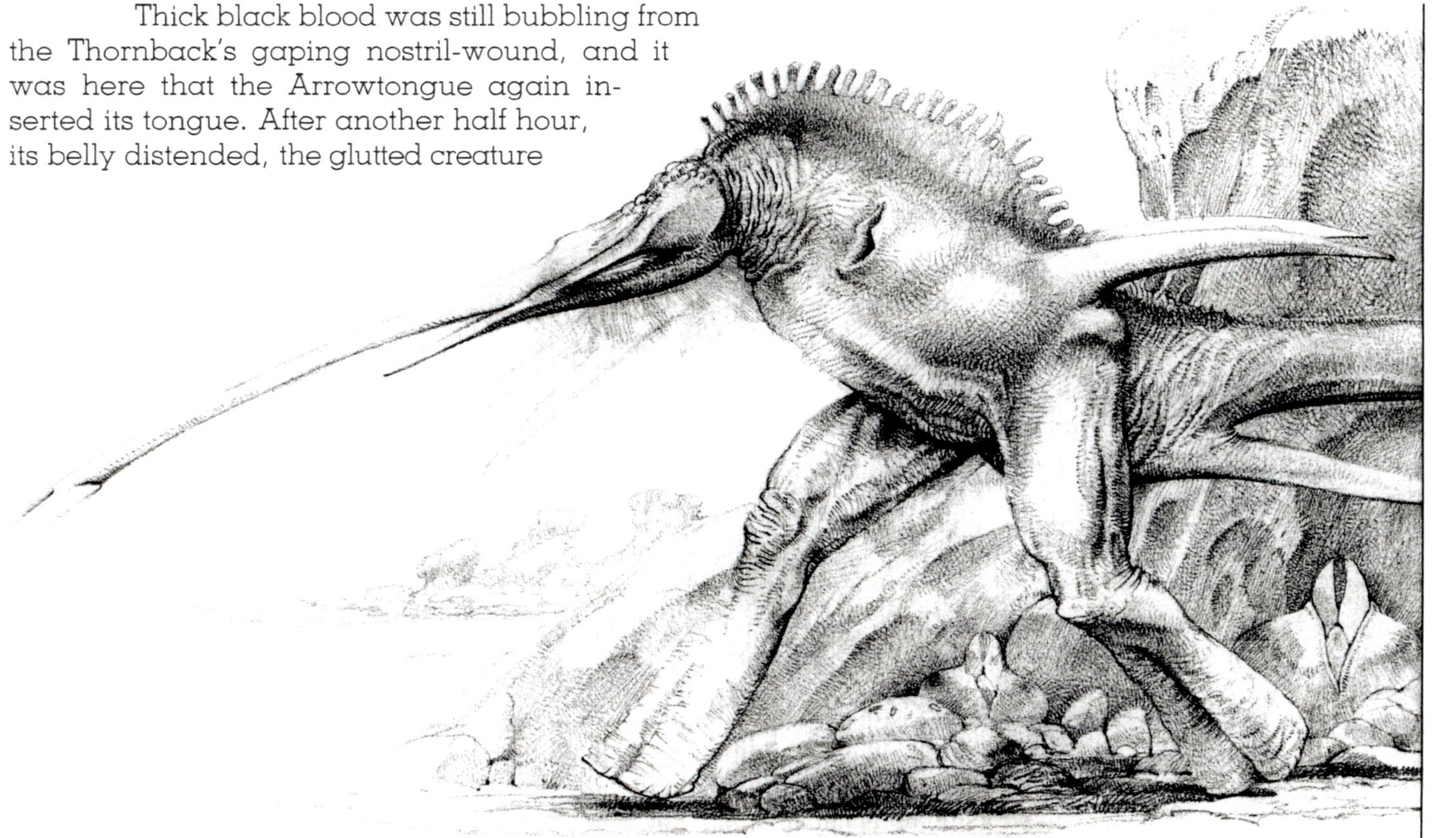

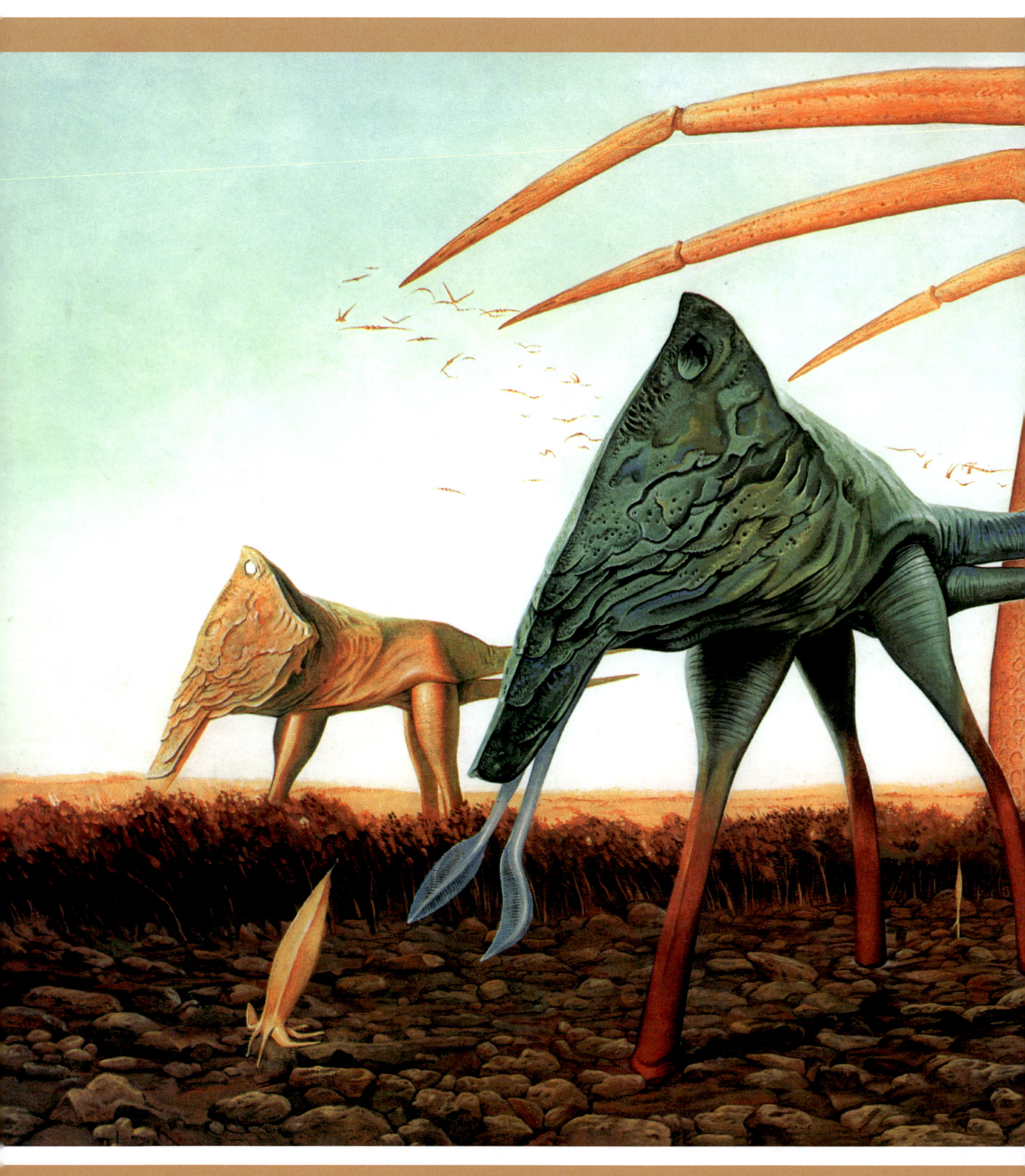

PLATE VII. *"A splendid tripedalien bounded over a nearby hedge."*

BUTCHERTREE AND PRISMALOPE

Late one afternoon, during the course of my southern desert exploration, I decided to get a closer look at the curious "trees" we had observed during our medium altitude passes over the Chasma Cook. Opinion was divided as to their botanical or animal lineage. Their tree-like appearance was belied by the behavior we had witnessed from our altitude of two hundred meters. These sightings had shown us a possibly predatory organism very different from any tree we had ever seen. On several occasions I had watched one of the "trees" folding and opening its long, sharp limbs in a grotesque slow-motion pantomime of a kill. Often, too, I had seen dried carcasses stuck on their spear-point branches.

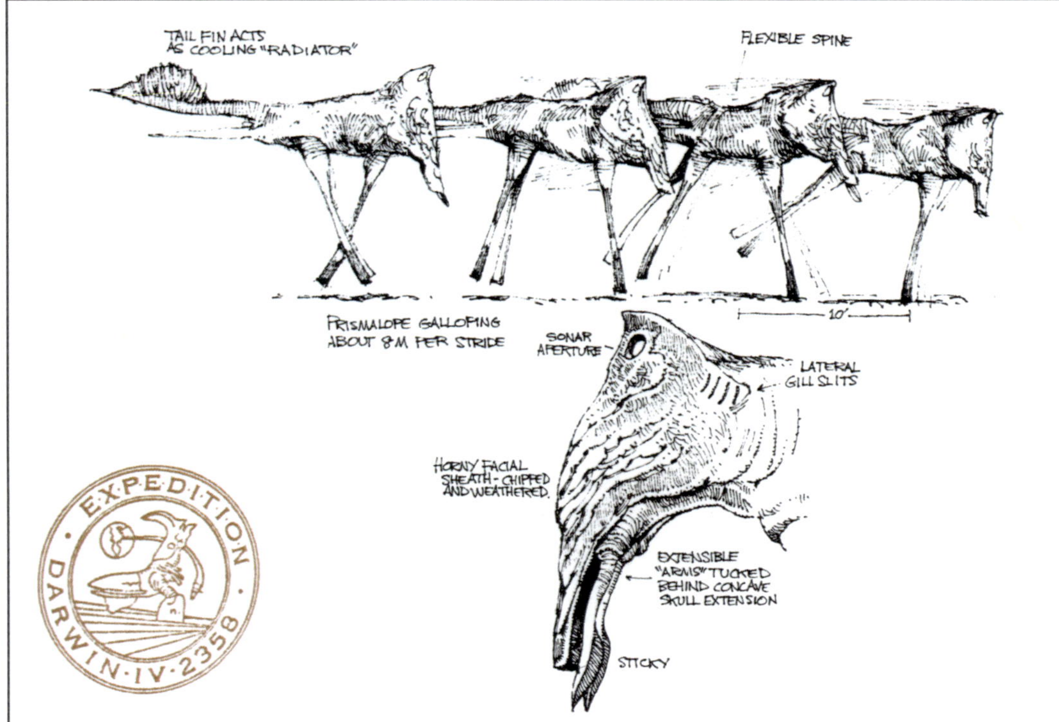

When one day I found myself in a position to investigate the bizarre "trees," I jumped at the chance. I had been on the move for a week with three other Expedition members, and we had stopped only to sleep. I was delighted by the opportunity to "park" after our lengthy peregrinations and did not even watch the shrinking specks of my fellow travelers as they disappeared over the horizon. I set my radio on "Emergency Only" and hovered near a small stand of the "trees."

My first task was to run a series of scans on the organisms in order to determine their true nature. Within minutes I had my answer: I was unequivocally watching a group of animals. One large "tree" was surrounded by four smaller ones. Surrounding their wide trunk-bases were a number of yellow lanceolate growths, seemingly rooted beneath the rocky soil. An hour or so into my vigil these growths started to move, swaying on some imaginary zephyr (for there was no wind). Then, riding on the still, warm air, a small flyer insinuated itself amidst these dancing growths. The flyer blended in remarkably well, its color, shape, and movements causing it to disappear in the surrounding yellow fronds.

The cause for this mimicry became immediately obvious when a splendid tripedalien bounded over a nearby hedge in hot pursuit of another identical flyer. This flyer, too, hid itself among the waving fronds. The Prismalope (as we had named the creatures when observing them in herds from the air) skidded to a halt. It was panting hard through the eight vents on the sides of its massive, bony head. It paced delicately around the base of the trunk, *pinging* slowly and flicking out its two grasping tongues in a parody of bewilderment. The rapid pacing spiraled into tighter circles until the creature was quite close to the largest "tree."

The flyer was difficult to spot under the hanging branches. Its flying pattern alternated between freezing near the fronds and darting rapidly from one frond to another. When it froze it was very difficult to tell from the growths. The Prismalope was clever, though, and drew closer, *pinging* more rapidly as its confidence grew. It could probably already taste the airborne treat.

So absorbed was the tripedalien in its small prey that it failed to see the lightning descent of the spear-like arm. The limb pierced the Prismalope with such force that a full meter was exposed on its other side, dripping with blood. The flyer darted back out of sight. The powerful arm lifted the kicking beast high into the air where, for the next three quarters of an hour, it died, as its fluids were slowly drained.

I saw the beautiful colors on the dying creature's body fade; I saw its carcass shrivel perceptibly as pores in the impaling arm sucked it dry. It became apparent that the tree-like predator was finished when the remains were tossed down to land, in a cloud of dust, near the desiccated corpse of another Prismalope.

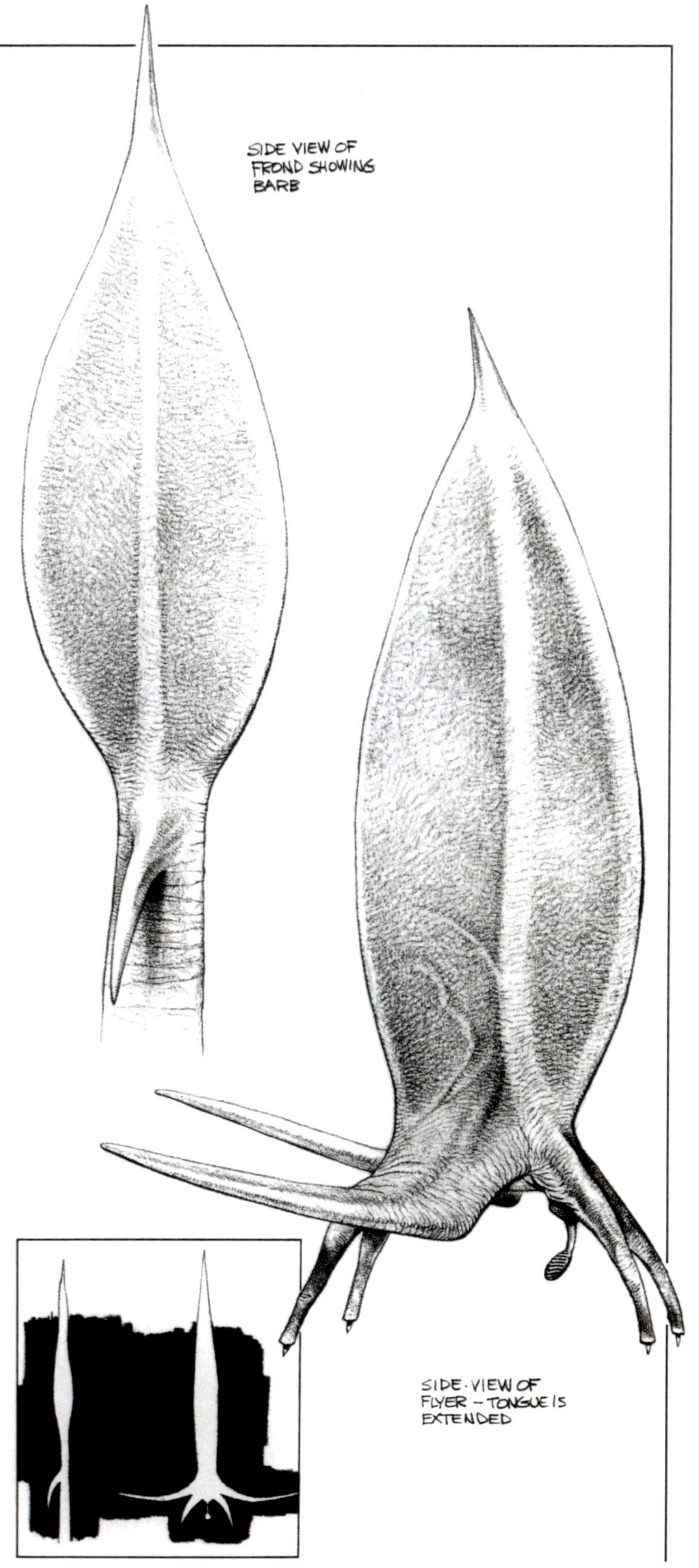

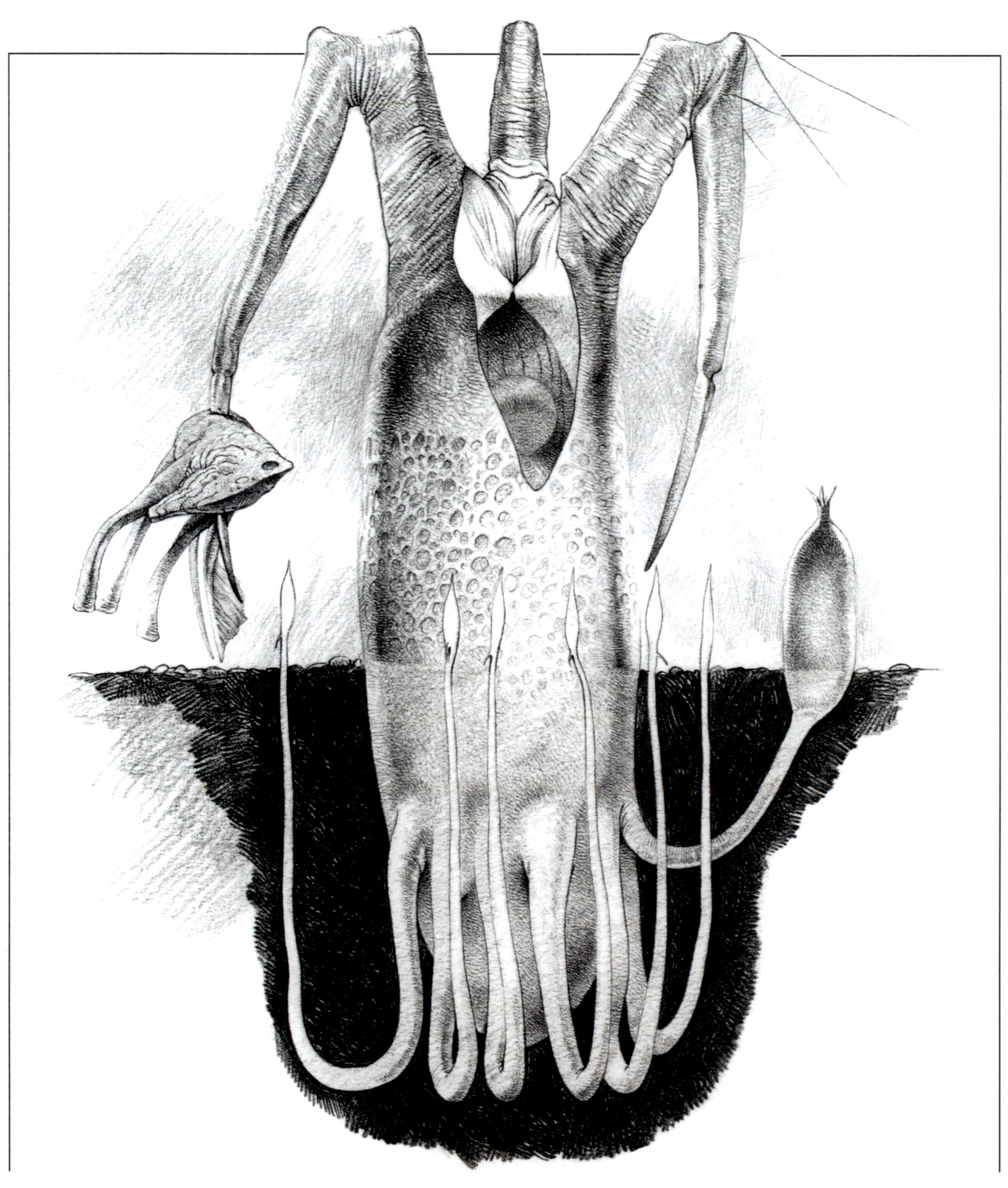

The Butchertree forms a stationary extended family with a radius of a few yards. It spawns its young in the form of still-connected buds, feeding them through umbilici until they have developed their own hooking fronds and spear-tipped limbs and can hunt for themselves.

In the remaining three hours before dusk I watched as the Butchertree (for I so named it) dispatched five more of the beautifully-colored tripedaliens. And with each kill the lure was, again, the small yellow flyer. One Prismalope, chasing the wily flyer in circles, caught its tongue on the barb near the base of one of the yellow fronds. I was surprised to see, in the ensuing struggle, that this frond was attached to the trunk by a stretchy, underground tentacle. Not that this mattered to the Prismalope, which was still impaled and hefted into the air; apparently this position allowed the fluids from the dying animal to flow more easily down its gullet.

At one point three of the luckless prey were simultaneously held high in the air, in various stages of desiccation. It was a gruesome scene that is still etched on my memory, the tree and its victims silhouetted against the darkening sky.

My interest was piqued by the underground tentacles, and I ran another series of scans. I discovered that the largest of the Butchertrees was connected to the four smaller ones by thick umbilici. Since only the larger one had made kills, I surmised that the others in the group were its offspring and that it was probably still sustaining them with nourishment until the day their own limbs were powerful enough to kill prey. We later learned that this takes about two years, depending upon the size and migratory patterns of the herds, since during periods of decreased prey, the Butchertrees' metabolic level drops leaving only passive systems, such as the infrared receptor pits on its sides, active.

I remain, to this day, uncertain as to how these odd, stationary creatures mate. The intimacy that the Butchertree shares with the yellow flyer led me to speculate on a few possibilities. The flyer may be nothing more than an opportunistic symbiote gleaning morsels from the Butchertree's kills. But somehow I am not convinced. My guess is that the flyer is, in some way, responsible for the continuance of the species. It acts as a lure for the Butchertree; this is its most obvious contribution. It is also, however, an ideal candidate to carry sperm or eggs from one Butchertree to the next. Or (and this is my favorite theory) perhaps the flyer is itself the second sex, a sexually dimorphic extreme. Unfortunately the Expedition did not collect enough data to confirm any of these theories.

PLATE VIII. A Rayback at dusk.

THE FOREST
AND
PERIPHERY

PLATE IX. "Pulling itself over the crest of a hill was a huge, dark form."

GROVE-BACK

I was awakened late one night by the alarm beeping on my hovercone's open radio channel. Dr. Vinogradov, one of our geologists, had detected a seismic disturbance in the Sinus Columbus, the great pass through the equatorial mountains. Because I was nearer the moving "epicenter," he asked me, very politely, to investigate it. He claimed that the tremors were local and steadily moving toward me. In his opinion, this intimated a non-geological origin and possibly zoological source. He apologized again for waking me, asked me to keep him informed, and signed off.

I rubbed the sleep out of my eyes and trained a couple of my instruments in the general direction of the tremors. The geolo-

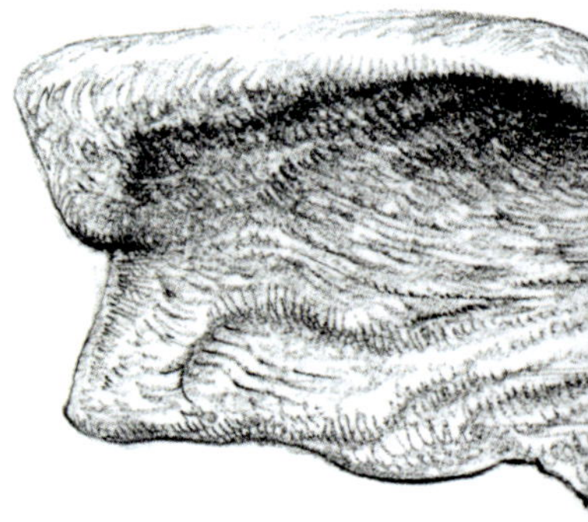

gist's conclusions were correct; a very large creature, some seven kilometers distant, was headed toward my "parked" 'cone. Infrared and sonar confirmed this.

After converting my warm bed back into a not-so-warm chair, I synthed a cup of tea and a doughnut. I sat back in the chair and stared into the moonslit darkness, waiting. Forty-five minutes passed as the "tremors" grew in intensity. Not much, however, had changed outside. The moons were a little more separated, and a long flight of glowing Diskflyers had passed in front of me. But the gloom had not yielded anything more. Suddenly, coalescing out of the darkness, I saw the red biolights of an Arrowtongue as it headed toward me.

The powerful bipedalien was coming from the direction of my expected guest, and as it padded down the slope in front of me I could barely see its dark head swinging back and forth in the characteristic manner of its kind. It was *pinging* continuously. Clearly this animal was not responsible for the ground-shaking tremors I was monitoring. As it disappeared into the night, a second Arrowtongue strode into view, followed closely by a third and a fourth. A hunting pack? Other predators, such as Raybacks, had been seen hunting in packs, but I had not personally seen social behavior in Arrowtongues.

Then I heard, in the distance, a faint scraping. It was a low sound, but growing against the background of slow, ground-trembling thuds. I decided to climb to a greater altitude to get a look over the hills that obscured my vision. As the 'cone climbed to one hundred meters I realized that I had been prudent to move when I did.

Before me, pulling itself over the crest of the hill and blotting out the moons behind it, was a huge, dark form. Silhouetted against the noctilucent clouds was a gigantic wedge-shaped creature, biolights aglow, supported on two, thick pillar-like legs. I estimated that it was at least sixty meters tall, but the darkness made an accurate appraisal impossible. It hesitated at the top of the hill, almost as if it were gathering itself for

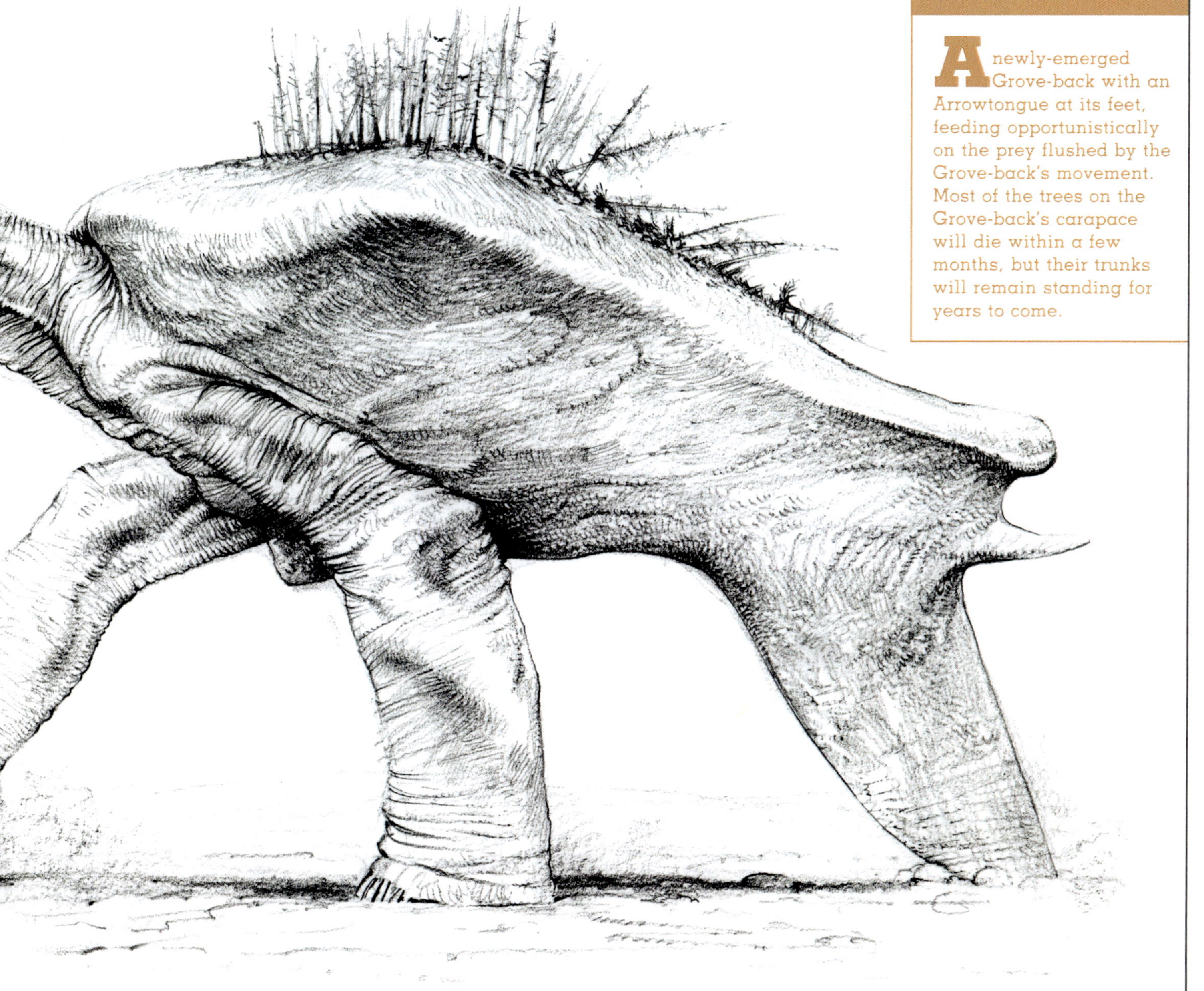

the downward plunge. As I watched, another Arrowtongue darted into view between the behemoth's legs. Just then, the larger animal started forward and caught the Arrowtongue under the enormous skid that made up the rear of its body. The Arrowtongue was crushed like a grape and passed over without the slightest notice from the looming giant.

As the beast came down the hill, I could see more clearly the enormous skid that carried the rear two-thirds of its body. I realized that it was this plow-like growth that I had heard scraping over the hilly terrain. But the most remarkable aspect of this already remarkable beast was the dying forest of young plaque-bark trees growing out of its dorsal carapace. At first I speculated that this might be some kind of protective adaptation that would enable it to hide; this seemed

unlikely, though, given the creature's bulk. I later learned that once the Keeled Grove-back (for so I called it) reached this size and age it had no true enemies and did not fear predation.

As the Grove-back topped the next hill, I could very clearly hear the suction of its breath as it inhaled the luminous clouds of minute, airborne animals that made up its diet. These tiny creatures are consumed in prodigious numbers by Darwin IV's placid air-sifters. Born pregnant, these microflyers complete their life cycles as eggs in the excreta of the animals that eat them.

My questions about the Arrowtongues accompanying the Grove-back were soon resolved. A predictable side-effect of the travels of so large a creature as the Grove-back is the flushing of enormous quantities of game. The Arrowtongues opportunistically follow the huge beast, preying upon this game—even at great risk to themselves. I found this commensalism in a predator as fierce and independent as the Arrowtongues fascinating, and watching them dart and

stab into the moonslit undergrowth, I gained a new respect for their adaptability.

The Grove-back, for its part, placidly continued on its journey, raising and lowering its broad ax-shaped head, unaware of the dramas being played out at its feet. The creature's breath whistled out of generous gills aft of its nose. The trees on its back

The Arrowtongue and Prismalope roam the vast grasslands of Darwin IV. While the Grove-back is also a creature of the plains, it carries a forest on its vast dorsal carapace categorizing it as a forest peripheral.

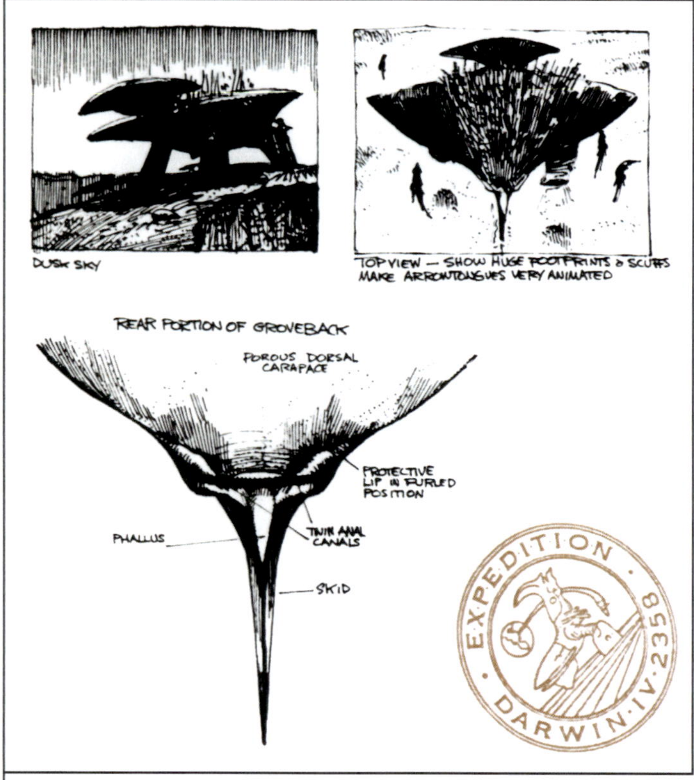

The young Grove-back (far right), unlike the lumbering behemoth it will become, is graceful and fast on its feet: The complex and delicate anatomy of the adult is usually hidden under the soil that covers its carapace.

cracked and rustled with each ponderous, lurching footfall, while the enormous skid turned the ground with a clatter of upturned boulders. The noise of the animal's passage was substantial and, when I finally gave up my pursuit, I could hear it receding into the distance long after it had dropped out of sight.

During my three years on Darwin IV, I had several opportunities to observe this extraordinary creature and to piece together the stages of its life. It was my good fortune to come across a nesting Grove-back during my second spring. It was submerged in a pit and grown over with underbrush and small trees. Had I been skimming the ground under treetop level I would have passed it by. It looked like nothing more than a small, tree-covered hill.

Based on the growth of the trees, I estimated that the animal had been buried and immobile for at least ten years. In fact, I scanned the Grove-back for vital signs, not entirely convinced that the animal was alive. My instruments' readings were so weak that I had to conclude that the animal was hibernating. During the course of its prolonged stasis, small creatures, as well as plants, had accumulated on the behemoth's porous dorsal shell. Infrared indicated a large colony of Bush-Jumpstars as well as a polyhedral Cobalt Jetdarter hive.

I monitored this particular specimen for two and a half weeks. Each day I returned to find the faint life-signs growing stronger. On the ninth day I was surprised to find that a fifteen-meter-long tunnel had been excavated beneath the animal. Its long ovipositor was slowly squeezing eggs into a small chamber at the tunnel's end.

Five days after laying its eggs, the Keeled Grove-back rose shakily amidst a great cloud of debris and soil. Its stiffened legs, trembling under the immense, forgotten weight, tentatively took their first steps in more than ten years. The tangled forest on the creature's back shook like reeds in the wind as it moved forward.

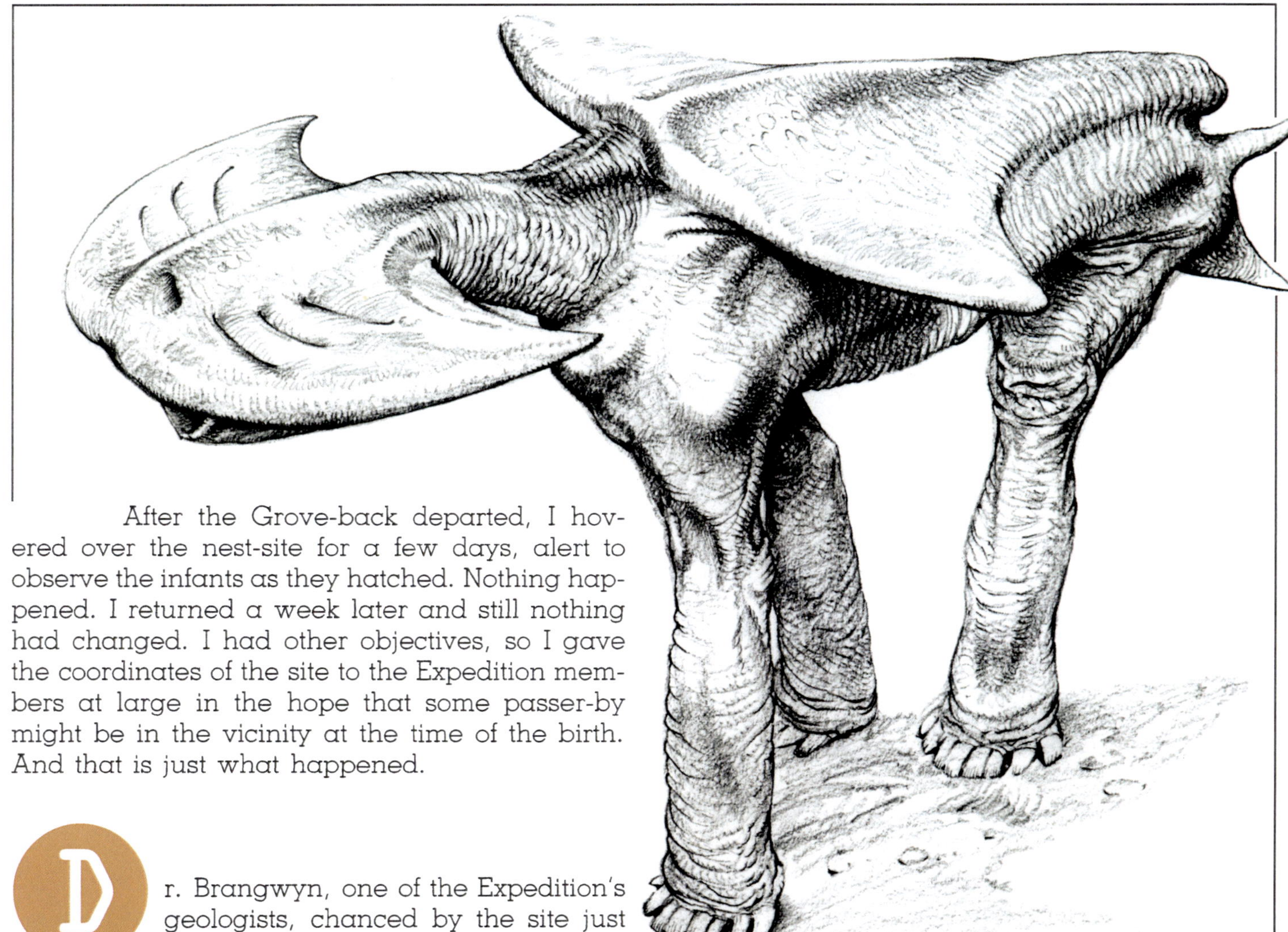

After the Grove-back departed, I hovered over the nest-site for a few days, alert to observe the infants as they hatched. Nothing happened. I returned a week later and still nothing had changed. I had other objectives, so I gave the coordinates of the site to the Expedition members at large in the hope that some passer-by might be in the vicinity at the time of the birth. And that is just what happened.

D r. Brangwyn, one of the Expedition's geologists, chanced by the site just as the birth occurred. He described each small Grove-back emerging from the sandy soil, covered by sticky amniotal fluids and *pinging* feebly. An hour after hatching, the young, which have three functional limbs, dart off in all directions. They are fully independent and seem to delight in their speed, an ironic counterpoint to their slow-paced parent. Only later will their hind limb atrophy to be replaced by the familiar skid, as with the other keeled inhabitants of Darwin IV.

It was only after I encountered the peripatetic Grove-backs that I realized that the odd twin fecal trails I had been noticing strewn about were their product. These ruddy, ropey excrescences lay on the ground, on either side of a deep trench, like double weals, often a meter high and many meters long; and before becoming aware of their true origin, I had suspected them of being an artifact, possibly of intelligent creatures. They frequently spiralled into tight coils or perfect ovoids, which I saw as a sign of their artificiality. To me they seemed like lures meant to direct and trap unwary game. It was with more than a little embarrassment that I was proven wrong, and I received many good-natured jibes from my fellow Expedition members who had, of course, developed their own fair share of not-quite-accurate theories on Darwin IV.

PLATE X. "Without warning, the cylindrical animals launched themselves into the sky."

hile sketching in the northern moors near Lacus Parry one afternoon, I received word from Dr. Evan Tenbroeck, head of the Geological Survey Team, of some extraordinary creatures twenty kilometers downrange. Since Dr. Tenbroeck was not known for his excitability, I dropped what I was doing and pointed my navigational grid toward the GST's transmitted coordinates.

Three kilometers from my objective I spotted the creatures in question. Standing at an impressive height of sixty meters, four very odd tubular animals were swaying and bending slightly in the gentle breeze. Their globe-tipped balance-organs were easily the most developed gyroscopic mechanoreceptors I had seen, and for a brief

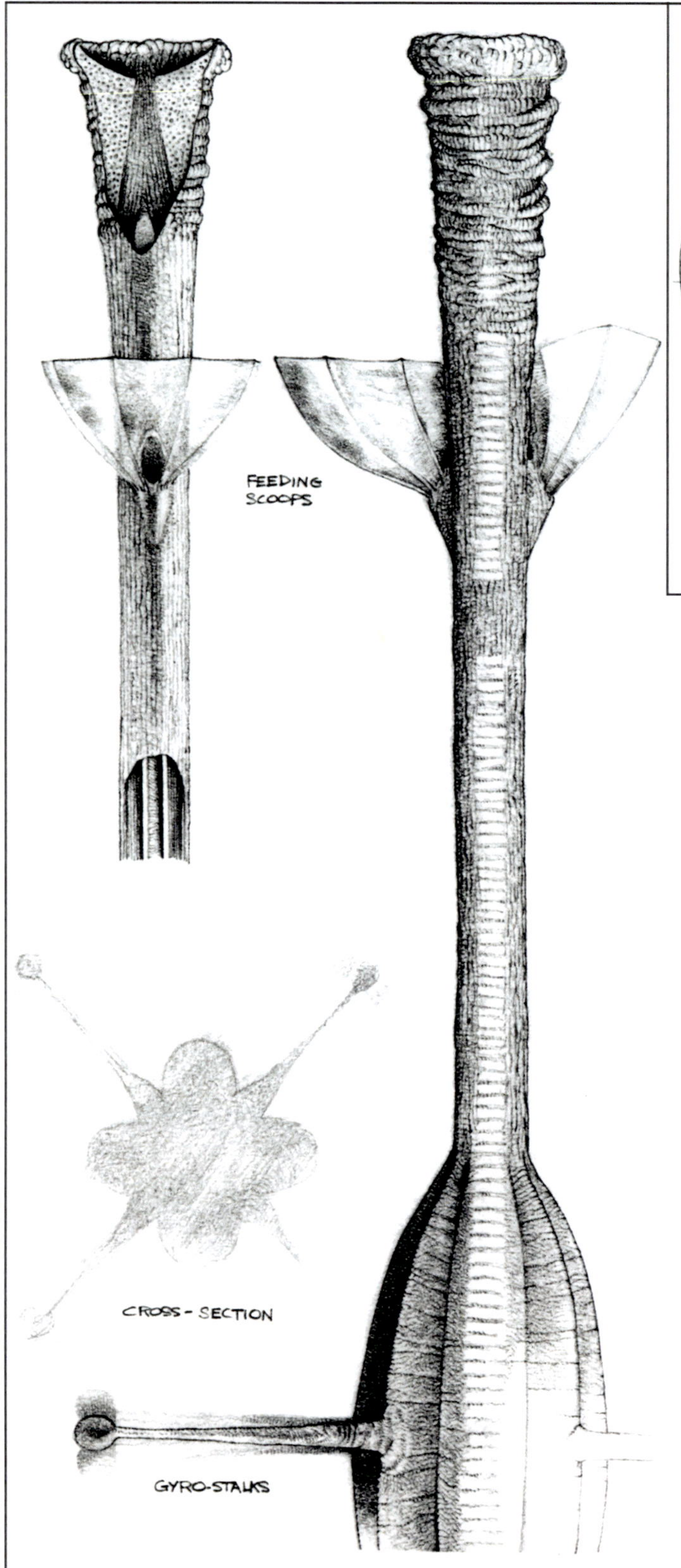

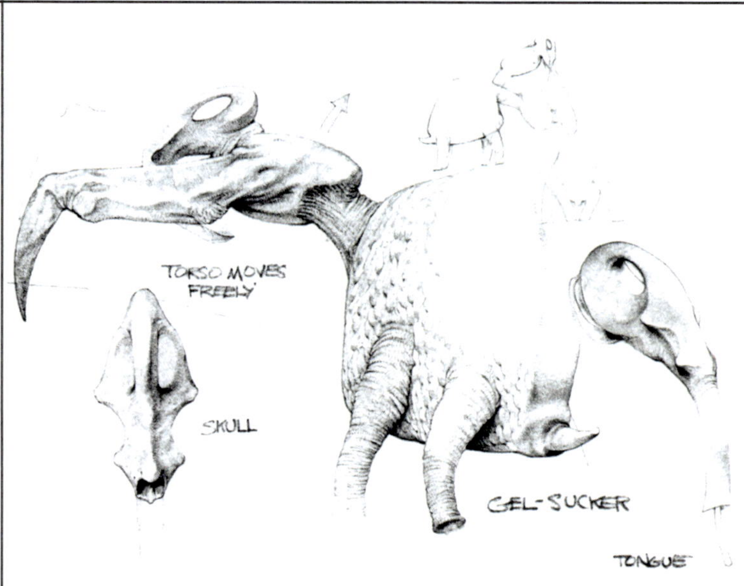

moment I wondered why the animals needed them. Then, as I drew to within a thousand meters, I saw the great beast's fleshy feet begin to wrinkle and compress, and I heard a rushing of air as of a great, deep inhalation. Without warning, the four cylindrical animals launched themselves into the hazy sky. Backlit by Darwin IV's twin suns, their darkened sides flickered with rainbow biolights as they performed complete somersaults and landed upright. I understood the necessity for the overdeveloped balance-organs; it was an incredible display of coordination.

No sooner had the Flipsticks, as I termed them, landed than they were airborne again. This singular mode of locomotion was what had undoubtedly excited the unflappable Dr. Tenbroeck. I, too, was impressed.

The object of their activity soon became visible as I saw a cloud of small micro-flyers trying to elude the tubiform predators. The speed of this chase was remarkable, due to the distances covered with each bound, and I was hard-pressed to keep up.

Then I saw one Flipstick, after some incredible maneuvering, plunge straight through the swarm of flyers. It unfurled two giant umbrella-like scoops, which had been previously folded flat, and simultaneously emitted an oscillating sonar jamming tone. The tone created enormous confusion amidst the swarm, so that they fell easy victim to the vacuuming scoops of the air-sifter. In seconds, three-quarters of the swarm had been sucked into the animal while the rest dispersed in chaos.

As the clouds of micro-flyers headed in every direction, the Flipsticks resumed their precariously balanced stationary posture. Fearing that I might alarm them, I "parked" about three hundred meters away, near a circular stand of curious, post-like plants which had a puzzling gnawed look to them. Strangest of all, a large, intact Arrowtongue head lay in the center of this ring. It almost seemed to have been seized by giant, taloned hands and twisted off, as there were claw marks on the dried skin and bone and ropy tendons trailed from the stump of the neck. The long, barbed tongue was missing, evidently wrenched free by the same unknown creature that had decapitated it. I watched over my shoulder as I sketched this scene, nervous about meeting a creature that could so easily dispatch one of Darwin IV's fiercest liquivores.

During the course of my high-speed

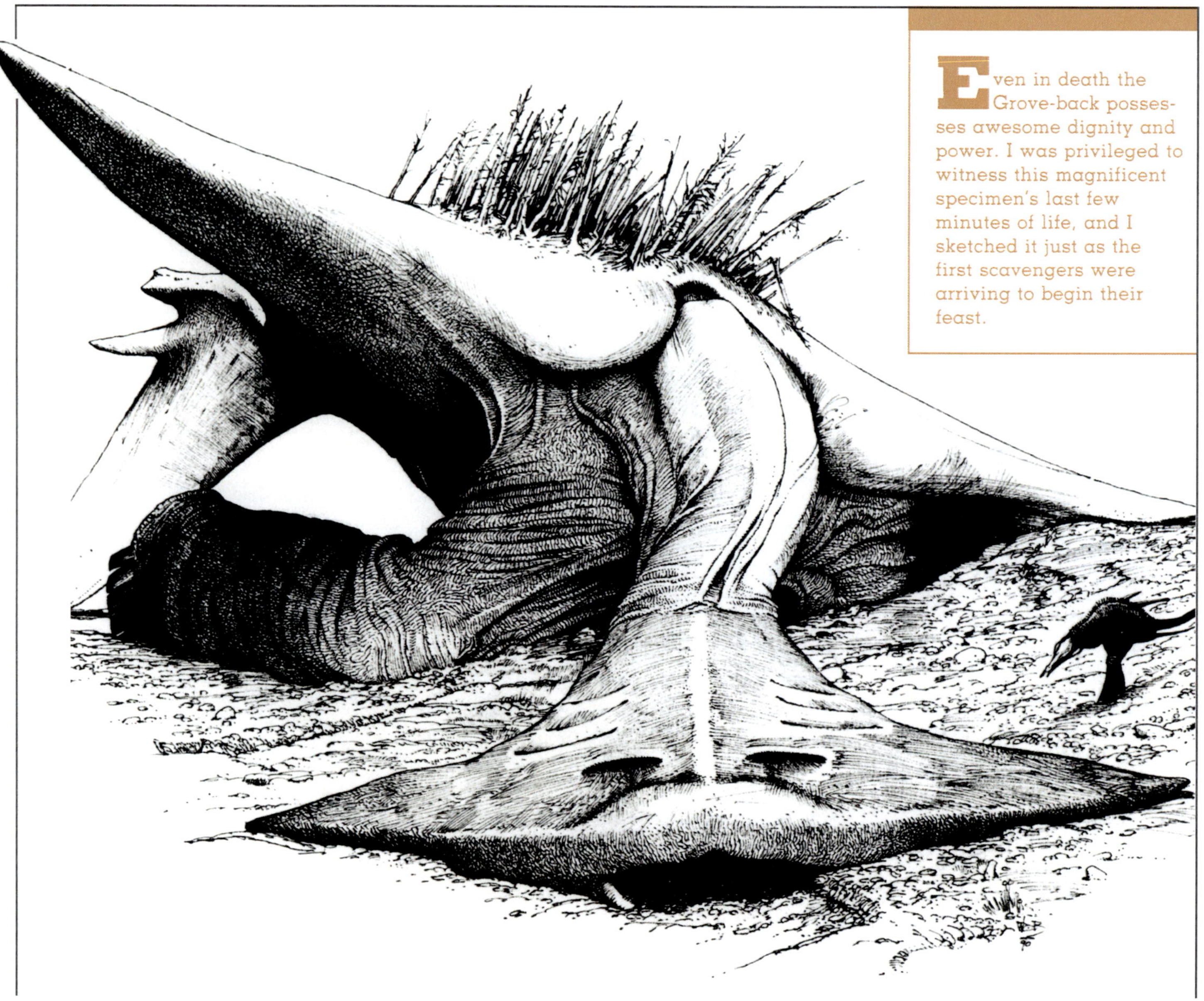

chase, I had noticed an especially large Grove-back stumbling across a meadow. At the time, the creature's difficulty with the easy terrain had not registered on me, as I was caught up in the chase. Then I circled around and found the Grove-back struggling feebly to negotiate a small rise. At once I realized that the behemoth was sick, possibly even dying. This was something I had not yet encountered upon Darwin IV; I had never before witnessed a death by natural causes.

The Grove-back repeatedly attempted the two-meter rise, never quite getting its enormous foot high enough. It paused and I saw a tremor pass through it. Suddenly, with a great, roaring exhalation, the huge animal pitched forward, digging its massive head into the loamy soil. Brittle trees cracked and flew, javelin-like, from the animal's back. It seemed to take forever for the beast to settle into what I knew was to be its final resting place; its feet pawed sadly at the ground until at last all was still. I decided to sketch this poignant scene, to honor so great a creature's passing.

Short moments after the Grove-back's death, an Arrowtongue appeared, the first of many opportunistic liquivores to arrive at this easy banquet. By the time I was finished sketching, at least a dozen larger animals and hosts of smaller scavengers were feeding, all in apparent harmony. The Flipsticks were just as I had left them an hour earlier.

I studied the Flipsticks for about an hour as they rested on their compressed feet, their six-sided mid-bodies heaving rapidly from their recent chase. Now that I was closer I could see that their bodies were of very light construction, with a latticework of muscles apparently lying in thin layers over the surface.

I found myself distracted by a pair of lumbering Gel-suckers that had stumbled into a patch of jelly-bladder plants. With greedy abandon, the awkward creatures ripped into the wobbly bags of vegetable gel and drank their fill through their hyper-extended proboscises. It was not long before the first bladders were shriveled husks, their liquid drained or spilled.

The glutted Gel-suckers then moved methodically from one bladder to the next, ripping them apart, apparently for sport. Gel tumbled and cascaded out in big chunks, melting into lumpy puddles on the ground. As each jelly-bladder was destroyed, dozens of small, *pinging* Hoppercones appeared from their tunnel nests to snatch pieces of semisolid bladder skin.

A group of silvery, barrel-shaped Finlegs waddled into view, headed toward the motionless Flipsticks. I decided to follow them, to see how close I could get to the huge monopedaliens. I thought that if I stayed behind the Finlegs, they might not notice me, so I skimmed at a low altitude of ten meters. I was sure that my plan had been successful as I came to within thirty meters of the giant tubes. Suddenly all four creatures compressed, inhaled, and leapt into the air. They were gone in a moment, tumbling and twisting toward the horizon, and I kicked my 'cone into a fast and furious pursuit.

Five minutes into the chase, however, a chime rang to warn me that I was in danger of running out of fuel. I broke off my pursuit and thus saved my pride, for I probably did not have a chance of catching the Flipsticks. I transmitted my coordinates to Orbitstar Control and waited for them to synchronize the descent of a fuel pod and arrange the rendezvous. Two hours later the pod dropped down within a kilometer of my position.

FOREST SLIDER AND GULPER

Darwin IV's many small pocket-forests proved to be our greatest frustration and largest failure. We were grossly unprepared for exploration within these tiny, dense woodlands; our hovercones were far too bulky for us to wend our way through the mazes of vines and tree-trunks. One day, however, I did manage to penetrate a stand of plaque-barks to an unprecedented distance of four kilometers. Once within the emerald confines of the forest, I discovered the magical nature of these pocket biomes. Golden filtered light pierced the shadows, picking out clusters of leaves, patches of bark, or the foliage-carpeted floor. Small, four-winged flyers fluttered in and out of the sunlight, flashing vivid blue against the forest's gloom. Enhancing these and other

PLATE XI. "Three Hook-tailed Flyers burst out of the foliage and startled the Forest Sliders."

Forest Sliders seem genuinely unperturbed by the loss of their hind limbs. In fact, I noticed an increase in mobility once the legs were shed. While the body may appear ponderous, it is actually lightweight and can be lifted from the ground to execute rapid turns.

images were the delicate xylophone tones of thousands of striker-nuts, the bell-like seeds of the plaque-bark tree. Each of these is formed with two small bark strikers that beat upon its shell, eventually loosening the nut and sending it to the forest floor. The sound of these nuts is like some beautiful arboreal symphony.

I decided to follow a small stream, reasoning that the foliage would be less dense above it. I also felt that my chances were good of encountering creatures on the rocky banks. As I guided my 'cone deeper into the forest, I was rewarded with the sight of two creatures shambling to the waterside. I "parked" the 'cone and watched as the larger of the pair sniffed the air with its purple, hyperextended oral tubes. The animal seemed aware of me, and yet, as with so many of Darwin IV's creatures, ignored me totally. This behavior, in which of course any naturalist would delight, is a result of the animals' inexperience with outsiders. Pleased by this indifference, I settled down to observe this pair of Forest Sliders, as I came to call them. I speculated that this was a parent and its offspring, and noticed that between them there was a discrepancy both in size and in the number of limbs. The parent possessed only two

legs and a skid, but when it turned I noticed a dangling, wrinkled flap of tissue where one of the juvenile's hind legs was to be found. This apparent deformity held my interest even as a trio of Hook-tailed Flyers burst out of the foliage overhead and startled the Forest Sliders. The parent lurched backward into a tree, scraping the "deformed" leg completely off. Unperturbed by its loss, the animal shook itself and headed back to the water. Amazed to see that there was no wound, I concluded that this growth had been the neotonous remains of a limb used during the creature's early life, before it gained the control of its pronged pelvic skid.

The three Hook-tails dropped to a sun-dappled branch, hooked it, and dangled inverted, folding their leathery wings around themselves. On the bank below, the juvenile Forest Slider hobbled after its parent, which was drinking copiously midway out in the stream. Wet sides heaving as it sucked down water, the larger Slider began to emit warning *pings* as its child approached the slick rocks of the bank. Warned, the child went no further. After a quarter of an hour, they both disappeared into the forest's gloom.

I took my 'cone out of "park" and slowly continued my journey, hovering seven meters above the stream. Branches and vines whipped across the glass, leaving pollen in a sticky, yel-

lowish filigree. The screen-clean spray did little to improve viewing conditions, which left me no choice but to switch to remote video.

As I debated whether I should press on, I heard a strange ululating cry which seemed to be a true vocalization rather than the sonar calls to which I had become accustomed. I was intrigued, and resolved to continue my journey to find its source.

PLATE XII. "The silence was broken by the same wailing cry I had heard upstream."

As I floated along the heavily overgrown banks, watching the underbrush moving with the passings of furtive, unseen creatures, I could see luminous biolights fractured by twigs into strange abstract patterns. I passed a stand of short, glowing stalks with alternating black and red stripes that pulsed rhythmically; they were, in turn, surrounded by a moving carpet of tiny blue lights that, on closer inspection, belonged to a huge colony of nearly transparent Ghost Bracken-hoppers. They seemed to me a phantom army in a dark sylvan kingdom; there were hundreds of them circling the stalks, which they eventually cut down and carried off into the green darkness. Each stalk still glowed as it was borne away, a diminishing red effulgence in a river of blue creatures.

I continued downstream, pausing at intervals to peer into the murky forest, until I arrived at a shadowy, tree-circled clearing. There, lying still amidst the leaves and detritus of the surrounding plaque-barks, was a large, bloated organism. It was about three meters high and fifteen long, the bulk of its length composed of a thick, intestine-shaped tail that lay curled on the ground. Above and behind the creature's distended, yawning mouth, a pair of shrunken winglets beat the still forest air in an almost comical manner. The entire creature was an unlovely shade of yellow-green, translucent in the mouth

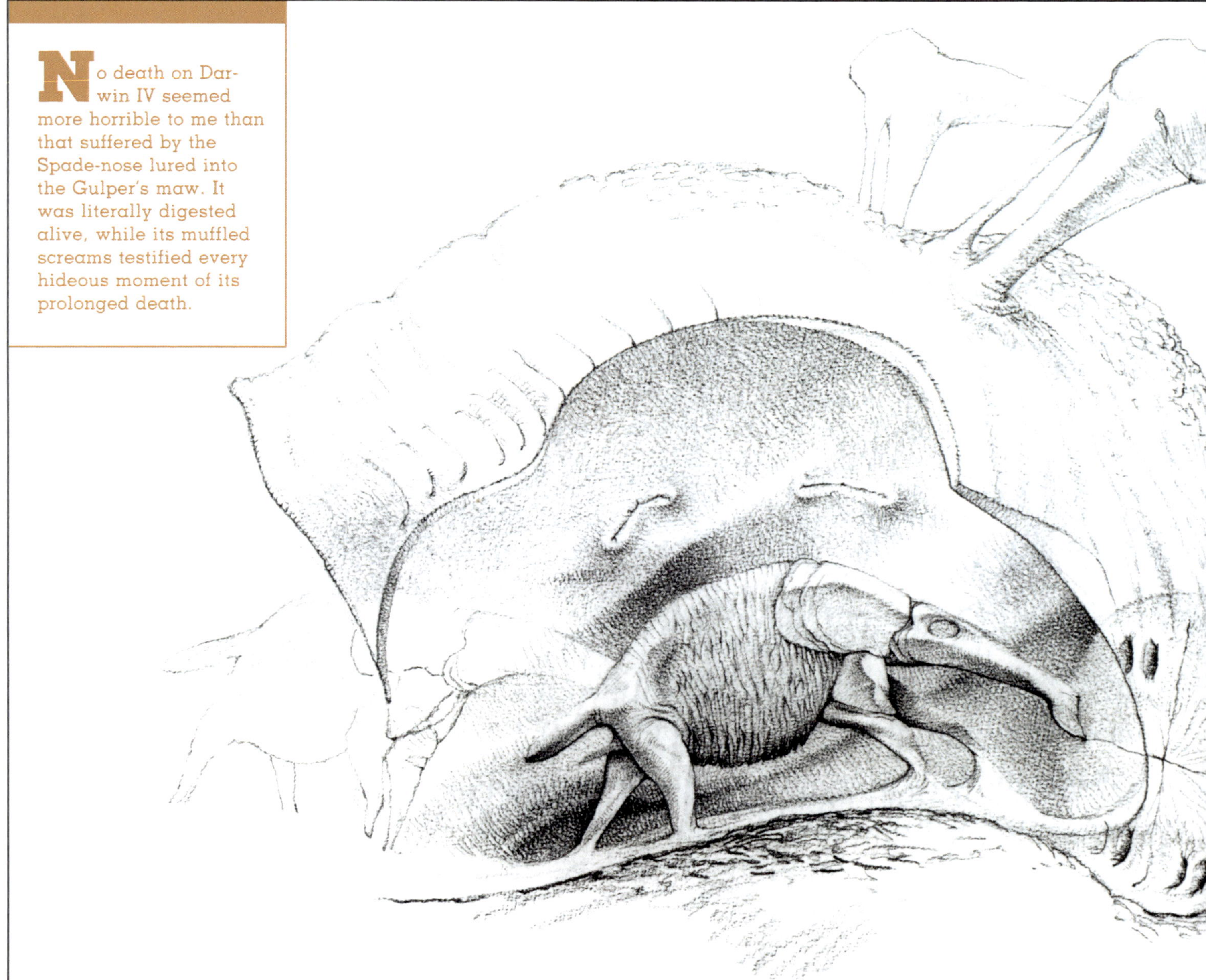

No death on Darwin IV seemed more horrible to me than that suffered by the Spade-nose lured into the Gulper's maw. It was literally digested alive, while its muffled screams testified every hideous moment of its prolonged death.

cavity, where the dappled light touched its wrinkled skin.

While I observed it, the creature roused itself with a series of rippling shudders that shook fallen twigs and leaves from its back; the silence was broken by the same wailing cry I had heard upstream. It seemed that a series of nostril-like holes inside the creature's oral cavity produced the strange keening, for even as I watched they puckered, drawing in air, and burst forth with their incongruous lament. Along with the cry, a fine cloud of pungent gas was exhaled to drift through the trees.

In a manner of minutes, either the cry or the scented air, or both, had attracted a blue-headed Spade-nose, a small barrel-bodied creature that came snuffling and *pinging* to within a meter of the prone organism. This latter barely moved; only the barely perceptible expansion and contraction of its sides betrayed the fact that

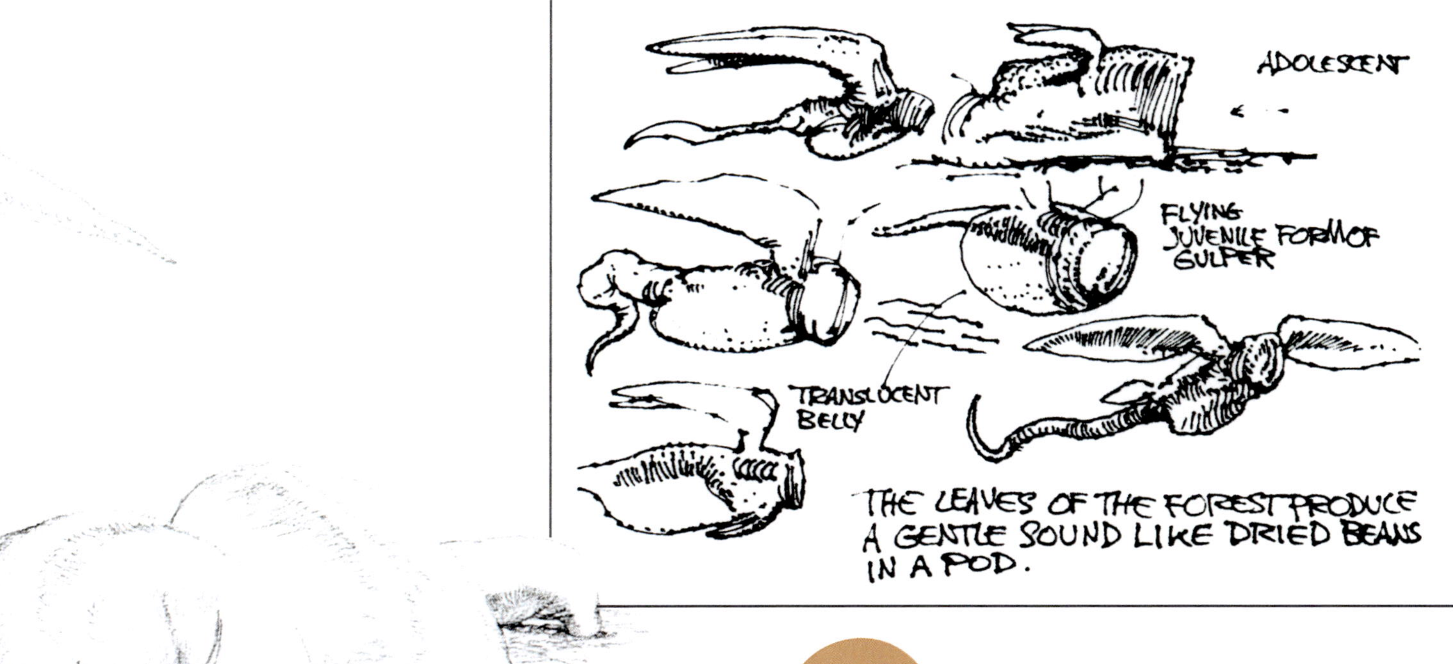

it was alive. The small mouthlets silently puffed out a thin stream of gas that enveloped the Spade-nose — which, without further deliberation, marched directly into the open maw!

Within seconds its feet were stuck to the floor, trapped in some glutinous secretion. As I watched the small beast struggle, its captor's mouth snapped slowly shut. I could discern two sounds from within: the pathetic, muffled *ping-ings* of the frantic Spade-nose, and the gurgling of digestive fluids. Soon both sounds ceased, and the forest surrounding the beast I decided to call the Gulper was again silent — except for the incongruous bell-like tones of the striker-nuts.

Perhaps affected by this brief drama, I was beginning to feel claustrophobic within the dark, tangled confines of the woods. I felt a growing desire to be in the open, so at the next relatively open area I began to ascend slowly through the branches. When I broke through the leafy forest canopy, I was greeted by a strange vista of buoyant green bubbles, each tethered like a child's balloon to the crown of a tree. Superimposed against the expanse of leaves, these two-meter-wide bobbing floatballs, as we came to call them, gleamed in the afternoon light. I remain to this day uncertain if they are plant or animal, or if they might be some kind of tree parasite or spore sac. My readings indicated that they are filled with some kind of light gas, the composition of which remains a mystery.

As I floated free above the forest a *pinging* flight of Hook-tails rose noisily from the trees below and skimmed away toward the open grasslands. Not having any immediate destination, and feeling relieved to be out of the pocket-forest, I swung my 'cone around and followed them until they were lost in the purple dusk.

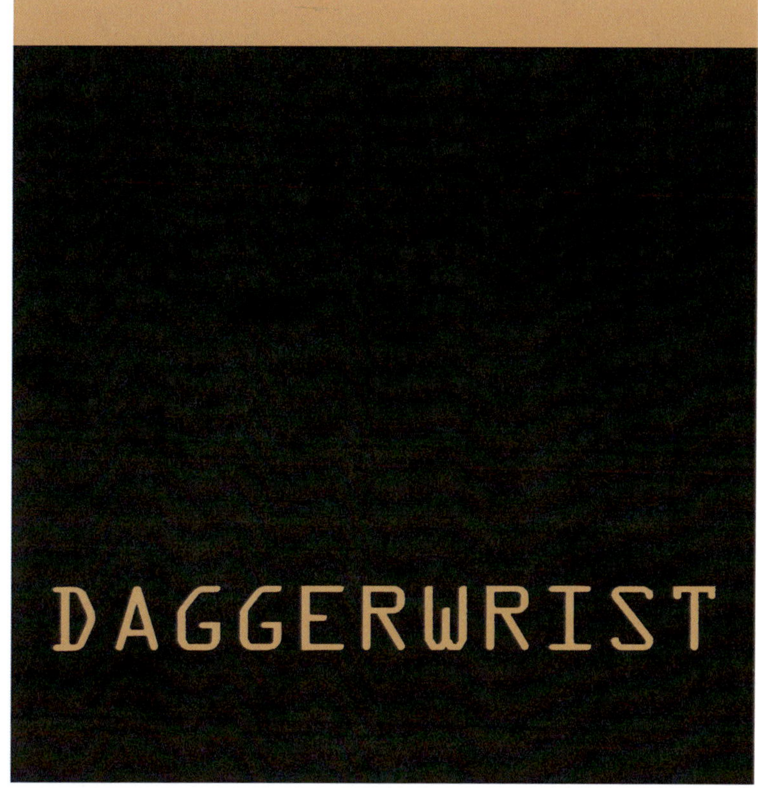

DAGGERWRIST

The most overtly social creature I encountered on Darwin IV was the arboreal Daggerwrist. As these are denizens of the upper treetops, I discovered their presence only by chance.

One morning, tiring of the plains' flatness, I set my navigational grid for one of the largest pocket-forests that the Expedition had found and surveyed. It was a relatively short distance from the Planum Pytheas where I had been sketching, and by noon I was hovering some ten meters above the forest's canopy. As I weaved my way between the strange, bubble-like Floatballs that hung above the trees, I noticed a creature below, partially hidden in the leaves. It was motionless, and had it not been for the breeze that riffled through the treetops,

PLATE XIII. "Each creature began to hone its daggers on the rough bark."

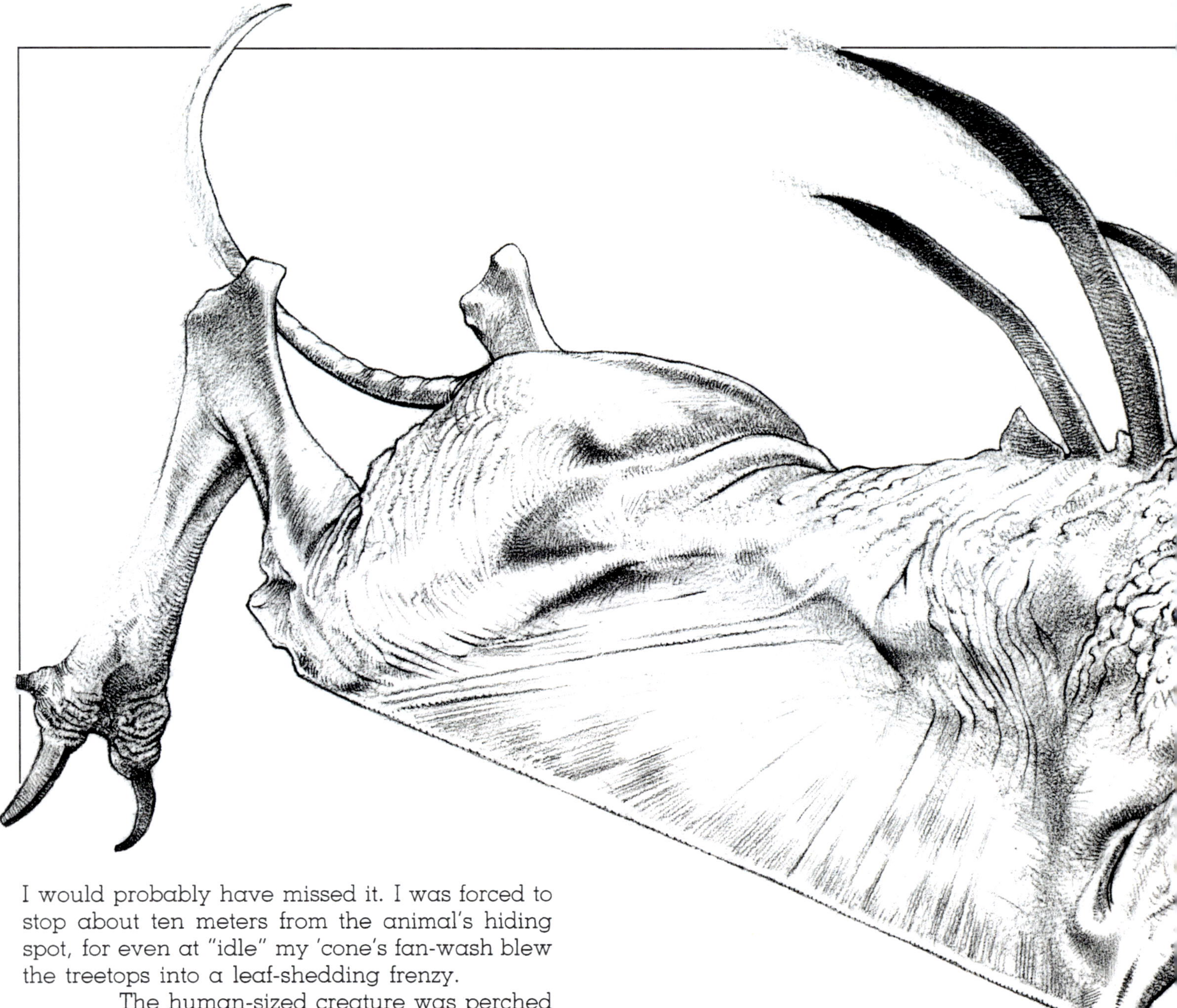

I would probably have missed it. I was forced to stop about ten meters from the animal's hiding spot, for even at "idle" my 'cone's fan-wash blew the treetops into a leaf-shedding frenzy.

The human-sized creature was perched rigidly on a thick branch with its two dagger-terminated arms held out before it in a menacing state of readiness. It was obvious that the Dagger-wrist (for so I named it) had sensed my presence and instinctively assumed this defensive threat posture. It accompanied this fierce stance with an intermittent and somewhat raucous *pinging* which, on an impulse, I decided to record and play back on the external speakers. This experiment garnered instant and startling results.

ithout hesitating, the Daggerwrist attacked me! Extending its long arms to expose a substantial gliding membrane, and propelled by its powerful hind legs, it leapt straight for me and covered the ten meters between us in one shocking bound. Striking the surface of the 'cone, it hung by its two curved

While there are many parachuting herbivores in Darwin IV's forests, the Daggerwrist is the only gliding predator known to date. Any injury to the glide-membrane is serious, and large tears result in an inability to hunt and, thus, survive.

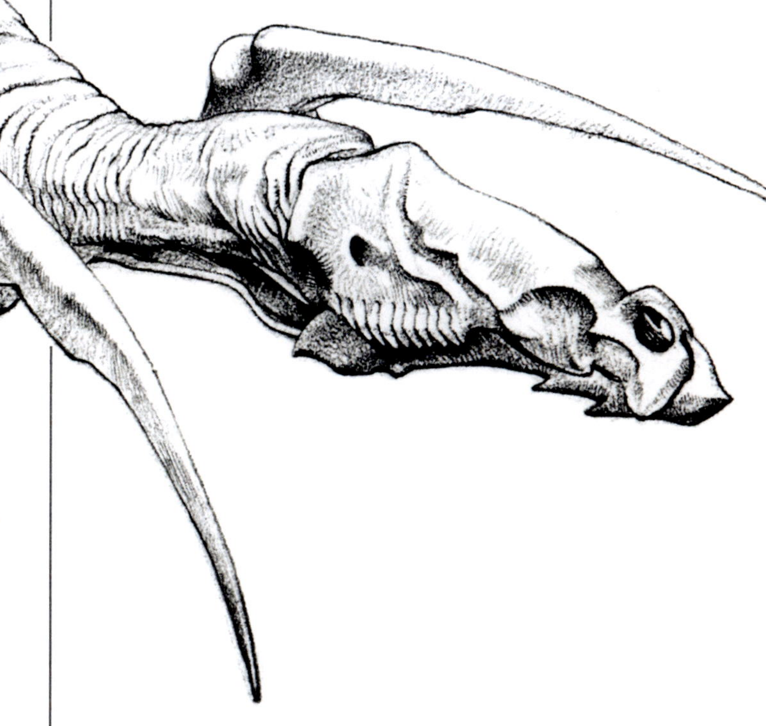

and horny daggers: somehow it had managed to hook them into the fifteen-centimeter-wide channel that accommodated the 'cone's revolving long-range antenna. I could see its hind legs clawing and scrabbling at the optical blisters, trying to gain a foothold to pull itself up, to better its attack on me. I could not help but shiver at the blind anger of the animal as it dangled in the air above the trees. I could not help but wonder what it thought it had attacked.

Though I knew I did not have much time, I took the opportunity to study the Daggerwrist close up. It was a fierce-looking beast with sinewy muscles that covered its two-meter-long body from its neck to its whipping tail. Great purple veins bulged on its distended belly, filled (I was sure) with its last huge meal.

As it struggled, its bony head came into view and I realized that what had appeared to be a complete skull with an attached jaw was, in reality, two separate and unattached pieces. The "cranium" obviously housed the brain and the well-developed sonar projector-receiver. The hooked "jaw" was connected directly to the creature's breast by three thick muscle-covered tubes. For brief instants this pseudo-jaw would separate from the "cranium" and writhe and probe about in a snake-like manner. It would seem that this was the closest any creature on Darwin came to actually possessing a working jaw: for I could see that when the two pieces did come together, a razor-sharp, scissors-like interface was created.

The Daggerwrist gave no indication of loosening its grip on my 'cone, and since I could not hover around all day with an enraged animal clinging to my vehicle, I decided to liberate myself. This was actually an easier task than it might appear. I hit the switch to activate the radio's signal finder, and as the long antenna swung around in its track it hit the points of the animal's twin daggers. The Daggerwrist's grip was loosened, and as it fell it opened its gliding membranes, arched its back and flipped over backward to parachute to the foliage below.

This display of aerobatics was even more impressive than the attacking leap. I decided to try to keep up with the agile creature as best as I could. I found this to be a greater challenge than I had first envisioned as the Daggerwrist descended and ascended through the trees. In addition, the numerous translucent floatballs, which bobbed on the breeze above the trees, were unpredictable in their movement and made my passage more difficult. I was on numerous occasions sure that I had lost the Daggerwrist in the leaves, but fortunately, the plaque-bark's vegetation is somewhat sparser in the upper canopy; and since I almost never lost IR contact with the animal, I somehow managed to keep up.

Periodically, the fleeing Daggerwrist would stop and pivot on a branch and, amidst a flurry of leaves, assume its threat posture in a vain attempt to shake me off its trail. I was not that easily discouraged, however, and eventually we came to an open area that surrounded a massive, hollowed plaque-bark. Here, in exactly the same threat posture, were a dozen or more Daggerwrists perched on branches that de-

scended into the darkness of the forest's lower levels. I could just barely discern their red biolights in the gloom of the forest floor some thirty meters below.

I "parked" the 'cone and watched as the Daggerwrists climbed with incredible rapidity to the uppermost branches. Some used their hooked "hands" to swing from branch to branch, while others hammered them into the trunks to climb as if with pitons. Their climbing abilities were truly as-tonishing. Within a minute they had encircled me at a respectful distance, careful to avoid my craft's fan-wash. My earlier companion, which I had named Scar-chest for the tracery of thin scars that crossed its breast, had regained some of its composure. It methodically *pinged* at me, probing with its sonar as it cocked its head to and fro. I imagined it felt more secure in its own territory surrounded by its compatriots.

I wanted to spend some time observing the Daggerwrists, so I called up to the Orbitstar for clearance. This was granted, with the usual warnings and provisos regarding physical contact. (I found these fairly amusing in light of my

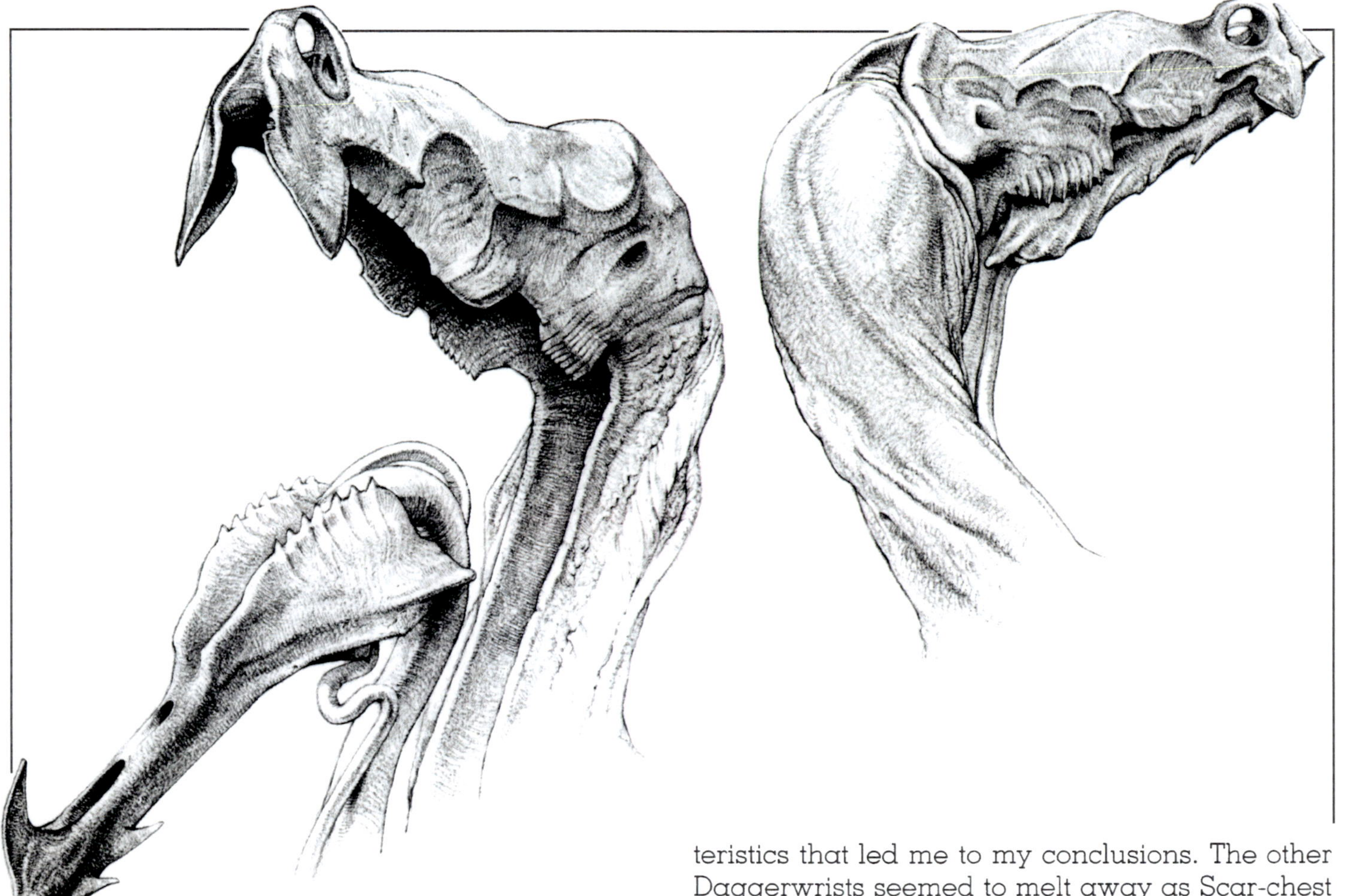

warm introduction to the species. I could not be blamed if some of my subjects were as eager to meet me as I was to meet them!)

The Daggerwrist troupe must have sat studying me for the greater part of an hour before making any significant moves. Then, as I might have expected, Scar-chest was the first to lose interest in me, descending from its perch to disappear into the foliage. I had, by then, guessed that it was the dominant animal. The creature was larger than most of its companions and had appeared to be older, but it was not just these physical charac-

teristics that led me to my conclusions. The other Daggerwrists seemed to melt away as Scar-chest approached, and I began to wonder why this single animal held such sway over them.

With Scar-chest's departure, the troupe relaxed and resumed what I presumed was its normal activities. Each creature began to hone its daggers on the rough bark, producing a couple of harsh scraping sounds. I named a few more individuals for quite obvious physical characteristics in evidence—Bent-tail, Broken-dagger, Split-spine, Twisted-neck, and so forth.

As I was naming them I began to realize that nearly every individual showed some degree of physical damage. I found it hard to believe that so many injuries were the results of falls, especially after I had seen the creatures' ease in the branches. In addition, many of the scars seemed to be from punctures and slices. All this led me to theorize that the Daggerwrists were a fairly aggressive breed and that their wounds were the results of ritualistic combat. At that moment I had no idea that I was about to witness just such a combat.

Arrayed as they were in the branches circling their huge, lightning-blasted tree-home, the Daggerwrists were easily able to guard against unwanted visitors. Any twig that snapped brought the high-strung creatures to attention; any unfamiliar *pings* sent them into defensive threat postures. These interruptions were seldom the result of anything truly threatening, and it took very little time for the troupe to resume its activities.

About two hours after my arrival I picked up the *pings* of a single Daggerwrist as it approached the nest-tree. By this time many of the animals had withdrawn into the hollowed trunk of the ancient plaque-bark and were curled up resting. As the area was swept by the newcomer's sonar, they poked their heads out, inquiringly, from the many meter-wide holes in the trunk. Some climbed out and settled into the branches, while others continued to doze. Scar-chest emerged from the trunk and climbed to a high position to survey the entire leafy amphi-

theatre around the tree. The powerful animal seemed almost expectant as it began to hone its long daggers.

Moments later the approaching Daggerwrist came into view and, hesitating at the edge of the clearing, sat down upon a gnarled tree limb. It was as large as Scar-chest. Its head had a long notch cut into it, obviously the result of some old combat. It, too, began to noisily sharpen its daggers.

Scar-chest appeared to grow more agitated as some of the other Daggerwrists such as Bent-tail and Rough-back came out to watch. The newcomer (which I named Cleft-head) raised itself upon its hindlegs, opened its membranes and sprang to a branch closer to Scar-chest. This move was too much for my old friend.

Scar-chest emitted a shrill *ping* and, with daggers extended, dove down upon the upraised torso of its opponent, knocking Cleft-head to a lower branch. I must have missed the actual penetration of the daggers, for as the creatures separated, I was surprised to see two small geysers of arterial blood spewing from both sides of Cleft-head's neck.

Scar-chest was already poised for a second attack. Cleft-head was twisting its head in agony, slipping downward from branch to branch. Scar-chest gauged its next attack and hurled itself upon its staggering opponent. But instead of going for the throat, this time the animal sank its daggers deep into Cleft-head's blood-slicked sides and held on. Almost simultaneously it used both "jaws" to tear out an ugly, ragged hole under its victim's arm. Scar-chest then inserted and anchored its hooked feeding jaw and began to pump digestive fluids into the dying Daggerwrist's chest-cavity.

For the next twenty minutes, accompanied by the frenzied *pinging* and leaping of the Daggerwrist troupe, Scar-chest proceeded to noisily suck the liquified insides out of its victim. The other animals seemed disturbed by this cannibalistic display, making tentative mock attacks on the feeding Daggerwrist. Each attack, however, was rebuffed by Scar-chest who emitted a string of ominous, low frequency *pings*.

As this scene unfolded, I realized that there might be nothing unusual about this form of feeding for Daggerwrists. I was not familiar enough with these creatures to judge. My only clue that this might be aberrant behavior was the hostile manner in which the troupe dealt with and maddened Scar-chest.

Later that day, though, I did observe that the other Daggerwrists did not eat their own kind, but preferred a diet of Trunk-suckers — small plump gliders that soared from tree to tree, attaching themselves with a powerful suction organ. Once attached to a trunk, the Trunk-suckers were apparently impossible for the Daggerwrists to remove. It was necessary for the hunters to hook them on the wing, using their honed wrists or lower jaws, a feat which challenged both species' aerobatic survival skills.

I was left with the impression that Scar-chest's behavior was aberrant. I formulated a few possible explanations, among them that the creature was deranged, that there was some environmental reason for its needs, or that it was the result of its elevated status among its fellows. Whatever the cause, the troupe seemed uncomfortable with the gruesome result.

I watched the Daggerwrists for a few days, sketching them in various attitudes of repose and conflict. They were an energetic species with interesting habits. I was also intrigued by them on a purely aesthetic level; their grotesque appearance struck some responsive chord within me, and I found myself sketching them even when they were not at hand.

On the fourth day of my Daggerwrist watch, an extraordinary event took place. I was

PLATE XIV. *"It was necessary for the hunters to hook them on the wing."*

Daggerwrists are extremely active animals and can assume both quadrupedal as well as bipedal stances. They frequently use their daggers to hang and swing from branches.

following the troupe as it headed for a flock of Trunk-suckers on the outskirts of the forest. Again I marveled at their supreme confidence in the forest as they swung from bough to bough, then glided through the air between the trees. Nothing impeded their progress and they covered the kilometer to their goal in five minutes, which was quite remarkable considering the density of the foliage.

Scar-chest, who led the pack, indicated (with a signal to which I had grown accustomed) that the prey was near. The troupe gathered silently in a circle around the Trunk-sucker's roost-tree in preparation for their ambush. It would be each individual Daggerwrist for itself, with little or no team effort beyond the first surprise assault.

I suspected that Scar-chest's blood-lust was up; the creature had not eaten in the four days since its cannibalistic episode. Oddly, its belly seemed to still be digesting that last meal, for it still protruded grotesquely. Upon reflection, I realized that the volume of liquid Scar-chest had ingested at that meal must have been at least three times what the other Daggerwrists were accustomed to take in a day.

As Bent-tail stalked up alongside Scar-chest, I could sense a sudden shift in the latter's attitude. The other Daggerwrist's proximity had apparently triggered the same uncontrollable craving that had proven to be Cleft-head's undoing. In an unbelievably fast move, Scar-chest scimitared off Bent-tail's head, leaving only the lower jaw attached to the trunk. The creature's headless body spasmed once and pitched forward, plunging through the snapping branches as it went down. Scar-chest was poised to follow, presumably to feed again, when suddenly the Trunk-suckers took to the air in a noisy flurry of frightened bodies and wings. The element of surprise was gone, the ambush was spoiled, and the Daggerwrists turned their attention toward Scar-chest.

In the confusion caused by the fleeing Trunk-suckers, Scar-chest's sonar had been effectively jammed. The animal had no idea where its new victim's body had landed. As it grew more frustrated, it began to rock in a frenzy of anger on the branch.

The Daggerwrist troupe had, by now, closed in a tight circle around Scar-chest. For a moment they were still — and then, as if with one mind, they began to rain lethal blows upon the enraged animal, gradually turning it on its back in the process. Spread-eagled and dying, the Daggerwrist began to convulse. I could barely watch what appeared to be the beginning of a protracted death scene; though I felt that a certain justice had been dealt, the creature's agonies were not a pleasant sight. The troupe, I thought, must be deriving some vengeful satisfaction from its work. I could not have been more incorrect.

A reddish Daggerwrist, one I called Long-dagger, leaped onto the branch and climbed to a position directly over the dying beast. With almost surgical precision, it slit Scar-chest's distended belly from crotch to breastbone. I nearly gagged; but then, to my utter astonishment, out popped a blood-soaked infant Daggerwrist. It was shaky and uncertain, but clearly alive and well. It hopped upon the waiting back of Long-dagger, dug its soft unformed daggers into the rugose skin, and clung with all its might as the Daggerwrists turned and disappeared into the forest.

I was so shocked that I could not follow. Instead, I decided to remain where I was, hovering above the forest, contemplating the unpredictability of it all. I had never even considered the possibility that Scar-chest's cannibalistic behavior was the result of pregnancy. As I hung above the treetops I watched the gentle winds riffling through the foliage. The late afternoon sunslight burnished the sea of leaves below me to a coppery luster.

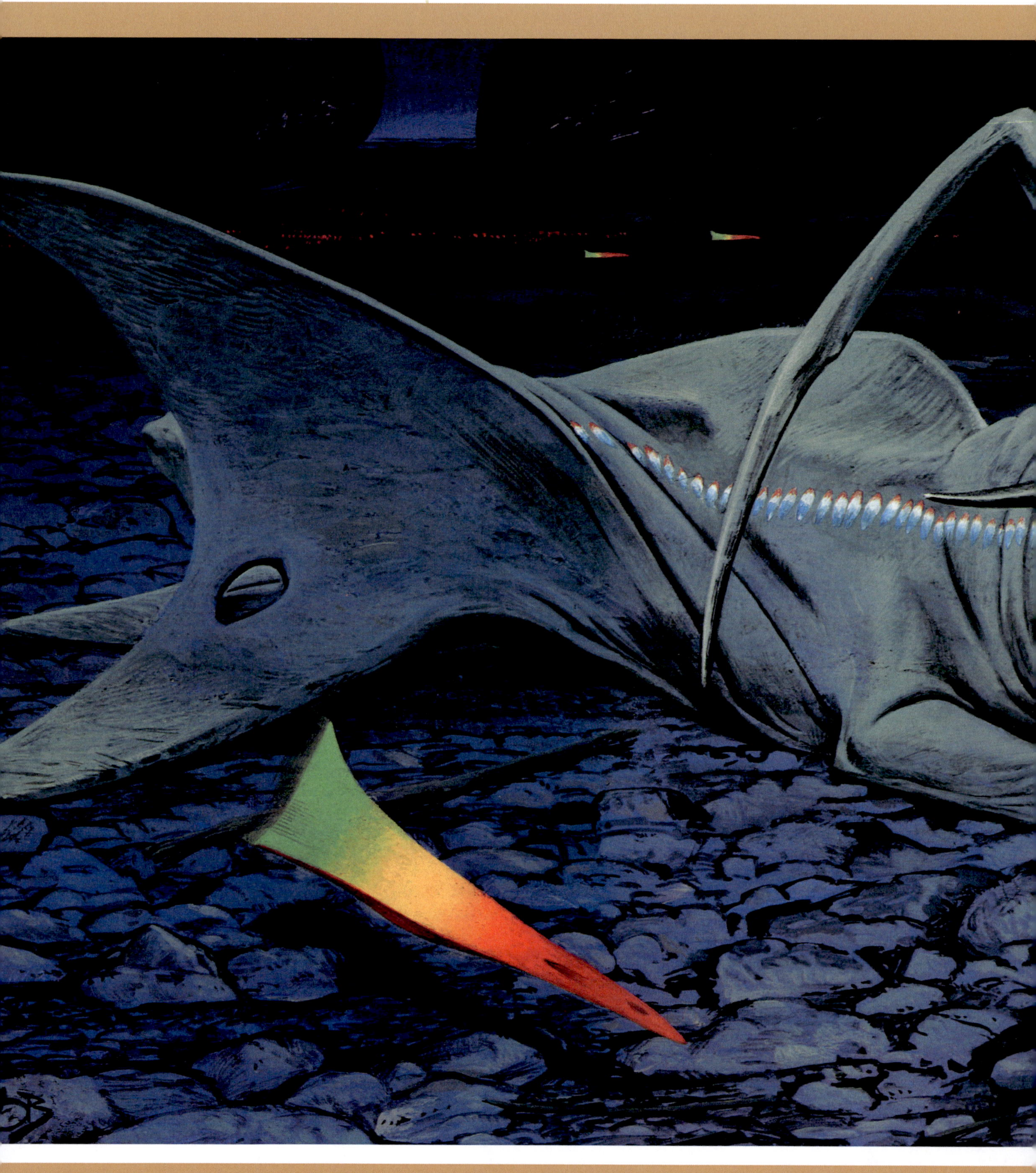

PLATE XV. "The arm is so quick that it virtually disappears when striking."

This delicate predator, with its elegant airfoil body and streamlined legs, snaps up its main prey, the Jetdarter, with amazing ease. Finned Snappers live around the edges of Darwin IV's pocket-forests, where Jetdarter hives are to be readily found. They are cooperative predators, often hunting in pods of six or eight individuals.

The Finned Snapper is capable of impaling up to half a dozen flyers on its single, jointed hunting arm. This arm, which extends to about two meters, is so quick that it virtually disappears when it is striking. It is also rather dextrous; I watched one Snapper spend about ten minutes working a fallen 'Darter out of a seemingly inaccessible crevice.

Air is drawn in through the Finned Snapper's grille-like frontal intake and forced out under high pressure through vents under the trailing edge of its fins and tail.

The grille-like frontal region of the Finned Snapper's head serves to channel air (as well as scent) into the finned portions of the animal's torso; it is then forced through small escape holes on the trailing edges of the fins, enabling the creature to skim so lightly when it runs that, at times, I wondered if its feet actually touched the ground.

On an evening early in my explorations, I had an unfortunate mishap with a Snapper. It was pursuing several 'Darters across a stretch of dried riverbed near Lacus Hedin toward four polyhedral Jetdarter nests. I followed, but as I caught up I overshot my goal, and in my haste to brake created a fan-wash that sent the Snapper tumbling. Its light body was blown a dozen meters or more and I knew that it had to have sustained some sort of injury.

When I finally swung around, I realized that the situation was worse than I had feared. The Finned Snapper had broken one of its lightweight legs and was hobbling around miserably, *pinging* with what I was certain was pain. My fan-wash had also disintegrated one of the nests and a stream of angry Jetdarters was harassing the crippled Snapper, diving and pecking at it.

The creature grew more and more distraught, its pain and terror clear to see. I watched in horror as it sank down and collapsed. I hovered, aware of my part in this tragedy. No amount of wishing on my part, however, could make the creature regain its feet, and I am sorry to say that it soon expired. Perhaps it had sustained some sort of internal injury as well. My only hope is that the Snapper was old or infirm and that I did no more than speed up its demise. I left the area burdened with an enormous sense of guilt.

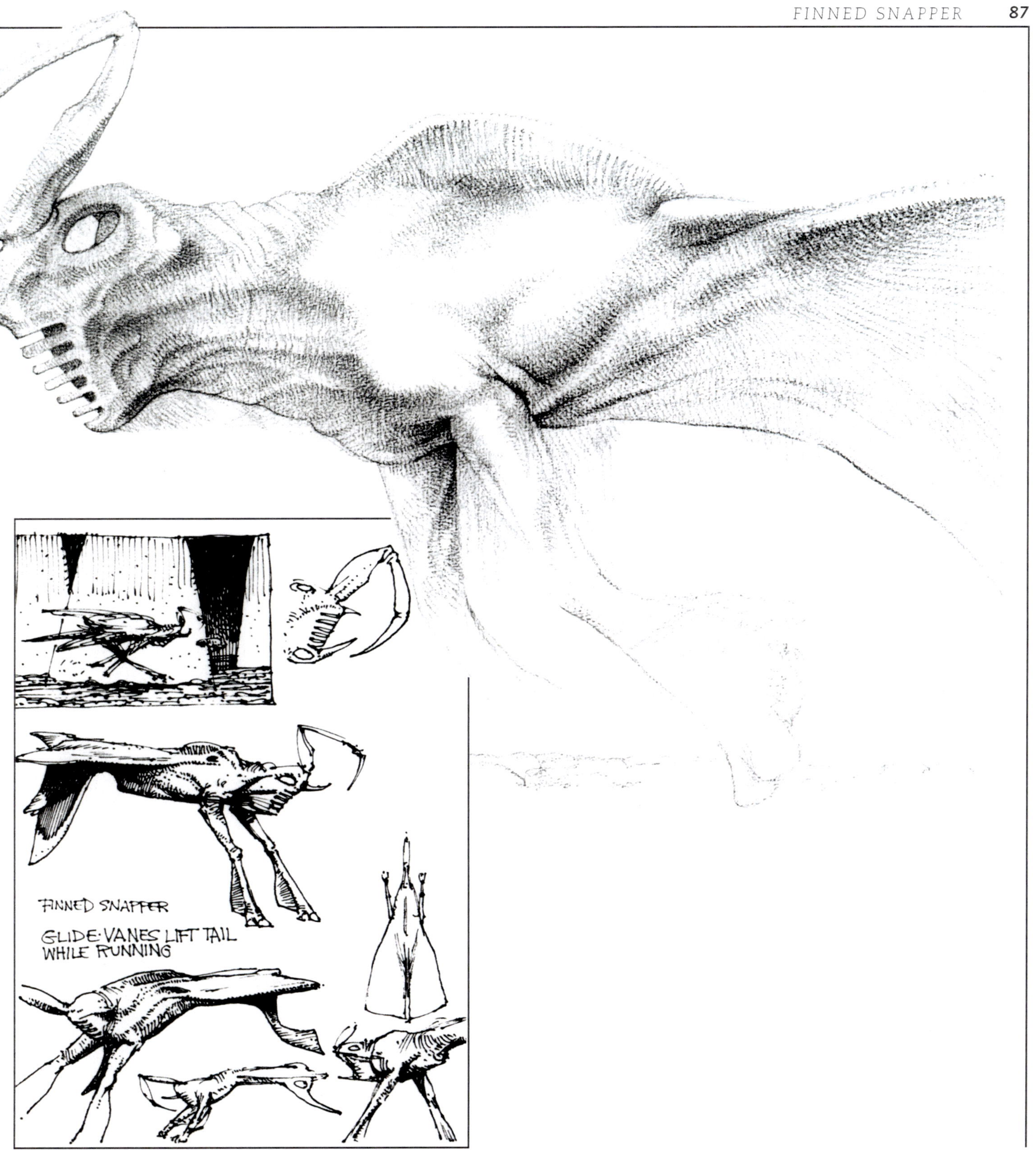
FINNED SNAPPER
GLIDE-VANES LIFT TAIL
WHILE RUNNING

PLATE XVI. A storm over the "sea."

THE AMOEBIC SEA
AND
LITTORAL ZONE

PLATE XVII. "Here was a rare moment of tenderness on a world where fierceness seemed the rule."

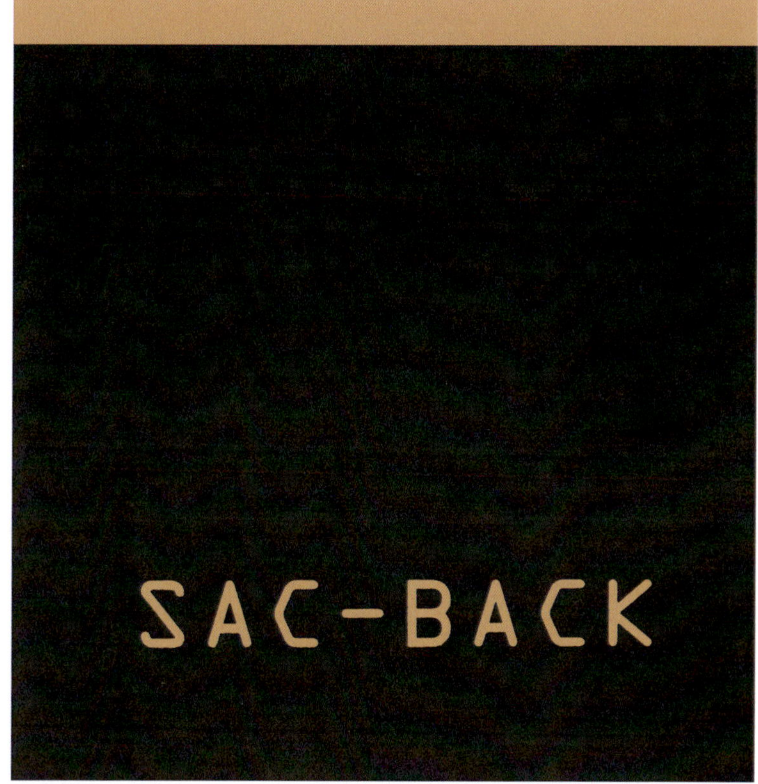

One day, close to the middle of my stay on Darwin IV, I received a request from Orbitstar Control to make an attempt at exploring the huge planetary surface feature known as the Amoebic Sea. At the time it was virgin territory; no other Expedition member had come this far north. My orders (if that is what one would call the politely worded request) were to head in a northerly direction until I reached the "sea's" edge and proceed directly into the heart of it. There was a certain note of urgency in the request; later I found out that the Yma had a particular interest in a huge creature photographed by their satellite some fifteen years earlier.

I ate my lunch to Prokofiev's Fifth, re-reading my "orders" and eagerly anticipat-

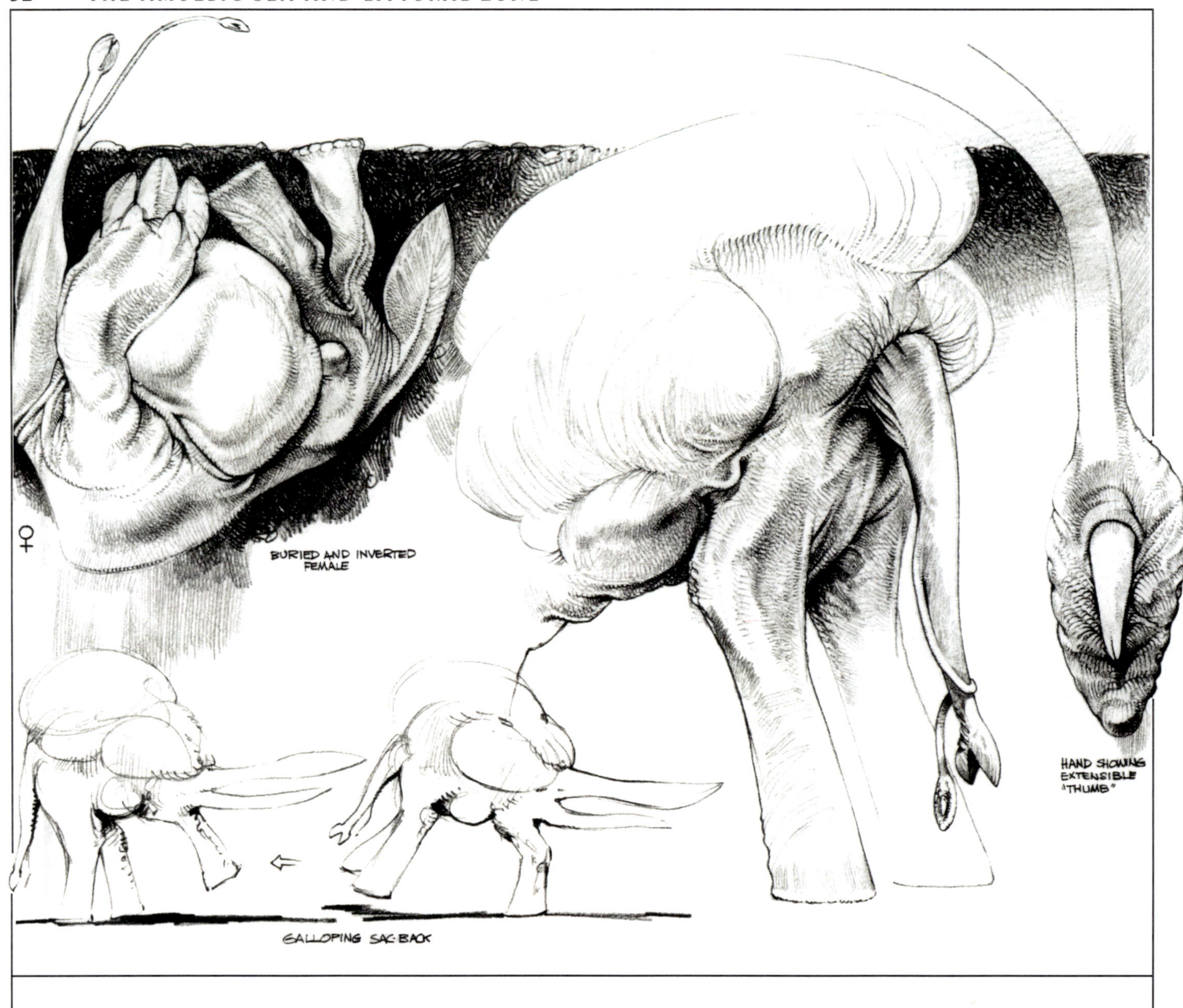

ing the change of scenery. The badlands I had been exploring were growing monotonous; at times, had not my navigational computer confirmed otherwise, I would have sworn I was traveling in circles.

Finishing lunch, I switched on the navigational grid and fed in my new destination. In moments the Yzar turbo-fan was whisking me across the desert at a fine pace. The striated mesas gave way to grasslands, which segued into the region immediately surrounding the "sea."

As luck would have it, just as I reached the raised edge of the "sea," something odd caught my attention. I slowed to a standstill and hovered about ten meters from the surface.

Below me, protruding from the level surface of the beach, were half a dozen bud-like forms. They were meter-high, semirigid stalks surmounted by horny, beak-like "mouths," each of which opened at regular intervals to exhale a cloud of steamy air. Adjacent to each stalk was a thinner, more flexible, tentacle, which writhed in constant motion. Each tentacle was terminated by a broad, flattened "hand" which I thought looked quite dextrous.

My aesthetic sense was sparked by the surreality of the scene and, with frequent glances at my canopy chronometer, I began to sketch. As I drew, I wondered: what were these creatures like below ground level? I put down my pencil and tried my IR scanner on the buried enigmas. Unfortunately, it had rained recently; the creatures were submerged in moist, cool soil and their heat images were indistinct on my screen.

I watched the stalks for two hours, hoping that some clue to their complete forms might be revealed. The stalks twitched, the mouths opened, the arms occasionally flicked some small, unwary creature into the mouths—and that was all.

Disappointed, I prepared to continue my journey into the "sea." Luck was with me, however, for just as I was about to punch in my course, I heard a low frequency *pinging*. I swiveled and saw something heading along the beach toward me. It was a bulky, red creature with a stalk, mouth, and tentacle similar to those I had been sketching for the past two hours. I

named the beast Sac-back, for it carried on its broad back a large transparent sac filled with colorless fluid. With each lumbering step this sac wobbled and the small, beaky mouth puffed out vapor. The creature seemed to be laboring under its heavy burden.

I watched, fascinated, as this ungainly animal slowly humped itself over to a stalk and settled above it. The great beast aligned its stalk with the one beneath it and reached out. With the most sensitive caresses, the two "hands" touched as if in greeting, stroked and then clasped each other. I was moved. Here was a rare moment of tenderness on a world where fierceness seemed the rule. I thought of my wife, unimaginably distant. How I missed her!

After the hands clasped, the Sac-back repositioned itself so that its beak was positioned over the stalk's. When this alignment was achieved, both mouths opened and the large creature poured a stream of clear liquid into the awaiting mouth below. (Later investigation proved this liquid to be broken-down "sea" material.) This took about three minutes. All the while, the Sac-back's emptying dorsal sac rippled in a kind of peristaltic spasm.

When the sac was entirely empty, both

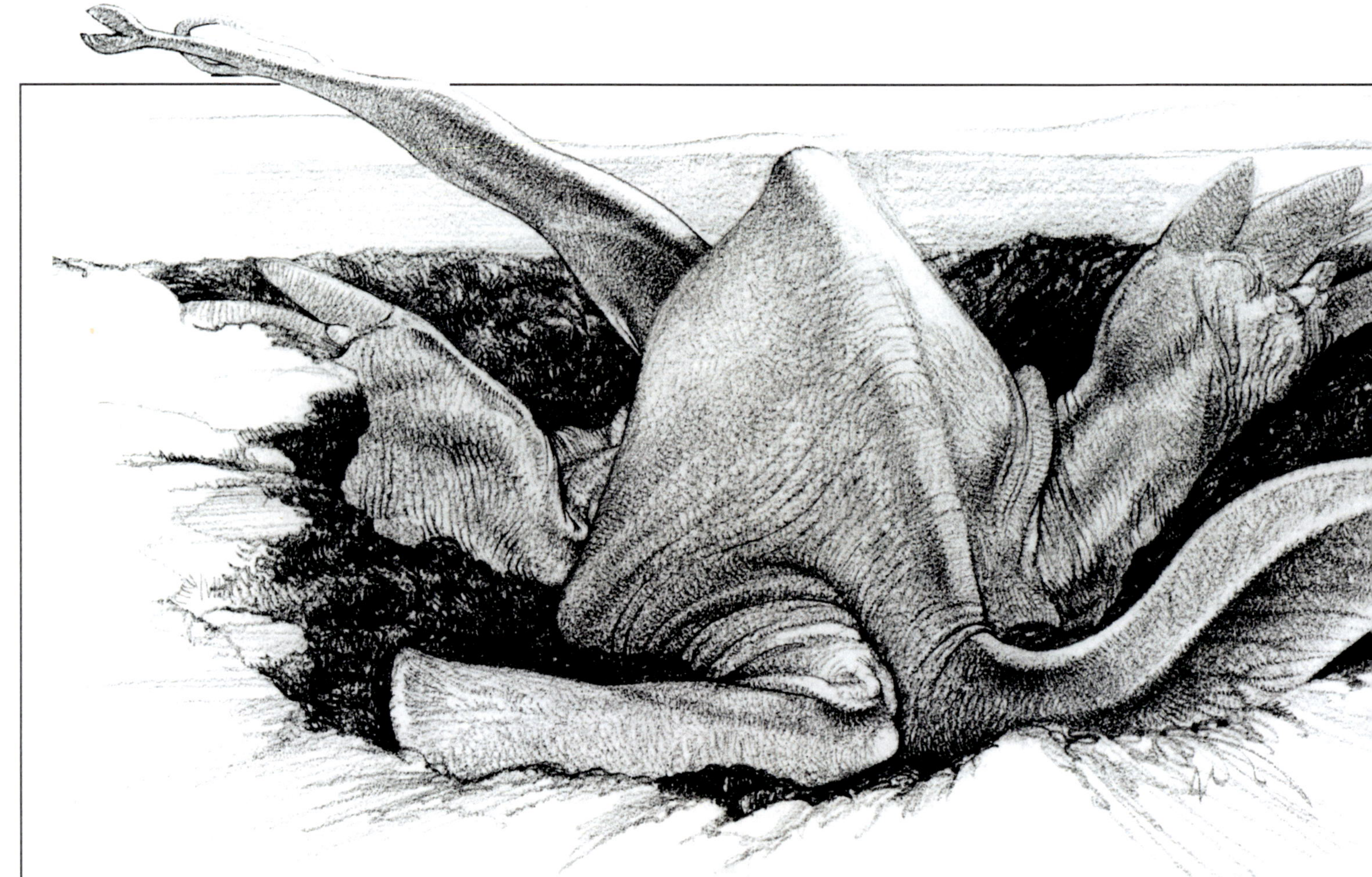

mouths snapped shut in unison. The caressing of the hands began anew and continued for about ten minutes. Then I noticed a movement on the ground directly under the Sac-back's flat tail. A small depression formed, and I thought I could glimpse a glistening-lipped tube within. At this point I concluded that the ambulatory Sac-back was a male, for a large phallus snaked out and probed the circular depression. This organ was wholly different from the standard sexual equipment I had seen on Darwin IV; it was a solid tube instead of the customary unfurling tube possessed by the majority of animals. More importantly, it seemed tangible proof of the existence of two sexes within this species.

In silence the Sac-back mated with its unseen partner. The actual coupling lasted about fifteen minutes, during which time I sketched furiously. I also contacted Orbitstar Control to explain what I was doing and why I was not, at the moment, pressing on into the heart of the "sea." No one in the orbiting vessel above seemed concerned, and I was told to take as long as I needed to complete my observations.

After its efforts, the Sac-back withdrew its flaccid organ and hunkered down, carefully avoiding crushing the protruding stalk. Its wrinkled sides were heaving and it expelled great clouds of vapor from its panting beak. Gradually quieting down, the animal remained motionless for about two hours. I imagined it was dozing. This was, of course, the best opportunity I could have asked for to draw the animal and I took full advantage.

When the creature awoke it got to its feet and, with muscles quivering, stretched. I could almost hear its joints popping back into place. Somewhat predictably, it moved over to the next stalk and over the next half an hour repeated its performance with no variation.

Two hours later, with the sky growing pink as dusk approached, the Sac-back was industriously copulating with a third female. I was not so eager to begin my travels into a strange and unfamiliar biome in darkness, so I settled in to observe through the night.

Over the next six hours the Sac-back mounted the remaining three submerged females. As total darkness descended I saw its biolights come to life with a soft effulgence. As I watched the creature finally wander off into the gloom, I wondered again about the lonely creatures buried in the moist soil. Did they ever emerge or were their entire lives spent underground? And what did they look like?

Answers to these questions would have to wait, for dawn found me hurtling out over the still-unexplored expanse of the colony creature that was Darwin IV's living "sea."

Weeks later, I returned to the site of the Sac-back matings and found, to my delight, that the ground was dry enough to permit accurate readings of what lay beneath the surface. Of the six females, four were pregnant, judging by the strong double readings I got from them. Some unknown calamity had claimed the life of one of the six, and when I looked closer I noticed that its protruding oral stalk was dry and withered.

My readings also gave me an idea of the females' appearance—an impression that was confirmed later by the discovery of a dead female that had been dug out of its home by an enterprising predator. The buried animals were similar to their male counterparts, with some major differences: the females were longer, and had digging flippers instead of pillar-like legs. They were also missing the large sac that so inelegantly graced the males' backs. The flippers apparently allowed the animals to excavate the living graves that they occupied. I tried to imagine the bulky creatures rolling over on their backs after digging out their holes, and covering themselves with dirt; for it is in that position that they remain for most of their lives. As the elements compact the dirt around them, only their inverted oral stalks remain protruding—a heat-radiating chimney that serves as a beacon to the males.

Oddly, in the remaining year and a half of our stay on Darwin IV, these females never gave birth. Our last check showed that all seemed well with their pregnancies, and we could only surmise that their gestation was quite long.

EMPEROR SEA STRIDER

The day after my encounter with the Sac-backs I set out to explore the vast Amoebic Sea, hoping to encounter the creature we had all seen in satellite image 848.28. It hardly seemed likely that such a large creature or its kin could be avoided.

My choice of day to begin this undertaking, as I later realized, could have been better; clouds had been building steadily overnight and by mid-morning it was still relatively dark. With my cabin lamps on, I ran through systems check, set my course on the navigational computer, punched up my HUD (head-up-display) on the angled glass canopy window and took the 'cone out of "park." I was off; below me was the dully shining surface of the Amoebic Sea. It was

PLATE XVIII. "Virtually no force in Nature could affect such a creature."

The Emperor Sea Strider in its nymph stage is not yet bipedal. The lower spur-like growths serve as stabilizers in flying; these gradually disappear as the feet develop into massive support and feeding platforms.

in fact neither amoebic nor a sea: those familiar terms having been applied to lend the comfort of familiarity to something so very alien. Darwin IV's only "sea" is really more a desert in the traditional sense, a place of little precipitation, harsh and inhospitable. Yet life exists in abundance, relegated primarily to the sub-Outer Membrane zone. Beneath the rubbery surface are unthinkable numbers of symbiotic organisms living within the matrix colony, tending in an almost proprietorial manner to its needs. When I peered down I could discern many layers of luminous creatures suspended in the gel, in such a variety of size and shape as to make cataloging them a lifelong endeavor.

An hour after taking the 'cone out of "park," I saw that the shoreline had disappeared behind me and I was deep into Darwin IV's strangest biome. The gel below seemed threatening, a slimy, amorphous entity eager, in my imagination, to enfold me and my small craft into its gelatinous bosom. I began to feel apprehensive, and yet rationally I knew that traveling here was no different than exploring any other region of the planet. My misgivings gradually diminished as I floated on, my 'cone's computer steering deeper into the heart of the "sea" while the HUD displayed a constant stream of data on the canopy. This flow of data was reassuring and distracting as the alien biomass slid in undulating mounds of sameness below. Occasionally a jagged island of volcanic rock would loom in front of me, and as the 'cone maneuvered past it I could see large communities of tiny, lighted creatures sidling around the rock to avoid being seen. Though in the gloom I could not discern their physical shape, I recorded them in infrared for later study. Perhaps they were trying to elude my exhaust or the dense clouds of small, disk-like flyers I encountered every four kilometers or so. I called them Diskflyers, and their dispersal seemed to indicate a territorial pattern, though I am still uncertain as to the actual nature of the territories involved. On one occasion I saw the Diskflyers at rest on the gel's surface, possibly feeding. I can only guess that the four-kilometer-wide territories represent the feeding radius of the odd flyers.

I "parked" for lunch and sent a request for meteorological projections up to the Orbitstar. Conditions had grown worse and I felt that I was going to be in the midst of some very serious weather. I watched the horizon as a ragged line of flickering thunderclouds advanced toward me. My reply came back garbled; to this day I am unsure if this was due to the electricity in the air or to some fault

in the 'cone's system. The Orbitstar's report later indicated that my request had also been distorted. Feeling quite cut off and having no desire to brave the elements, I hastily punched in the reverse course program to take me out of the "sea," and was just hitting the "execute" button when I saw a cloud of Diskflyers swirling around my 'cone. I was distressed to hear a brief grinding sound—and then silence; no steady hum of nuclear-driven rotors, and no indicators on the turbo-fan monitor at my feet. Instead, the 'cone began to plunge downward and the Emergency Systems klaxon went on. Though it seemed like minutes, only split seconds passed before the ES opened the Vertical Descent Brakes. Like the ceramalloy petals of some huge plummeting flower, the VDB successfully broke the fall and I jolted onto the surface of the "sea" much shaken. Luckily, the computer had not initiated the ejection sequence.

After calming myself, I set about transmitting my coordinates and request for assistance up to the Orbitstar. I was well aware that my signal might not be picked up until after the impending storm, and so, with thoughts of a prolonged stay, I launched a VAP (Video/Audio Pod) to keep me entertained. Before sending the remote flyer abroad, I had it focus on the hovercone. The 'cone was embedded up to its Directional Control Collar in gel, the slimy substance sucking gently at the titanium and ceramalloy fittings. Above, the VDB panels were splayed open, while further above them I discovered the cause of my trouble. The engine's air intakes were choked with dead and dying Diskflyers. My haste to leave the sea behind had assured me of a prolonged stay. I knew then that only a pick-up 'cone from the Orbitstar would get me airborne and underway again.

Dejected, I punched a course into the VAP and, not without envy, watched the small, silvery craft turn and head out over the "sea."

The storm was upon me in minutes, with winds and heat lightning of incredible ferocity.

My small ship bobbed nauseatingly on the jelly-like surface. The VAP, for all its diminutive size, performed beautifully, holding a reasonably straight course due to its great speed and sleek lines. Shortly it broke out of the ragged clouds and into brilliant sunlight—light that I knew I would not be seeing for hours. Before me, on the screen, was a fascinating vista. Hanging hundreds of meters above the Amoebic Sea were huge globules of gel, back-lit, looking like giant water droplets filled with spinning organelles. They poured upward in lazy slow-motion from a great puckered opening on the surface of the "sea." Even more fantastic were the creatures following their ascent. They were almost indescribable; the impression I had was of chitinous bodies, multiple flying bladders, huge pendulous arms and an array of unknown organs. The creatures appeared to be systematically puncturing the globules and inserting drinking tubes. I slowed the VAP and guided it cautiously toward them. I was so engrossed in my observations that I failed to notice my blinking warning light, and suddenly my screen went dark. I cursed aloud.

The storm had cut my electrical system down to auxiliary, leaving only enough energy for my distress signal. My VAP was floating blind, unable to return without my signal. I never recovered it.

The storm had grown in intensity, with

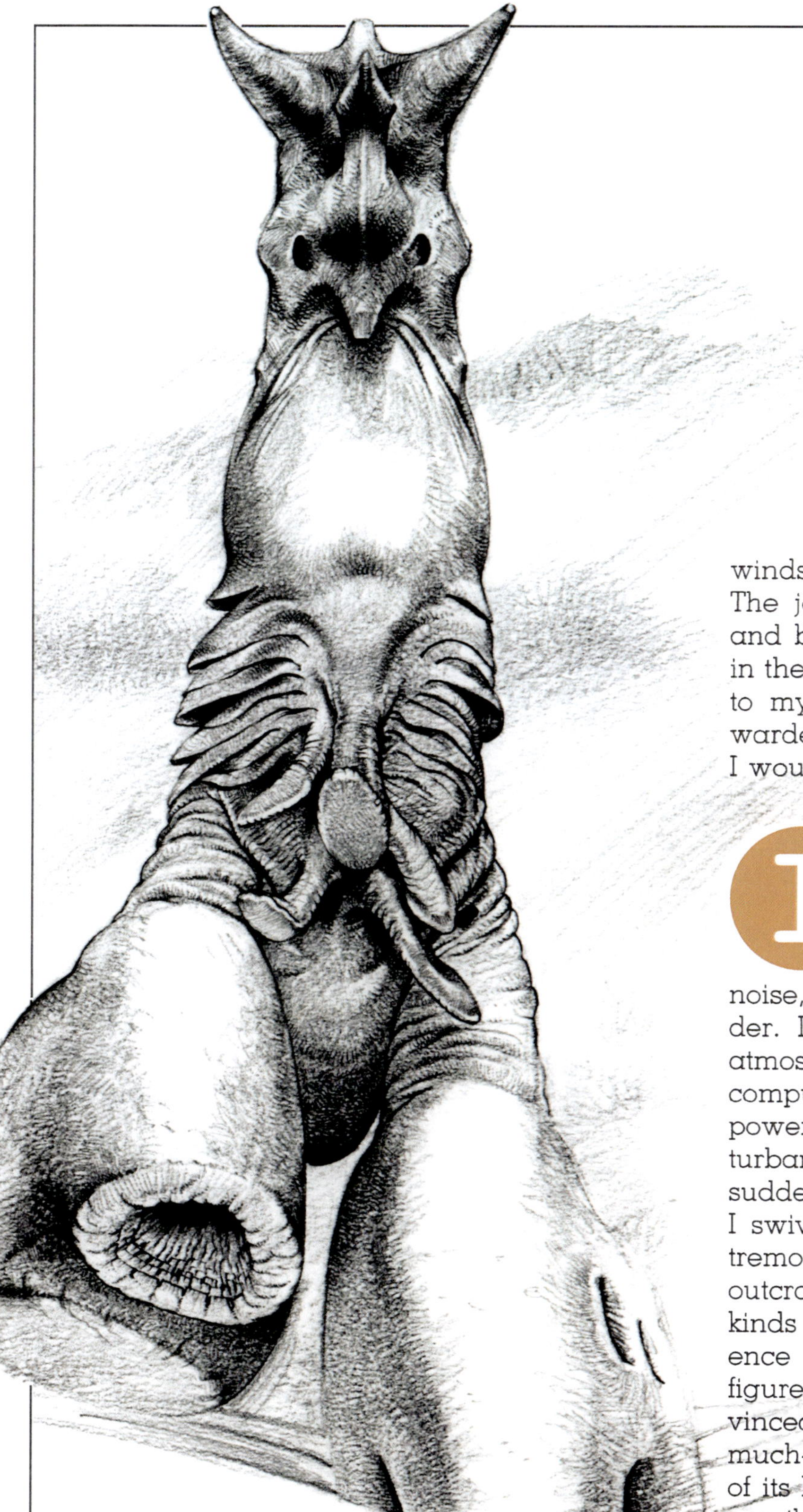

winds exceeding four hundred and thirty kph. The jelly-like surface of the "sea" was rippling and bouncing. Until the storm blew over, I was in the dark. As fortune would have it, this proved to my advantage, for an hour later I was rewarded with one of the most unforgettable sights I would witness on Darwin IV.

It began with a dull roaring. Luckily, my audio system was intact and gradually I became aware of a low noise, which at first I thought to be echoing thunder. It seemed, however, too continuous to be atmospheric, and again I swore at my loss of computer data. Running on the same auxiliary power line as audio, my extensible Seismic Disturbance Indicator was also functional, and it suddenly began registering rhythmic vibrations. I swiveled my seat toward the source of these tremors, but found my view blocked by a large outcropping of rock. I was familiar with these kinds of seismic readings from my past experience with the huge Grove-backs, but these figures indicated an even larger creature. Convinced that I would soon be encountering the much-celebrated creature from S.I.848.28, or one of its kin, I made as many preparations as were possible with the majority of my systems down.

These included readying the palm-sized Vidisc tourist camera from my personal kit. I turned the emergency cabin lamp off, dimmed the monitors and sat back to wait. The "sea" was dark and slick, wind-driven ripples occasionally revealing luminous patches of imbedded micro-animals. The SDI, now bleeping constantly in the background, indicated the ever-narrowing margin between myself and the incredible beast that had sparked so many imaginations years ago.

I rose from my chair and peered out into the gloom, hoping for a first glimpse. My view was all but blocked by the rocky island, with only a relatively small wedge of sky visible between two spires.

The roaring was so loud that I was forced to cut the audio volume. Under me, the gel's movement began to synchronize with the SDI's readout. I glanced out at the gap in the rock, only to see darkness; where sky had been there was now a moving form of great bulk. As I groped for my Vidisc, the behemoth cleared the outcropping. or more properly, stepped over it. I was stunned at the size of this magnificent animal. Apparently the rocks had shielded me from the impact of its footfalls, for now, unprotected, the 'cone bobbed horrifyingly on the rubbery surface. Somehow I held onto my camera and began filming. This was indeed the bizarre animal whose existence had catalyzed the formation of the Expedition. Its great crested head was licked by lightning; its sides, heaving with the enormous effort of its walking, were buffeted by the gale-force winds;

and I realized that virtually no force in Nature could affect such a creature.

The immense bipedalien's roaring was so loud that the glass in the 'cone's canopy retainers vibrated. I believe this sound originated from the two huge "gills" far up the torso in the bony collar. Meanwhile, frequent low-range sonar calls threatened to blow out every monitor I had, as their source — an array of blue-glowing pseudo-arms — waved wildly in the turbulent air. The sounds and sights flooded my mind and soul. I was completely transfixed by this creature; my euphoria was so complete that I had to actually shake myself back to reality. It strode slowly, measuring its vast footfalls, navigating like an ancient ship on some far-off, watery sea. I decided to call it an Emperor Sea Strider, although I felt awkward naming such a humbling animal.

My SDI registered a second Sea Strider, and with some difficulty I spotted it about fifteen kilometers downrange. Perhaps this was a mated pair; they were heading in the same direction. As I watched the second Sea Strider, a sharp whining overhead, similar to the scream of jet engines, made me duck reflexively in my cabin. A flight of small black creatures, faintly bio-lit, was headed directly toward the ponderous giant. They careened and banked and, oblivious to the gusting winds and lightning, steered straight into an opening in the front of the Sea Strider's carapace. They reappeared seconds later, having flown through the huge beast's chest and out the fiery exit "gill." The biolights on the small flyers blazed with renewed energy. Their tails alight with flaming exhaust, the creatures circled almost playfully, leaving behind long gray vapor trails that were twisted into sinuous corkscrews by the wind. As the flyers whisked by I noticed a distinct similarity between their crests and those of the Sea Striders, and I had a sudden flash of intuition that these small creatures were the nymph forms of the dark titans they attended. Somehow, as they entered their parents' bodies, they fed upon energy-rich secretions that renewed and nourished them. Later research, which included charting the nymphs' growth to massive adulthood, bore out this theory.

The exaggerated bouncing of the "sea" under me was beginning to subside as I watched the Sea Striders lumbering away. Their oversized feet, which I later learned were hollow and contained huge oral tubes, kicked up thin mists of minute jelly-shavings. Each oral tube, which led up through the thighs and into the torso, began as a mouth on the soles of the feet, where it was rimmed with thousands of sharp teeth. As the

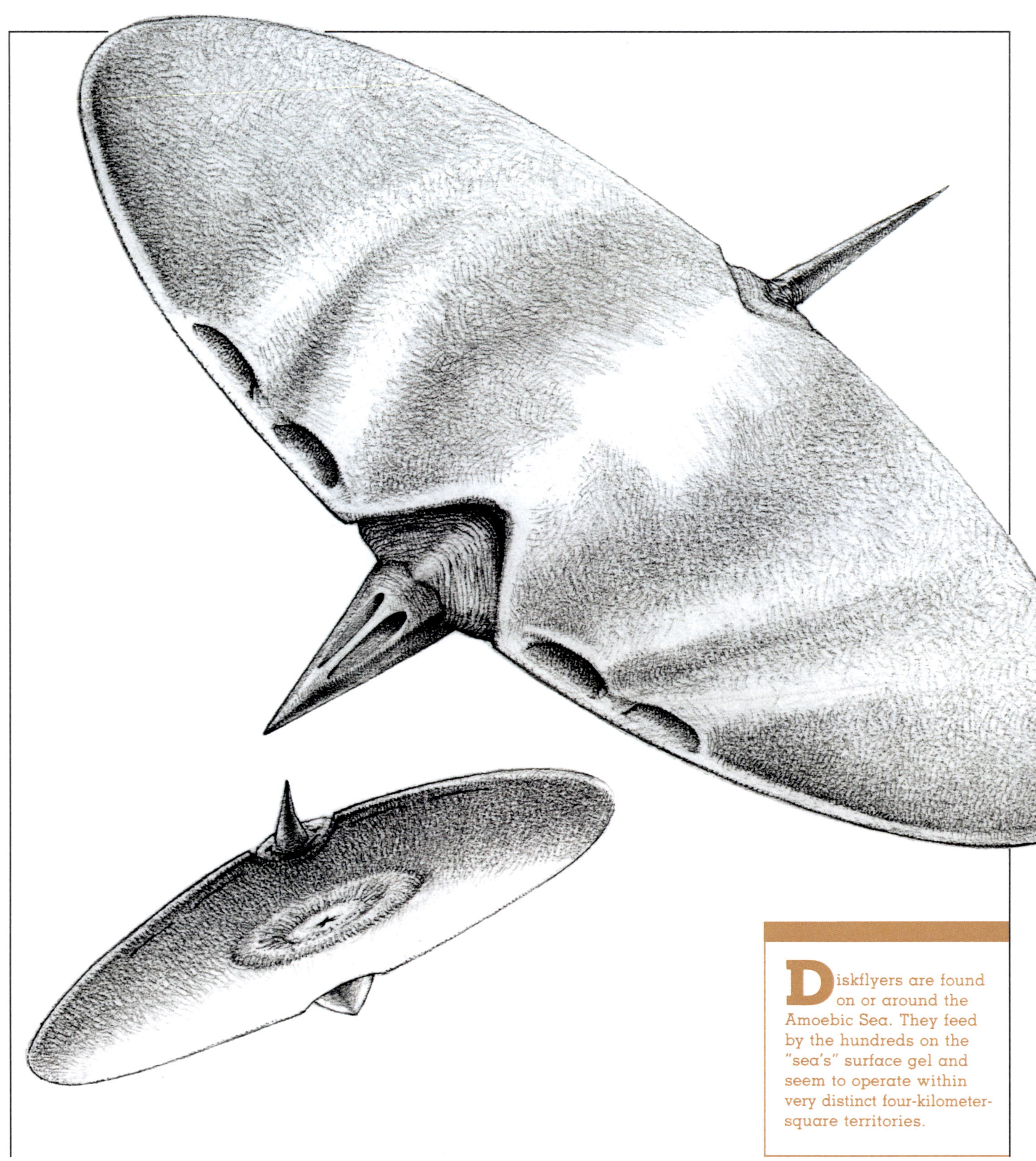

Diskflyers are found on or around the Amoebic Sea. They feed by the hundreds on the "sea's" surface gel and seem to operate within very distinct four-kilometer-square territories.

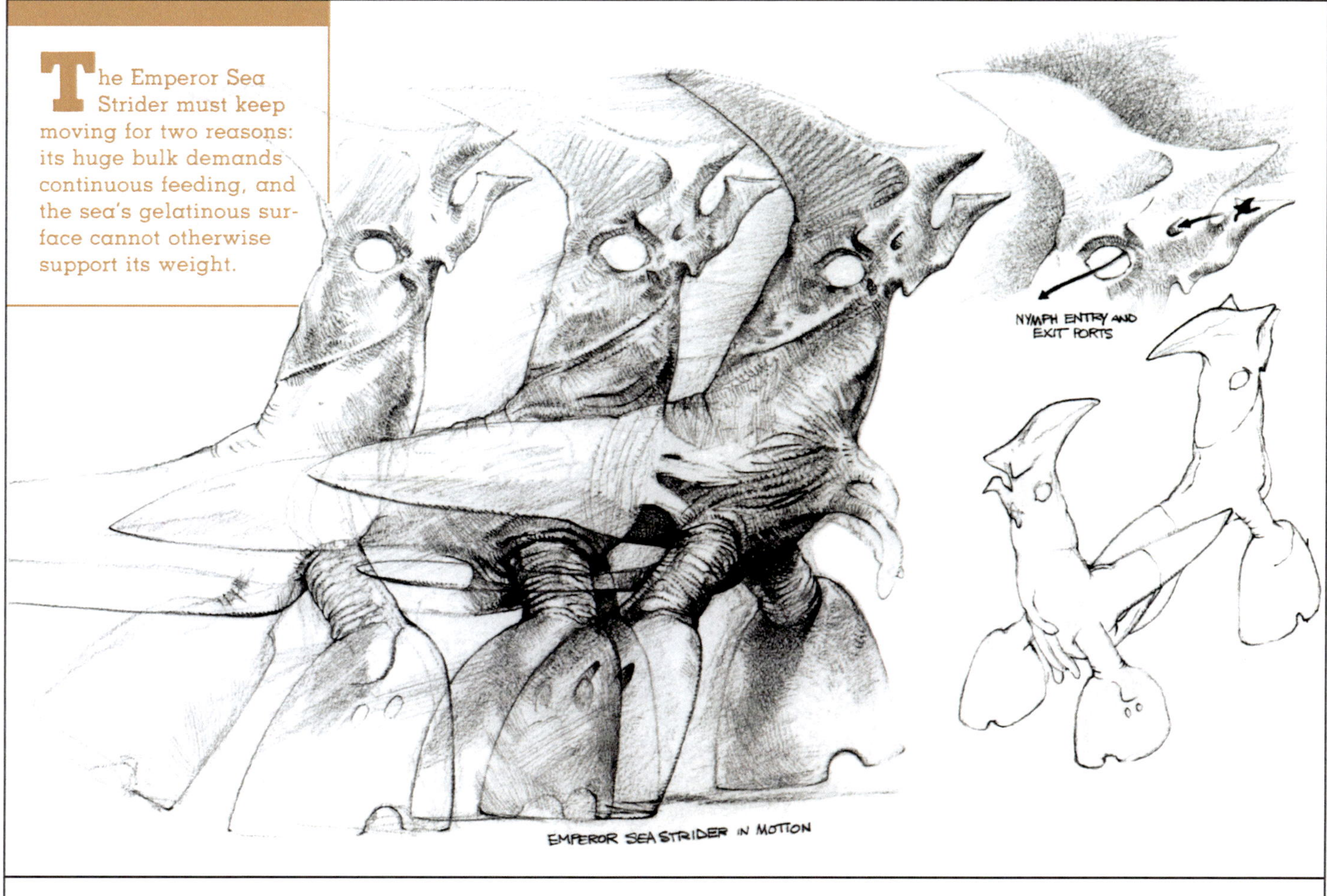

EMPEROR SEA STRIDER IN MOTION

beast walked, each sliding footfall shaved off a thin layer of gel, which was quickly sucked up and digested.

I was sorely disappointed as the Sea Striders ponderously plodded away from me. I was unable to follow or to even send a VAP after them; the pitiful best I could do was to follow them with my ridiculous hand-held Vidisc, zooming and readjusting my focus to take in their enormous size. My camera's rangefinder indicated that they were about one hundred ninety meters tall, but I was not certain of its accuracy. The impressions I gathered that day are still vivid today: huge "arms" gracefully swaying and pointing; irregular tiers of lateral breathing flaps, opening and closing with each footfall; gently glowing blue biolights accenting the smooth curve of a lightning-caressed crest; and the dull sheen of the sunlight as it filtered through the wild clouds and limned a swaying tail. I knew as I etched those images into my soul that I would come back to these creatures someday, not just to study them but to drink in the exhilarating nectar of otherworldliness. They embodied all that was Darwin IV.

A half an hour after the Sea Striders had appeared, they were specks on the distant horizon. I sat in silence on a now still and empty "sea." Two hours later the clouds broke and brilliant sunlight glinted off gently rolling gelatinous waves. An hour after that, the pick-up 'cone dropped down and pulled me free.

SEA STRIDER SKULL AND LITTORALOPE

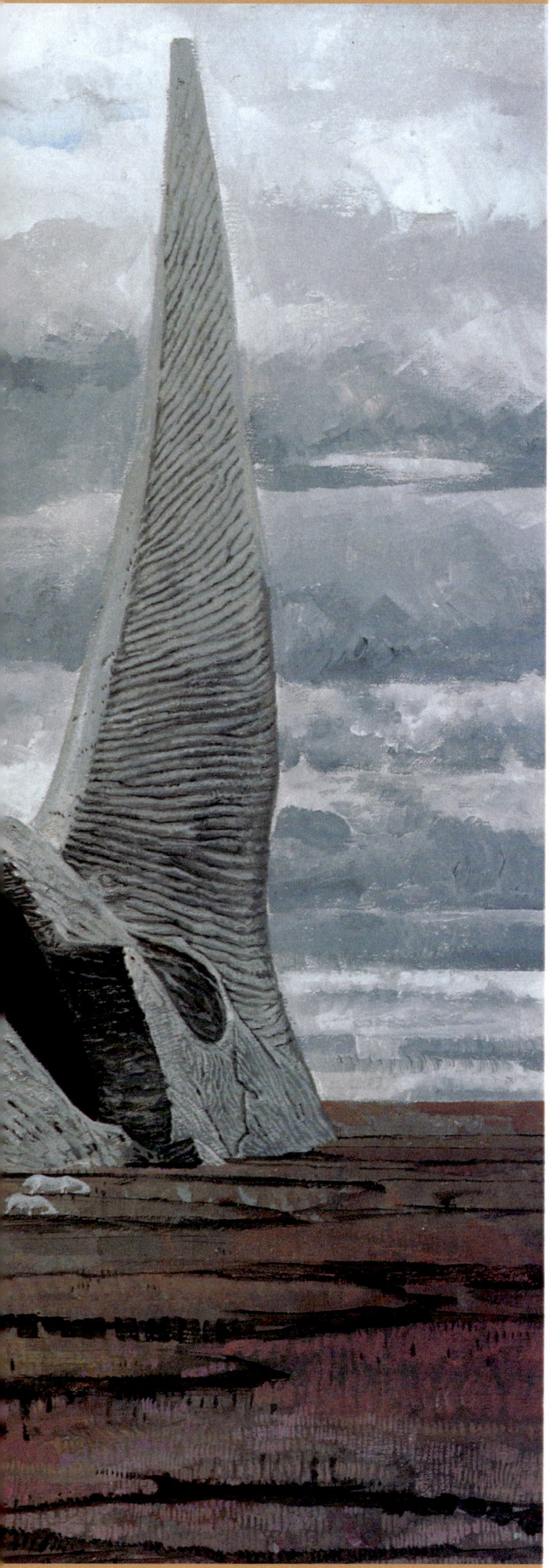

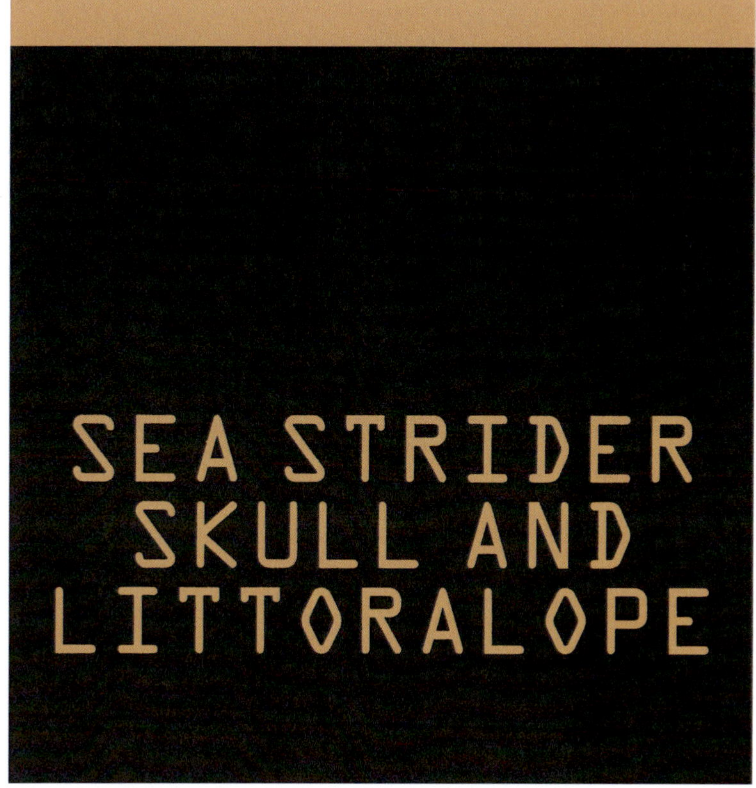

Darwin's single, unbroken littoral zone stretches for thousands of miles around the northern hemisphere's Amoebic Sea. It is by any standard a strange beach, with neither sand nor tidepools nor even waves lapping at its edge. Instead, one finds a constant slow expansion and contraction of the gelatinous matrix which sits about a meter atop the underlying beach. There is a genuinely surreal quality to this region: to the one side lies the vast expanse of the "sea" itself, rippling and undulating its jelly surface to winds that do not always exist; to the other side, sunken more than a meter, is the beach, so flat and still that it seems artificial. It is here that a silent war is waged between the colony creature we named the

PLATE XIX. "It looked like some bizarre organic cathedral."

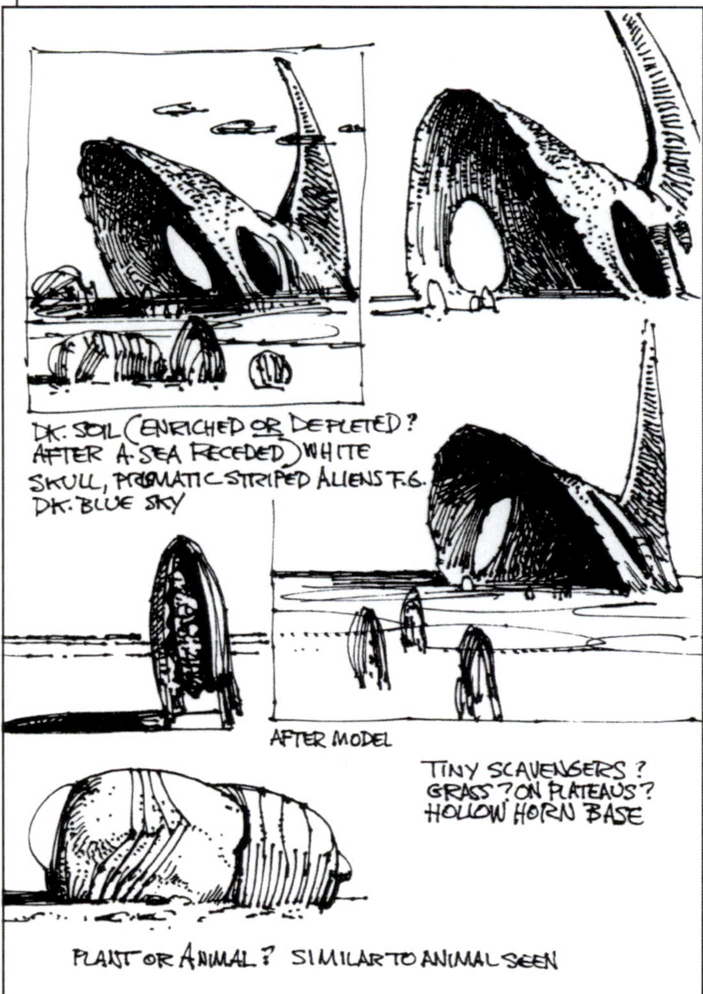

The awesome, cathedral-like cephalon of the Emperor Sea Strider captured my imagination as both architecture and biology. I found it hard to believe that such a creature could ever walk — until one almost walked over me!

and brown beachfingers, an extremely slow-growing and lovely succulent. The "sea's" recession is not a result of vegetable encroachment, however, but is the end product of the innumerable, specialized animals that dine on the vast, gelatinous colony's flank.

The apparent recession of the "sea" may be a cyclical process involving surges in the population of peripherals — the various species living around and dependent upon the colony. Most of these species spend many hours a day tearing at the gel's edges. They live quieter lives than their plains cousins, though there is still some threat from a small number of beach predators, for their ecosystem centers on the defenseless, protein-rich resources of the "sea." Their uses for the jelly-like matrix are many and varied. Most peripherals siphon up the morsels they collect for immediate nourishment, while others liquify pieces for storage either for themselves or their mates. Still others lay eggs on or in the resilient biomass, taking full advantage of the nourishment to their hatchlings and the protective insulation of the matrix. Finally, there are those creatures who make their home within the matrix and never set foot upon dry ground.

Amoebic Sea and the individual creatures of Darwin IV. The littoral zone is an ecological no-man's land, a place of flux and conflict between two silent armies, and the land bears their marks.

It would seem that the "sea" has been losing ground over the last few millennia. Evidence to support this includes the percentage of flattened beach ground that has either fresh plant growth or older, more established plants. Some contested areas have only the barest traces of fuzzy plant growth, while other, long-ago-fallen salients are heavily covered with lavender, pink,

The variety of lifeforms in the littoral zone provided me with hours of enjoyable observation. My inner aesthetics responded positively to the soothingly flat terrain and the strange creatures around me, and I found myself spending a greater amount of time in this region than was, perhaps, justifiable. It seemed to me that the beach was important; that I would not find another area where life had specialized to such an extent.

So I drifted above the beach zone with a quiet sense of contentment, that feeling that I imagine countless wanderers before me had experienced during their explorations of the wilderness. It was good to be alone, to see things no one had ever seen, to feel like a small part of some vast and universal scheme. Enjoying this sense of wonder, I traveled for many days around the edge of the Amoebic Sea.

O n one of these days I saw, from a distance, an immense and imposing artifact, the cracked and bleached skull of an Emperor Sea Strider. It lay partly submerged in the boggy ground with its gigantic crest pointing skyward, looking like some bizarre organic cathedral. As I drew closer I saw that its whitened surface was riddled with innumerable nerve holes and sutures; in many of these, small animals had made their homes, leaving behind nests of peaty vegetable matter and droppings that stained the ivory surface in long brown streaks. These exterior nests seemed to have been abandoned for some time, as I found no evidence of current occupation.

I circled the skull and entered it through one of its vast gill openings, finding myself floating in considerable gloom. For all its size, the skull's walls were remarkably thin, and all about me I could see huge panels of bone in the process of flaking off; below me, the floor of this artificial cavern was covered by a layer of shed bone flakes. Suspended from the "ceiling" was the huge and primitive braincase, which appeared to have been eaten away in many spots. As I studied it, I thought I could see tiny pinpoints of moving light, and so I decided to sweep it with my infrared scanners. I was immediately rewarded with the sight of hundreds of flyers squeezing their way in and out of the braincase. I flipped on my speakers and was nearly deafened by the cacophony of their chattering sonar; I flipped them off and resumed my explorations in silence.

I never did get a clear view of these creatures, for as I was circling within the skull a sudden jolt threw my 'cone off balance. An alarm klaxon went off, and as I sought to regain verticality I could see a large flake of bone tumbling toward the ground. This close call warned me of the dangers of a prolonged stay within the skull, and I hurriedly exited through the same opening I had entered.

As I was emerging I noticed that it was beginning to rain, and that a small herd of short-legged quadruped-aliens had gathered at the skull's base. They were placid, slow-moving beasts, smooth-skinned and white. As they then hobbled through the spongy beachfingers toward the skull's opening, I again turned on my audio system; this time, against a faint backdrop of flyer calls, I heard their soft, mewing *pings*.

Within a few minutes the entire herd of about twenty individuals was safely sheltered by the overhanging lip of the skull. I "parked" in the gill opening and was again forced to shut off my speakers, as their *pinging* was drowned out by the noisy flyers' calls. As they settled themselves in the gloom, I saw that their entire bodies glowed with a greenish lambency, a characteristic I had not seen before on Darwin IV. I named the creatures Littoralopes.

Suddenly my attention was directed toward a flock of small flyers that had taken wing with amazing rapidity. Within seconds the flock was circling crazily in the dark confines of the skull, their tiny orange biolights looking like the embers of some wind-whipped fire. I was engulfed in their streaming radiance as they flew past me and out the gill opening with incredible speed. By the time I had swung my chair around, they were nowhere to be seen, having been swallowed by the rain-laden clouds.

The Littoralopes were quietly waiting out the rain, and took little or no notice of the flyers' departure. With the noisy flyers gone, I switched my speakers back on. As before, the creatures were *pinging* and nodding their arrow-shaped heads; their exchanges seemed almost conversational. Beyond this impression, though, I had no evidence of intelligence among them.

The rain gradually tapered off and the small herd got to its feet and wandered out toward the open beach. It soon became obvious that they were headed for the "sea," which was in a state of moderate agitation with two- to four-meter pseudopodal waves on its surface. From past experience I knew this to be a reaction to the storm; but unlike watery seas, this reaction was always delayed about thirty minutes. The Expedition later learned that the agitation was a reaction to the introduction of water into the matrix.

As the Littoralopes approached the "sea," I noticed its edge shrink back a meter or

so in a parody of sentient apprehension. The herd gathered itself in a line along the edge and began, with broad, side-to-side swipes of their heads, to shave off long strips of clear matrix, which were quickly sucked lengthwise into the creatures' bellies.

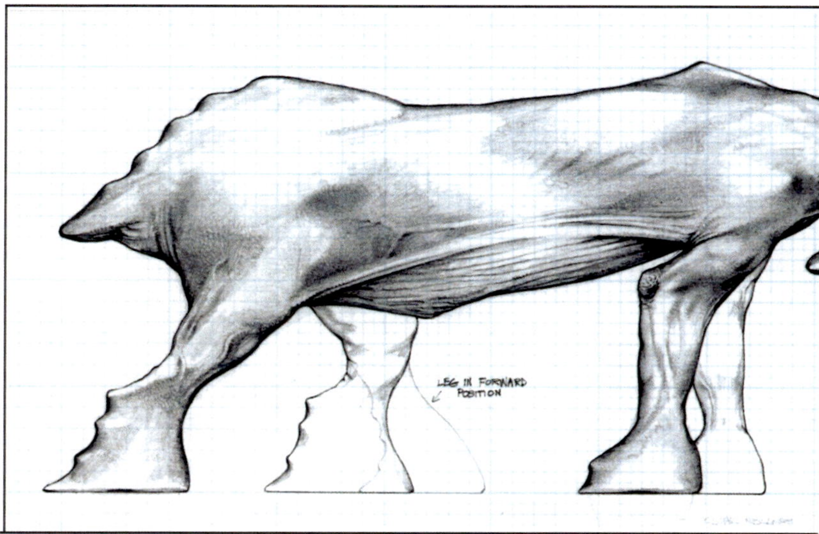

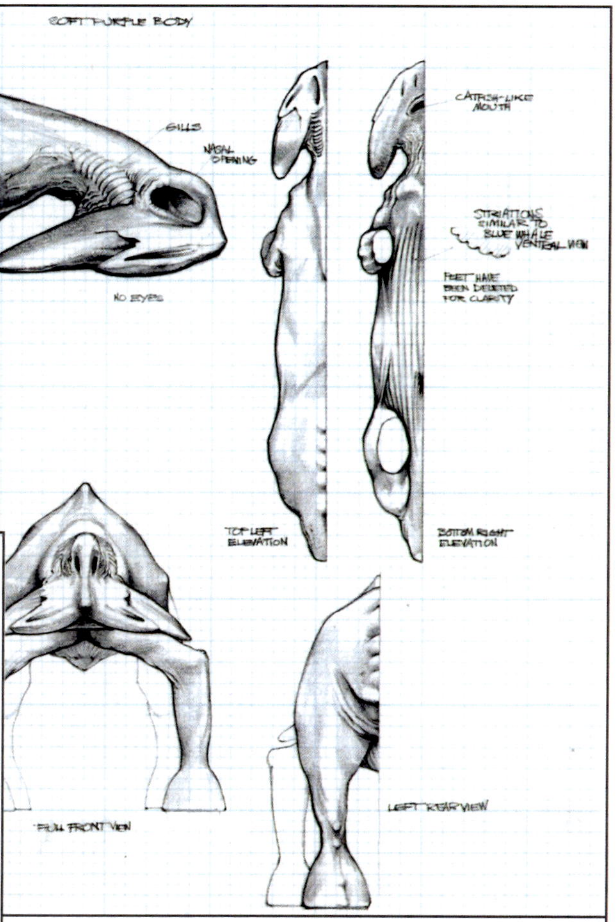

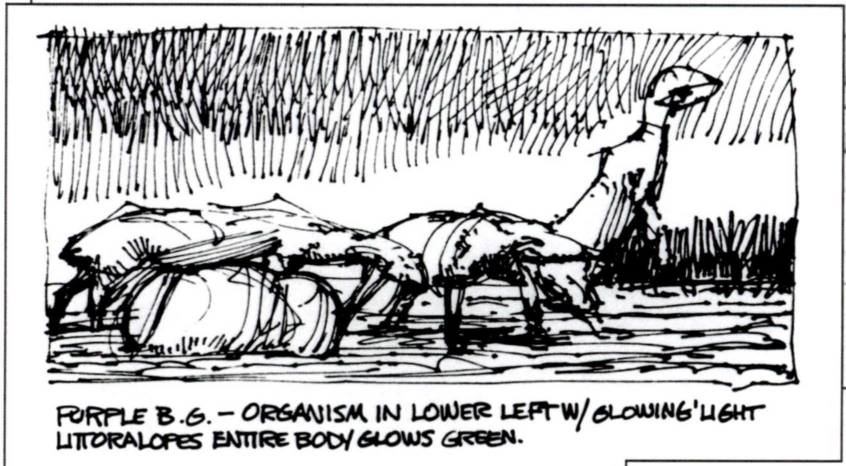

After about an hour, the satiated Littoralopes marched off down the beach and out of sight, their bellies distended, and I floated down to inspect the damage. An area of newly-exposed beach some forty meters by two gave

PLATE XX. "Fifty or so Beachquills suddenly burst from the ground."

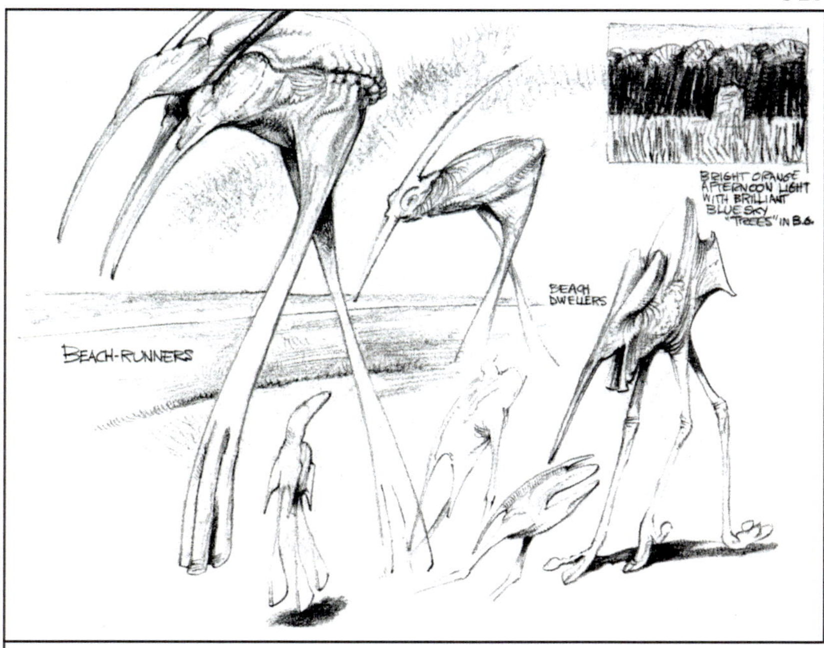

evidence to the quantity of matrix consumed by the herd. The "sea's" edge looked torn and raw, with partially shaved strips of matrix scattered about the beach. I hovered for about an hour doing studies of the surrounding terrain, and by the time I left the once-ragged edge was completely healed by new matrix.

Hidden about thirty centimeters beneath the soft soil of the littoral zone are rafts of communal hunters—the Beachquills. Often numbering in the scores, these dart-shaped creatures lie in wait for the unwary passerby to tread on the soil directly above them. As they rely primarily on their sensitive pressure receptors, their sonar is nearly nonexistent. These short-range attack hunters are able to propel themselves with enormous velocity over short distances. They launch themselves by means of a folded, muscular "foot" that snaps the individual animal through the concealing ground toward its target. After a kill, the Beachquills will instinc-

tively regroup and bury themselves, leaving no visual evidence of their existence. Their immobility and silence are perfectly evolved hunting techniques on a sonar-based planet. As the Beachquill's range is limited by the density and composition of the soil it lives in, it is found exclusively in the littoral zone.

On one occasion I followed a Beach-loper (a distant peripheral cousin of the Emperor Sea Strider) into a bed of Beachquills. It was not a pleasant scene: fifty or so Beachquills suddenly burst from the ground around the peripheral and within seconds had punctured it mercilessly. The force of their attack was so great that the creatures that missed the Beach-loper bounced harmlessly off my 'cone some twenty meters from their launch-bed. The Beach-loper was dead before it hit the ground. A bizarre feast followed, with those Beachquills that had struck home eating their way out of the carcass, and those that had missed eating their way in. An hour later the Beach-loper's bones lay exposed on the ground and the Beachquills had vanished, leaving no trace.

PLATE XXI. "With the onset of night, the Stripewings began to stir." (Preliminary sketch)

STRIPEWING

A day after my introduction to the Littoralopes, I came across another interesting flock of peripherals. These odd-looking animals appeared to be in evolutionary flux: they were winged and yet were unable to fly. When attempts were made—and these were not frequent—the two-meter-tall creatures would flap their stubby, beautifully striped wings in a vain effort to get airborne and would only manage a long hop. During the day the Stripewings, as I named them, seemed to lead a lazy life-style, bobbing on the undulating surface of the Amoebic Sea. At intervals they would simply extend their proboscises and begin to feed. The rest of the time, they did nothing but bob and doze.

But with the onset of night, the Stripe-

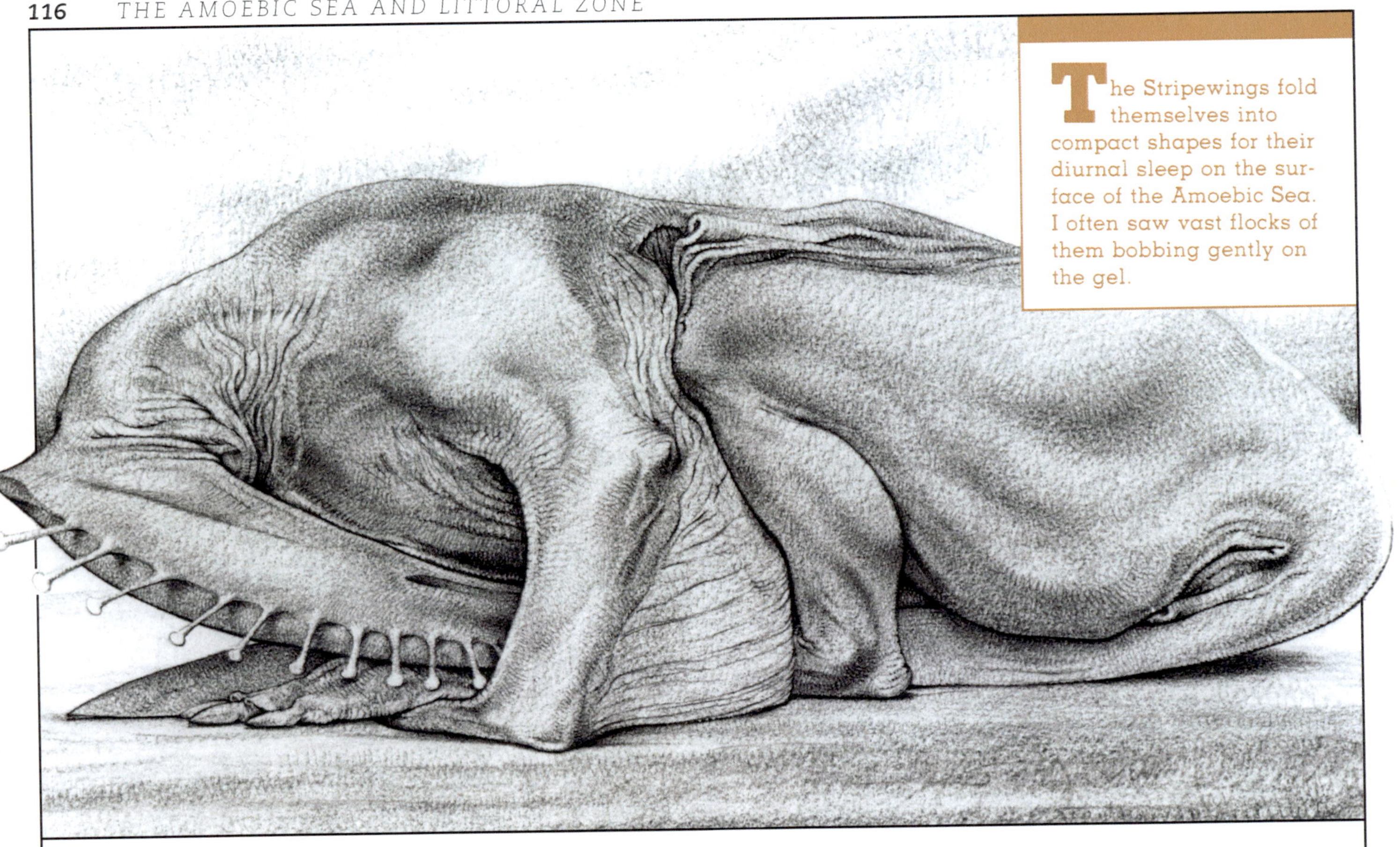

The Stripewings fold themselves into compact shapes for their diurnal sleep on the surface of the Amoebic Sea. I often saw vast flocks of them bobbing gently on the gel.

wings began to stir. Heads popped up, wonderfully glowing wings unfurled, and the creatures rose to their feet on the shimmering, quivering surface of the gel. In a moment, what had been a peaceful scene was now a riot of movement as the flock began its nocturnal rounds.

In all my time on Darwin IV, I did not again encounter anything quite as outlandish as the wild chase the Stripewings led me on that night. For hours this troupe of gaudy-winged lunatics flapped their way across the "sea's" surface in the most circuitous and erratic of patterns. All night the creatures hopped, bounded and cavorted through the darkness, a tumbling jumble of green-banded wings and bodies. I found it both exhilarating and exhausting keeping up with their unpredictable antics, and I would occa-

sionally rise to an altitude sufficient to keep the brightly lit line of them in sight over a large area.

All through the night I followed the Stripewings, puzzling over the strange behavior I was witnessing. With all my sophisticated equipment, I could still only speculate. Was I witnessing the pursuit of airborne micro-flyers? or a hormonally triggered courtship rite? I could reach no conclusions. By the time the sky began to silver, they had grown appreciably less energetic. So had I. As they slowed down I descended to about ten meters and "parked." Daybreak found the odd creatures wearily settled on the "sea's" surface, folding their wings and tucking their snouty heads down. From my vantage point I could see them gradually drop off to sleep, and I could not help but wonder if they were dreaming.

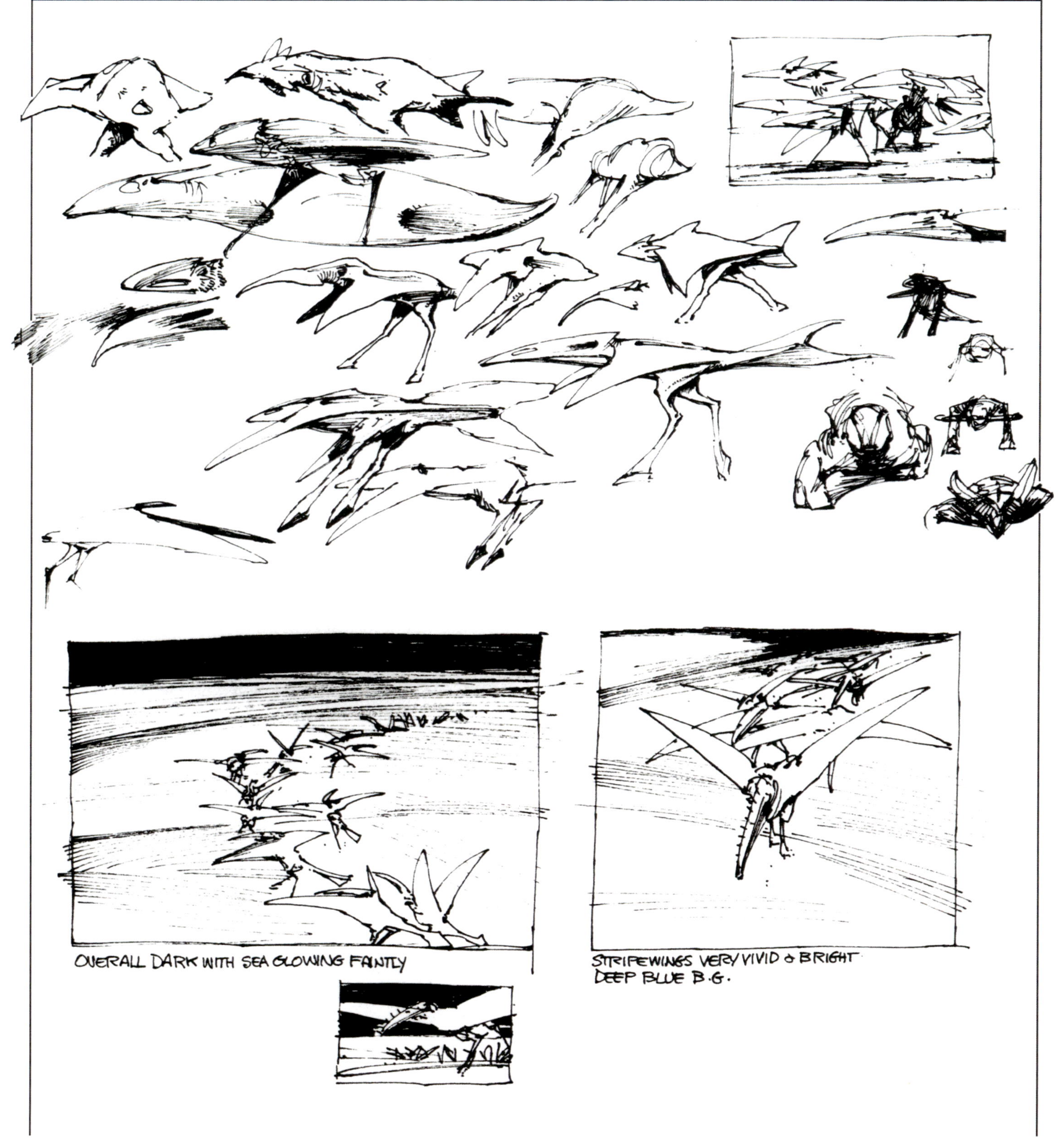
OVERALL DARK WITH SEA GLOWING FAINTLY
STRIPEWINGS VERY VIVID & BRIGHT
DEEP BLUE B.G.

PLATE XXII. *A Transalpine Floater near Mons Speke.*

THE MOUNTAINS

PLATE XXIII. "The secret egg chamber filled with rain and protective mud."

KEELED SLIDER

During the beginning of my second summer on Darwin IV I had my first glimpse of the foothill region that borders the great equatorial mountain range. As I crossed the Fugum Shingen, the gently rolling hills gradually gave way to a rougher, bleaker landscape in which mists and rain were not uncommon. In contrast to the plains' flatness and monotony, this hilly region offered wonderfully varied vistas, all with a distant backdrop of gray, mist-shrouded crags. Though there were occasional dense pockets of scrub-growth between the hills, the greater portion of ground was covered by short, blue plants no more than fifteen centimeters high and seemingly quite tenacious. This plant, which our botanist, Dr. Dorothea Kay, named hillvine, was seen to grow in very in-hospitable spots such as the undersides of over-hanging cliffs and along the steep sides of rocky fissures. A prolific plant, it covers the uplands right to the base of the mountains. Dotted all about on this beautiful, blue carpet were count-less grey, lichen-covered boulders, contrasting in color against the vine, whose tendrils could be seen braided amongst the boulders. The hilltops had the heaviest sprinkling of larger rocks, lead-ing me to speculate that these were the eroded remains of ancient volcanic plugs.

I floated at a mere eight meters over the rolling ground. The soil was satu-rated and very spongy, and in some areas I noticed a fine, rainbow mist hovering about a meter above the surface. Through a break in the lowering clouds, the suns picked out the exhalation mist of a bed of Peat-Bladders, curious pink ovoid creatures sunk upright in the boggy ground that served to moisten and protect their sensitive, wrinkled skins. The sounds of their wheezing voices were amusing as the animals' flabby, exposed lips puckered while they serenaded me. I recorded their cries for about a quarter of an hour.

Further into the highlands, I started to

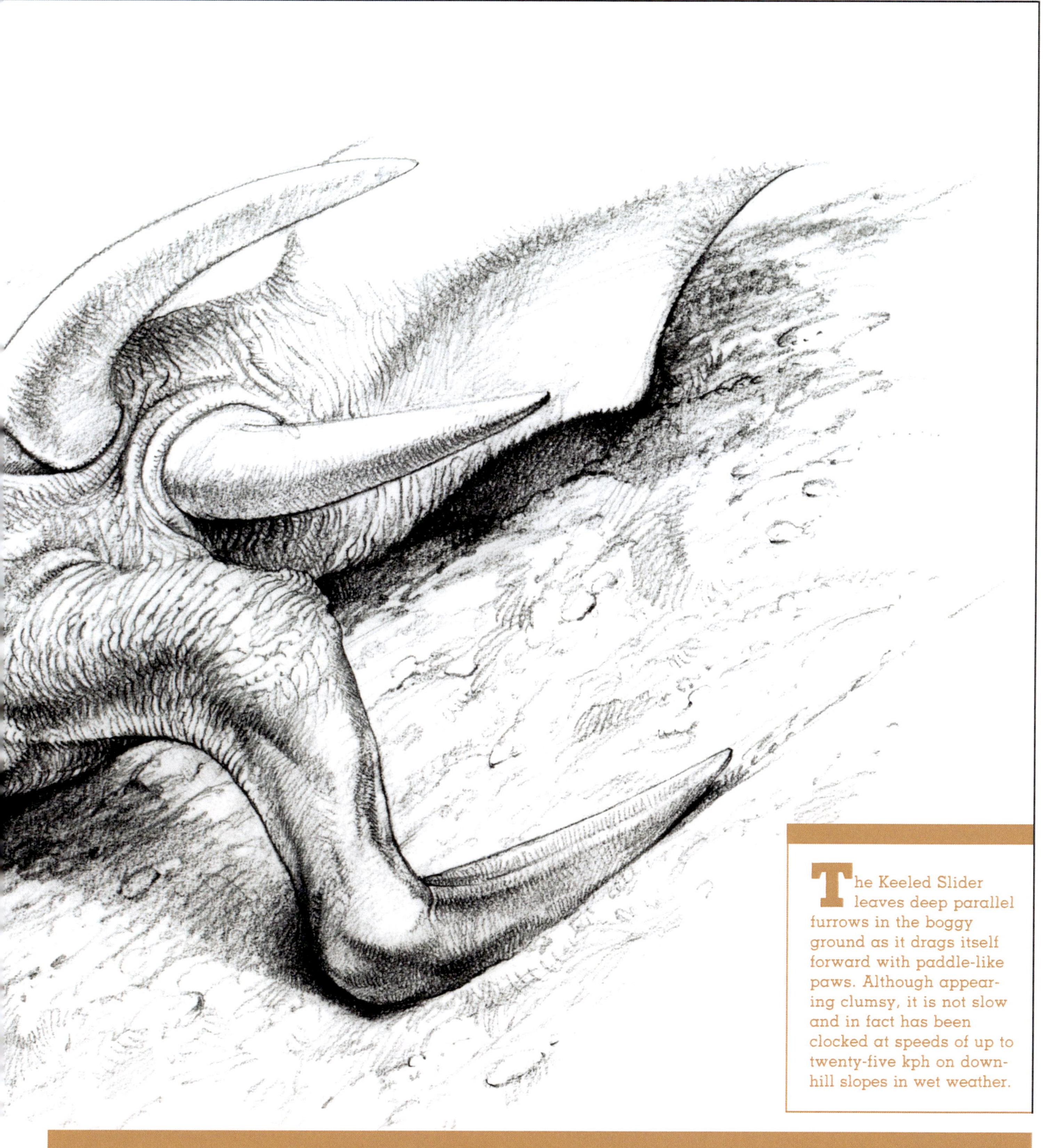

The Keeled Slider leaves deep parallel furrows in the boggy ground as it drags itself forward with paddle-like paws. Although appearing clumsy, it is not slow and in fact has been clocked at speeds of up to twenty-five kph on downhill slopes in wet weather.

The Keeled Slider's two facial feeding palps also are used in digging its egg chamber. The female then lays eggs far underground, where they are fertilized by the male — and apparently abandoned to their fate by both parents.

notice great furrows dug into the yielding turf, as if some giant had pulled his fingers through the blue foliage to reveal the brown soil beneath. The grooves crisscrossed the hills in seemingly random patterns. Accompanying them at intervals were deep scuff marks and the occasional clump of droppings, which made me conclude that the tracks were animal in origin. I followed the trace of what appeared to be two individuals heading due north, deducing their direction from the shape of the scuffs on either side of each furrow. The scuffs and the grooves seemed to indicate that these large creatures pulled themselves along, dragging a portion of their bodies. I was quite pleased when my guesswork proved correct.

High on a hilltop surmounted by a large igneous plug, a pair of creatures were huddled under an overhanging rock, motionless save for small movements of their crescent-shaped heads.

I picked up very little in the way of sonar; they *pinged* infrequently and for short duration.

The low clouds grew darker and it began to drizzle. I saw the creatures' brown, leathery skins get wetter as the rain became heavier. The rocks grew slick and the already-soaked turf began to form pools which, on the hillsides, overflowed and ran in muddy rivulets.

Suddenly a loud burst of high frequency *pings* broke the silence of my vigil. I saw one of the creatures (which I named Keeled Sliders) move back a meter or so, while the other appeared to grow restless, shifting from one muscular, paddle-like paw to the other. Its companion continued to move slowly backward until it finally settled directly under a large shelf of overhanging rock out of the pouring rain. I noticed its glistening sides beginning to swell with some inexplicable effort. With each spasm the creature gave voice to a piercing sonar squeal that seemed to increase the agitation of its mate, which by now was bobbing its huge head heavily. After twenty such squeals and much inquisitive scanning on my part, I determined that the Slider under the overhang was a female. She had excavated a long narrow channel underground with her tubular ovipositor and had laid twenty long eggs in a small chamber about five meters below. She eased herself off of the nest site and slowly slid forward into the rain, her limp, distended ovipositor trailing in the mud. The male Slider was by now in a positive frenzy of excitement and hurried without ceremony to the vacated tunnel. He quickly inserted his phallus into the opening made by his mate, and within two minutes completed the task of fertilizing the subterranean ova. Now also spent, he then slid off the nest to stand mutely next to his trembling partner, the rain bouncing off their broad backs. I watched as they shakily nuzzled each other, *pinging* gently. They settled down into the cradling mud, and by the gradual relaxing of their dorsal and lateral spines I guessed them to be dozing. Behind them, the narrow passageway and its secret egg chamber filled with rain and protective mud.

I realized later that rainstorms had softened the rich soil to exactly the right consistency to allow the Keeled Sliders to burrow out their nests; I found other pairs atop similar volcanic ridges after this downpour. Hours later, as the sunslight poured through the dissipating clouds and formed magnificent double rainbows, I returned to many of the nest sites. All were unoccupied by adult Sliders, the only sign of their presence being the parallel furrows cut into the ground. As for the egg chambers, virtually no sign of them could be found.

PLATE XXIV. "Arching its back, it snapped out over the abyss." (Preliminary sketch)

The mountains of Darwin IV are relatively young, sharp-edged and jagged, though not terribly high. Very few peaks remain sheathed in snow through the year. Looking all the more forbidding for their bareness, they form a planet-girdling band, evidence of Darwin IV's active sub-continental shield regions.

It was not without a sense of uneasiness that I entered this rough montane region near Mons Burton. Our hovercones, though extremely reliable and well engineered, were subject to the occasional malfunction, which I knew would not be tolerated by the unforgiving side of a mountain. Manual navigation in the tricky alpine updrafts was out of the question. All this I understood as I pointed my steering grid in toward the range, programming my computer to maintain a thirty-meter minimum altitude at all times.

As I topped the first summit, I was met with an impressive expanse of mountains receding into the early morning mists; sunrise had been about two hours before, and the mists which lent an ethereal quality to the brooding mountains had not yet burned off. I noticed occasional movements within the clouds, and as either my eyes grew sharper or the vapor dissipated, I could make out small winged creatures gliding expertly on the air currents. They banked deliberately to turn, never flapping their striped triangular wings. To descend, these strange creatures wheeled in increasingly tight spirals until they disappeared behind some peak.

Gradually the mists gave way and I got a clearer view of this aerial ballet. These two-meter-long animals, which I named Lesser Mountain Springwings, are indisputable masters of their habitat. The Springwings (of which there are numerous varieties) live in one of the most difficult regions on Darwin IV. They appear to be a species in transition, comfortable both on the jagged slopes and in the chill alpine air, moving from one element to the other so quickly as to seem uncertain of which domain they are a part. During the day I watched them light on the cliffs to feed, mate or simply climb about. Though they are expert mountaineers, making use of nearly invisible footholds, the bulk of their time is spent gliding between the peaks, following the pungent odor of alpine cliff-polyps, their sole forage. I found it a beautiful sight to see these gaily-colored mountain dwellers flitting from one escarpment to the next, in and out of the mountain's blue shadows. They filled the air with their metallic sonar *clicking*, a sound unlike the *pinging* of the majority of Darwin IV's fauna.

I watched as one Springwing steered for a particular ledge with remarkable aerodynamic precision. At the precise instant that its legs and hindspur touched down, it folded its leathery wings snug against its body, the leading-edge rib fitting tightly into a long lateral groove. Behind and on either side of its head, its large, well-developed balance fins twitched nervously. I could hear the creature taking short, deep breaths of the cold, scent-laden air as it explored the cliff. A moment later it was rewarded with a small clump of mauve cliff-polyps. The plants were clinging stubbornly to the rocks, each one, at intervals, puffing forth a yellowish cloud of strong-smelling spores. The Springwing pushed its beaked mouth into the cluster of plants and commenced to pop off the succulent, globular

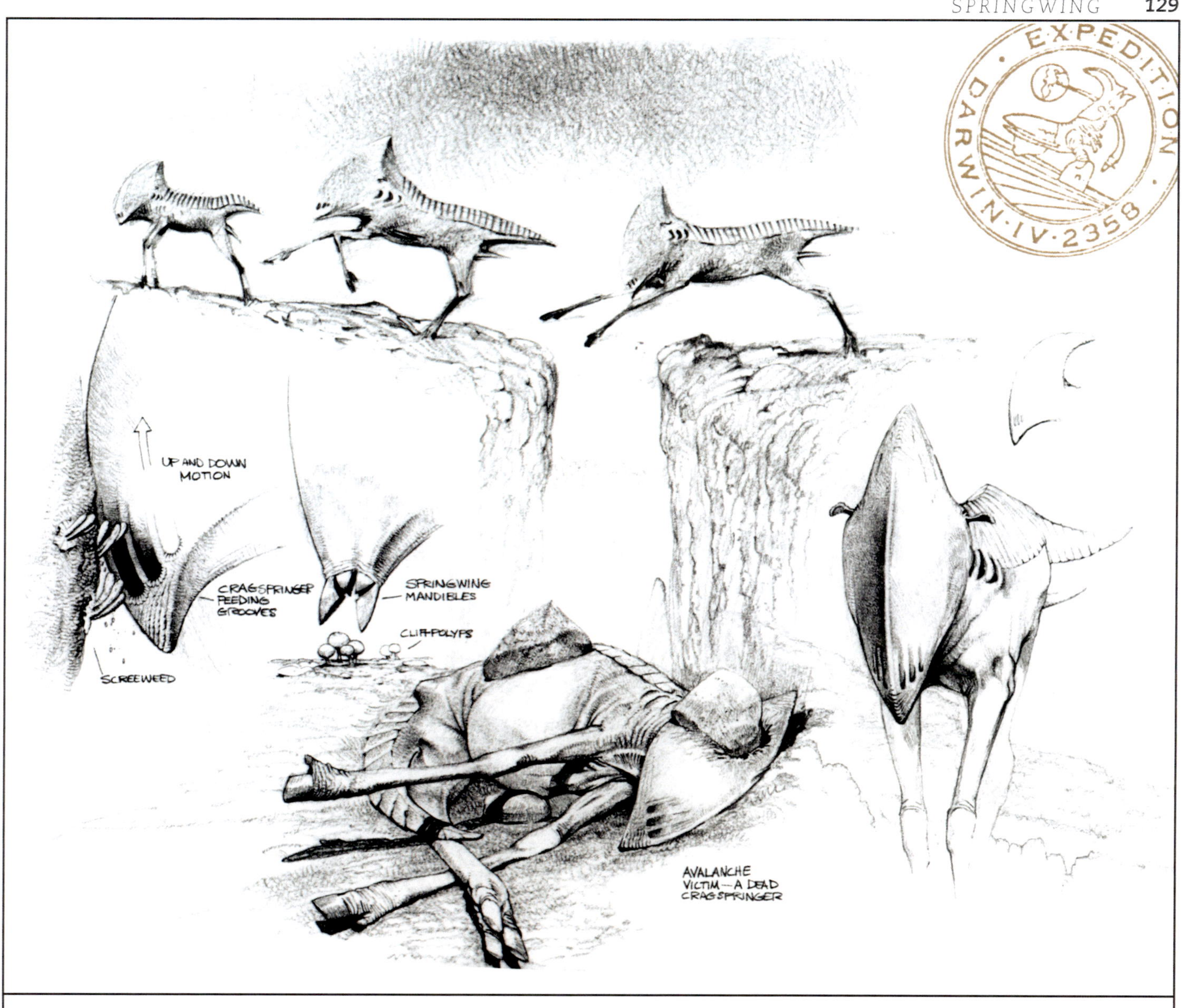

tips. It fed for a few minutes until a sudden hail of small pebbles from above spooked it. In a matter of seconds, the creature had turned to the shelf's edge and dug its hindspur into the ground. Then, arching its back, it snapped out over the abyss and, striped wings extended, sailed out of sight.

As the day wore on I encountered two more mountain dwellers, the Greater Mountain Springwing and the Cragspringer, each filling separate but similar niches in this biome. The former animal is half again as large as its lesser cousin and sports a cranial crest, which in some specimens curves nearly to the spine. I saw many instances of this massive crest being used in mid-flight dominance displays, often leading to seriously torn wings—a wound that is nearly always fatal, as it results in a crash on the rocks below.

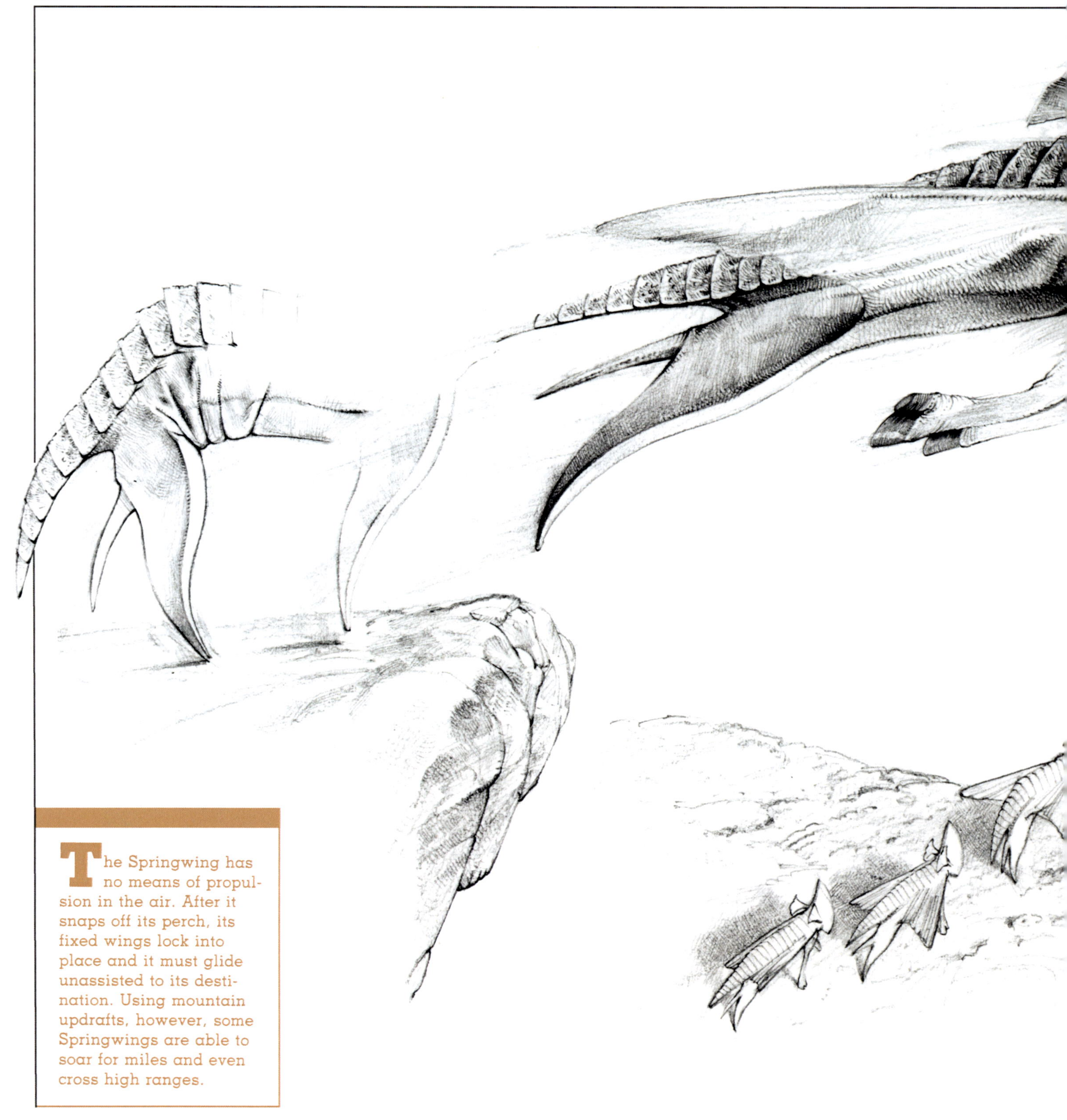

The Springwing has no means of propulsion in the air. After it snaps off its perch, its fixed wings lock into place and it must glide unassisted to its destination. Using mountain updrafts, however, some Springwings are able to soar for miles and even cross high ranges.

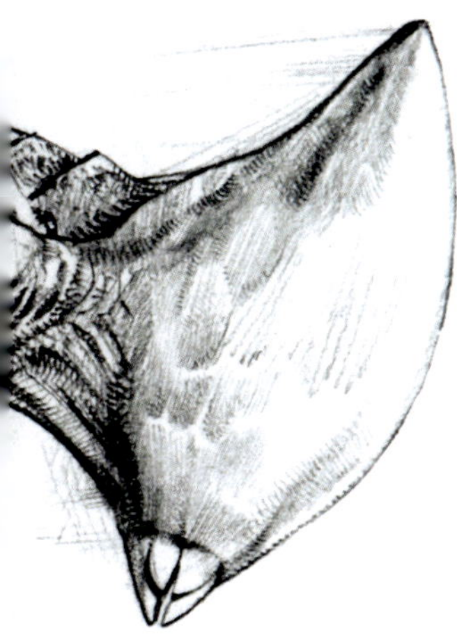

The Cragspringer lacks the wings of its distant relatives, the Springwings. It is incredibly nimble, with leaping abilities that took my breath away. I recorded many twenty-meter-plus chasm jumps and noticed very few injuries. It seems to be engaged in a continual search for food, choosing as its main diet the screeweed that covers the vertical rock faces. As with the cliff-polyps, the screeweed discharges its own odoriferous spores, sometimes in quantities sufficient to produce a haze over a large area of mountainside.

Toward the late afternoon of my first day in the mountains, I followed a troupe of Cragspringers into such a cloud of spores to watch them feed. The cloud must have triggered an instinctive feeding reflex, for the herd started to bob their large heads up and down. They continued this motion as they drew nearer the wall, producing loud sounds as they scraped their horny facial shells against the stones. Using a greater magnification on my screen, I could see that the creatures were actually shaving off the screeweed in long strips with their feeding grooves. Earlier, I had wondered about the mul-

tiple abrasion marks on the cliffs; observing these feeding habits provided me with an answer.

I watched the Cragspringers grazing for an hour, until dusk began to redden the peaks around me and deepen the shadows in the valleys below. Twilight in the mountains was beautiful. As the cliffs darkened I began to see traceries of delicate luminosities as the various mountain plants began to glow; the animals, too, outlined by their own biolights, were enchanting as they leapt from one ledge to another, twinkling like mobile versions of the emerging stars above.

Darkness generally brings about a slowing of activity among the mountain herbivores, with most Springwings and Cragspringers bedded down by nightfall. Whether this is due to their diurnal clocks winding down or to the increase of crepuscular predators, both flying and rockbound, I remain uncertain. As my first day in the mountains came to an end, I prepared dinner and sat looking out over the darkened peaks, reflecting on my needless worries about traveling through this majestic biome. As frequently happened during my travels on Darwin IV, I thought about the richness and abundance of Nature, of the blighted planet I call home, and of my wife and baby so far away.

BLADDERHORN

I was drawn to this mountain-stream dweller by its cry, an audible honk that is quite unusual on Darwin IV. This sound is the result of air being expelled from its twin bladders during their sudden deflation, a tone which echoes off the cliffsides and can be heard for kilometers. It is, I believe, a territorial signal.

Mountain streams on Darwin IV are not rich in plant life and these creatures, which I called Bladderhorns, are forced to spend up to three-quarters of their time searching for their aquatic forage, the red mountain-spike. As a result, Bladderhorns are extremely territorial and use their honking as well as their vivid biolight displays to frighten off challengers.

PLATE XXV. "It was a bit difficult to keep a straight face during these protracted encounters."

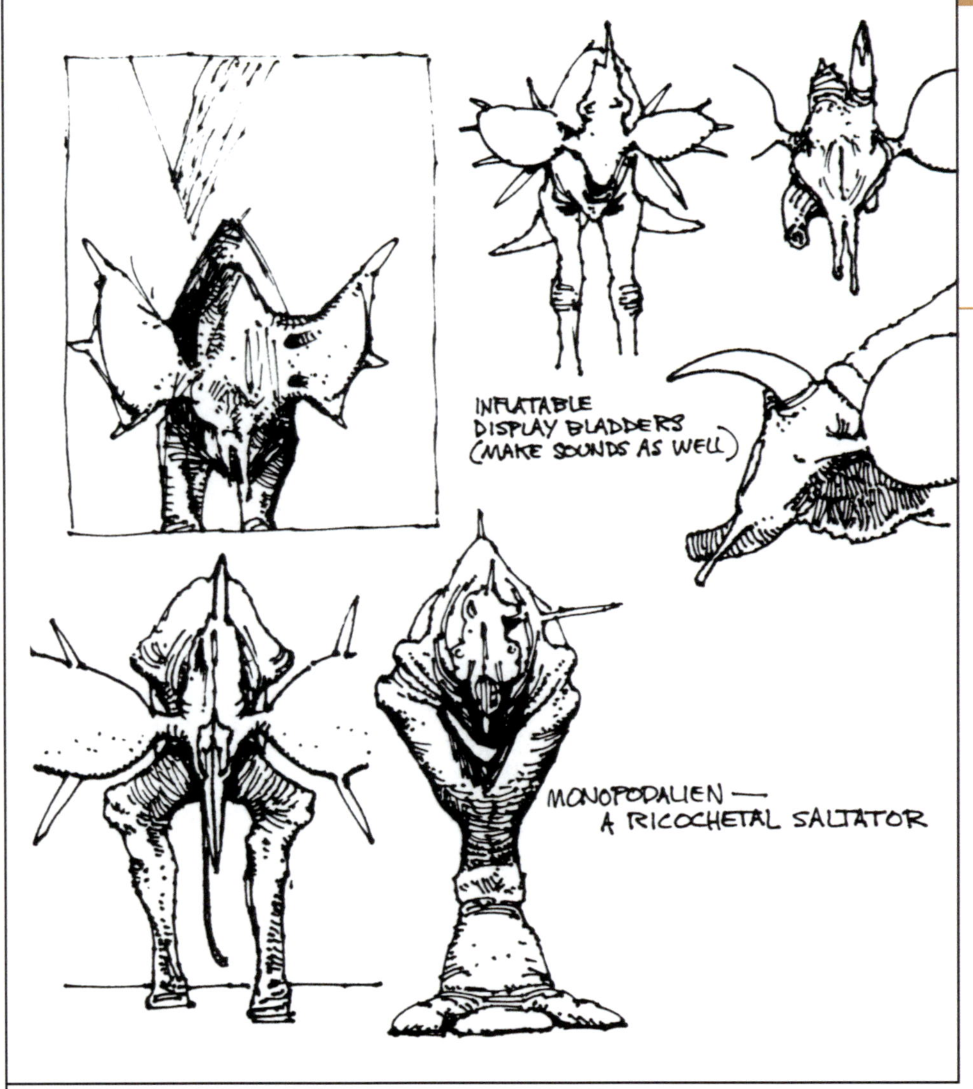

The Bladderhorn's deflated bladders ride its flanks on giant "antlers." Inflated, their eerie honking cry is one of the most haunting and easily identifiable sounds on the planet.

When confronted by a rival, the Bladderhorn will spread its "antlers," pumping up the large bladders in short, angry puffs. This is answered in kind by the challenger, who also begins to circle his rival in a slow and deliberate (as well as comical) tip-toe fashion. It was difficult to keep a straight face during these protracted encounters; I had to keep reminding myself that the two combatants were in deadly earnest. I never saw a fatality result from these territorial displays, but long bloody wounds were very common.

PLATE XXVI. Arctic polar-vanes rotating above the carcass of an Unth.

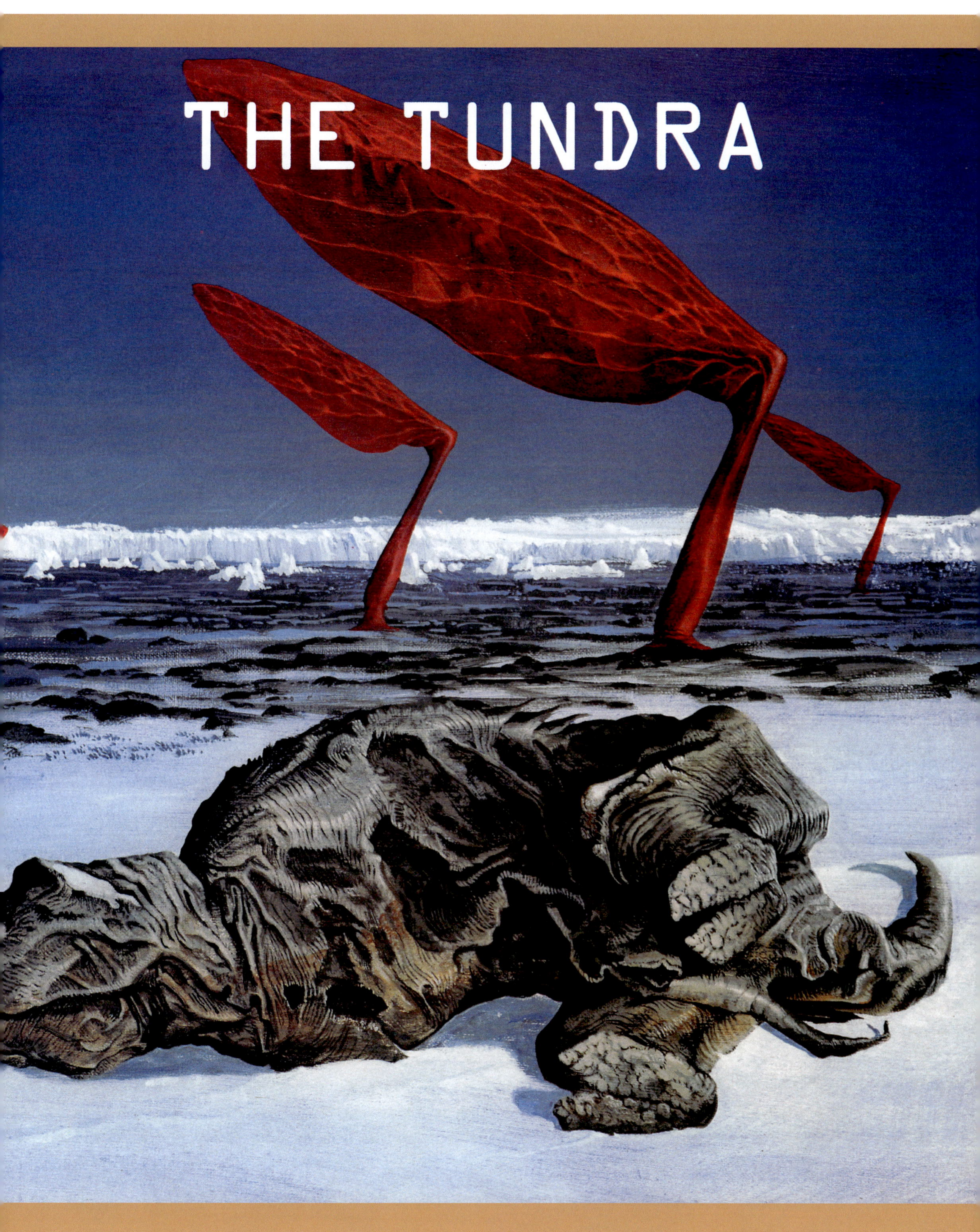
THE TUNDRA

PLATE XXVII. *"I decided to float along the glacier's edge surveying its fissured surface."*

ARCTIC SEDGE-SLIDER AND TUNDRA-PLOW

ragedy overtook the Expedition shortly after I left Darwin's montane region. I was traveling north with the idea of joining my fellow explorers, Drs. Ysud and Ysire, over the arctic wastes. As I skimmed above the boggy, pre-tundra moors I listened over long-range radio to the incomprehensible, untranslated conversation of the two alien xenogeologists. They were in separate 'cones some five hundred kilometers downrange, floating over the glacial shelf toward the magnetic pole. All seemed quite normal; the scientists' conversation was steady and seemingly lighthearted, punctuated by the rapid clicking I had come to recognize as the laughter of the Yma. I enjoyed listening to their strange language, all whistles and harmon-

ics, as I sped toward the rendezvous point. I estimated that I would join them in about an hour. And then, quite without warning, the radio became silent and the Homing Distress Indicator began blinking on my screen.

At first I assumed that the two xeno-geologists had simply ended their conversation and one had accidentally activated his homing distress beacon. But as the minutes of radio silence accumulated I grew more concerned. I ran a check on their position and discovered that it had not changed since my computer's last update, ten minutes earlier. This was ominous. It would be at least thirty minutes before I reached them; until then I could only sit and nervously watch the sub-arctic terrain streak below.

The flat tundra landscape of Darwin IV is an almost uniform olive-brown in color. Scattered patches of low-growing white and blue vegetation soften the bleak and monotonous aspect of this barren biome. Innumerable rounded boulders dot the

ground in growing numbers as one approaches the vast icecap.

Both of Darwin IV's poles are covered by glaciers of immense proportions. Glacier Cap North, toward which I was heading, differs from its southern counterpart by its greater thickness and by the jagged mountain peaks, B14 and B15, near its center. Glacier Cap South has no such visible peaks.

As the kilometers fell away, I began to discern a thin white line on the horizon. Brilliant against the gray-green clouds, the edge of the glacier appeared artificial, like an improbably long, whitewashed stucco wall extending to both horizons. I gained altitude and I could see the polar cap extending into the distance, a milky white ocean of ice shining in the suns' diminished light like a cracked and roughened lamina of ceramalloy. Even as I watched, a dense white cloud of frozen vapor began to steal across the surface of the ice, obscuring the suns and the icefields from view. Within moments I, too, was engulfed in a turbulent, hail-spitting cloud of total whiteness. I began to feel a growing sense of disorientation. In a state of near-panic, I called up the computer's topographic horizon; its

The high, humped back of the Sedge-slider contains its sonar bulge—one of the largest of any creature on Darwin IV. It is almost a second brain.

graphic linear display afforded me some measure of comfort.

It was all too easy for me to visualize what might have happened to my two associates: they would have been in close formation, performing their bi-instrument seismic surveys, when this squall or one like it roared down upon them. I could picture the two light 'cones thrown together, impacting, disintegrating . . . I hoped I was wrong, but as the storm grew in intensity around me I began to fear the worst.

Hovering at fifty meters I was buffeted about like a snowflake on the wind, with fine-grained hail blasting my windscreen. My 'cone's gyros strained to keep me level, but the artificial horizon projected on the windscreen pitched wildly. Then, almost as suddenly as it had appeared, the storm was gone. Below, the olive tundra became more and more distinct, while above the suns once again shone in the cobalt sky.

With the departure of the squall, I regained contact with the homing signal, and about ten minutes later was floating above the scientists' last coordinates. The evidence of their fate lay scattered on the ground and ice at the glacier's edge. Thousands of confetti-like bits of ceramalloy and titanium, orange-painted and twisted, lay in a broad smear about one hundred meters long. The two massive Yzar turbo-fan engines lay tangled together, their rotors interlocked. I saw no bodies, not even a shred of orange flight suit.

I patched-in to the Orbitstar and relayed the sad news of my discovery and the coordinates of the crash site. I was told that an investigation party would be down within the hour.

PLATE XXVIII. "It seemed a creature uncomfortable with its own method of movement."

Two hours later, after being fully debriefed (which included a complete downloading of my computer's records) I was sent to continue my explorations. As I pulled away from the crash site I could see on my rear screens the cleanup team's hoverpods, already in action. After they finished there would be no physical trace of my colleagues on Darwin IV. They would, I know, have appreciated that.

I had not really known the two xenogeologists very well, yet I was sorely depressed by their deaths. My mind kept wandering back to the crash site and its scattered remains. Instead of heading out to explore, I "parked," put Shostakovich's Fifth Symphony on the speakers, and sat back looking out over the stark tundra. It was, perhaps, my attempt at a memorial service.

When the symphony ended, I got back to work. I decided to float along the edge of the glacier, surveying its fissured surface as I went. Its blueish, icy face rose to varying heights, sometimes reaching thousands of meters, while other spots were no more than a few meters high. Strewn on the ground before it were fields of broken iceblocks calved off the fracturing parent glacier. These blocks, carved by wind and suns, attained the most bizarre forms. The tundra resembled a vast chessboard with hundreds of white, spired pieces slowly devolving in the thin, arctic sunlight.

The Sedge-slider's shovel-like beak can break through frozen ground to dig snow-bulbs from under the tundra. The hooked feet are equally adept on ice and boggy ground. The creature's head is fully retractable, a unique and valuable adaptation in this region of sudden, killing storms.

About an hour out from the crash sight, I rounded an outlet glacier and came across a half-dozen black creatures slowly dragging themselves along the near-frozen ground. They left behind long grooves that etched the tundra's surface for hundreds of yards. With these furrows in mind, I named the creatures Tundra-Plows. Two heavily-muscled arms terminated by flippers pulled the three-meter-long body with deliberate strokes, leaving both the furrow and small piles of dirt in its wake. Every stroke brought forth from the creature's nostril a tall plume of vapor that froze on contact with the frigid air and rained down as snow upon its back. Its heavy, black tegument glistened with this moisture as it heaved its laborious way along. It seemed a creature uncomfortable with its own method of movement, yet I knew that its very survival in this harsh environment proved me wrong.

I must have watched the group of Tundra-Plows (for so I was to call them when I learned their true nature) for at least an hour. They traveled very slowly. On occasion an individual would approach a clump of arctic cactus or polardots, and these would disappear from sight as if plucked from below; this puzzled me.

Ten meters apart and parallel to one another, the beasts traveled only about forty meters in the hour I watched them, squealing and belching vapor and turning the soil like harrows.

It was not until some time later, when I came across the mummified remains of a long-dead Tundra-Plow, that I understood that a significant portion of the Tundra-Plow's body remains unseen while the animal is alive. A large bony plow, triangular in shape, travels just below the surface, cutting and pushing the soil into six waiting mouth-grooves for moisture filtration. Extending from an opening in the bottom of the plow is a hollow, rigid tongue, terminated by a vertically hinged ovoid structure. This extensible mouth-pod is unquestionably the organ responsible for plucking the small arctic plants from below.

My examination of this mummified specimen was only moderately satisfying, since I was enclosed in a vehicle. My hovercone contained a complex battery of sensors and receptors designed to measure the vital signs of living creatures, but the Yma had not provided ways to

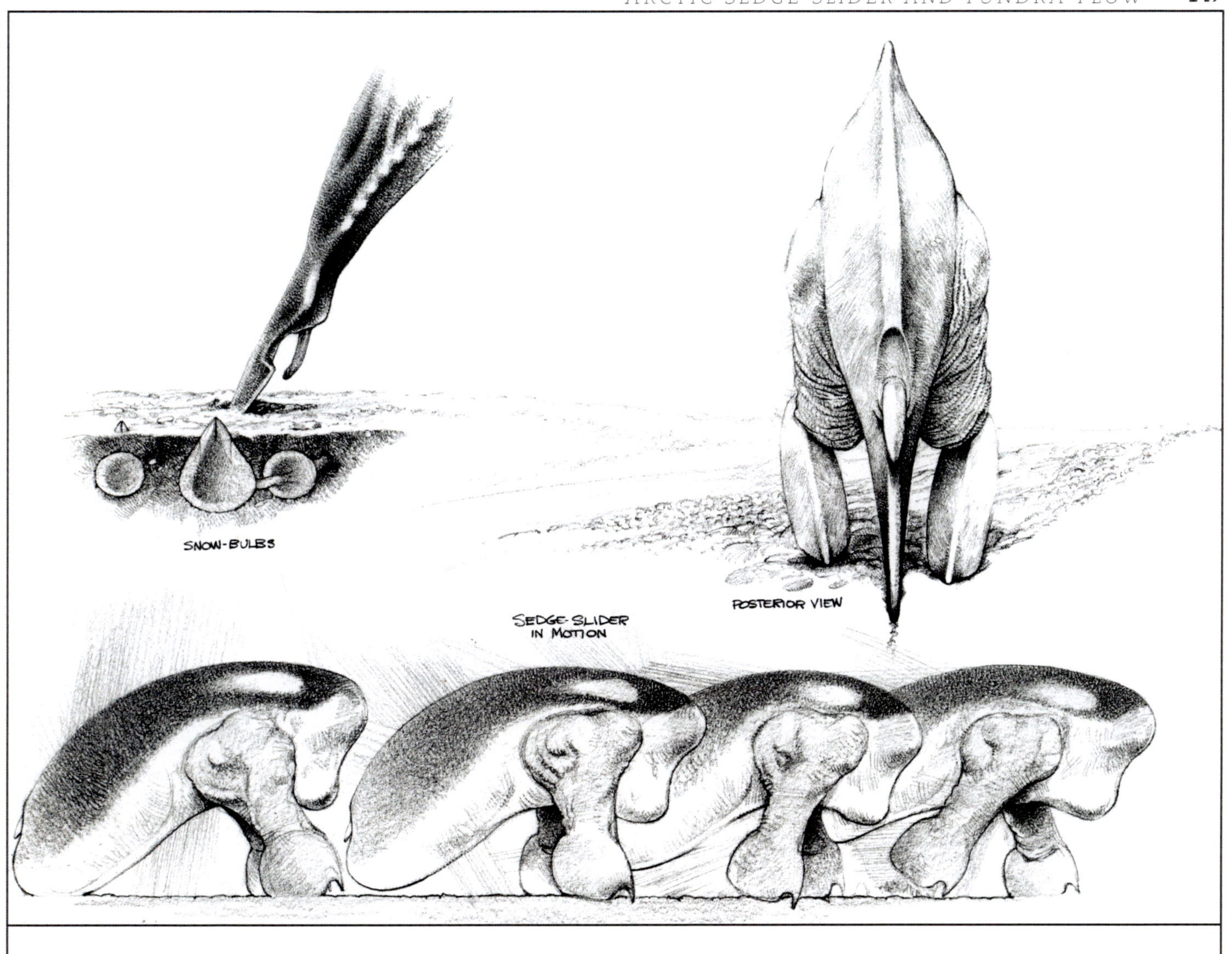

examine and preserve dead tissue. Perhaps this was an oversight, or perhaps it was part of their philosophy; at any rate, I felt that this moldering specimen might be a good candidate for collection and further study. The only possible source of conflict was the minimal microbial life within the carcass. But when I called the Orbitstar to ask permission, I inadvertently involved myself in a long-standing and bitter controversy. I was unaware that other members of the Expedition had made similar requests. They had all been answered with a flat refusal; and so was I. I re-member spending a good ten minutes muttering about the inflexibility of bureaucracy. Though we all thoroughly agreed with the Yma's objective of "preserving Darwin IV untouched," there were instances that pointed to a certain stubbornness within Expedition Control. Certainly Darwin IV was now and forevermore touched by the deaths of Drs. Ysud and Ysire.

A few kilometers from the crash site I heard some extremely loud *pings*; a few more kilometers and I came upon their source—three lumbering Sedge-sliders, their enormous pink

Over one-third of the Tundra-Plow travels underground, where it finds both food and moisture. Its long, deep furrows are a common feature of the sub-arctic landscape. The forward toothed pod pulls plants under by their roots, so that they seem to disappear magically from the herbivore's path as it travels.

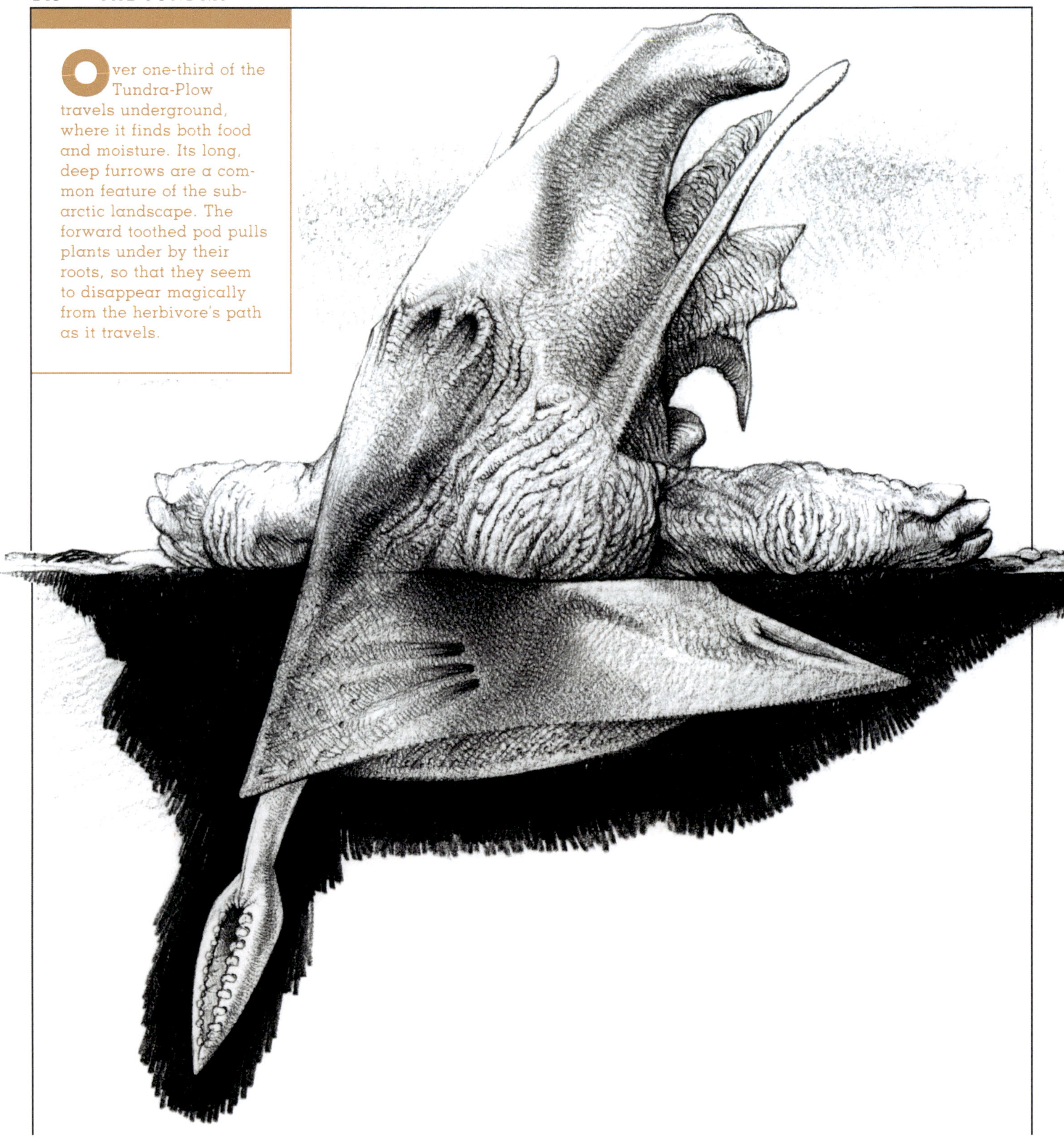

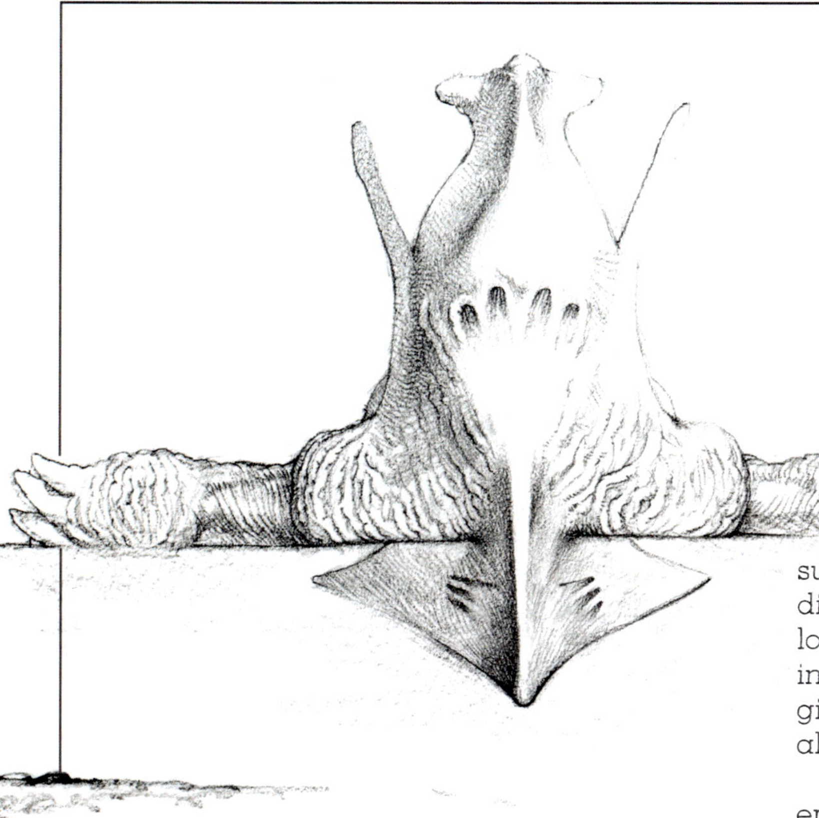

biolights shining like lanterns in the gloom of the receding storm. At first they appeared headless, but as the sky grew lighter I saw small dark beaks appear from beneath their anterior flaps. These gradually extended until an entire head was visible. The newly-emerged black heads steamed for a few moments in the frigid air until they cooled off. These large creatures had evolved a unique means of keeping their bare heads protected during arctic storms, by retracting them deep into their insulated body cavities.

The Sedge-sliders were anything but quick, pulling their ten-meter-tall bodies across the crunchy ground with laborious strokes of their huge, hooked feet. They were among the noisiest animals I found on Darwin IV, slamming out their *pings* with deafening regularity. I found the clamor annoying even after I shut down my internal speakers. The vibrations seemed to rattle every loose item within my 'cone.

The Sedge-sliders were placid animals, digging peacefully in the frozen arctic soil for the subterranean snowbulbs that comprised their diet. As they moved along I had the impression, looking at the ground behind them, that some indecisive paleontologist had been at work, digging here and there and leaving shallow holes all about.

A half hour into my sketching, I discovered the need for the creatures' exceptionally loud *pingings*. Because of the proximity of the glacier, the Sedge-slider has developed the ability to ricochet sonar signals off the ice wall; in fact, this seems to be its preferred means of echo-location. Over the hour or so that I watched the Sliders feed, one of them was always stationed near the glacier wall bouncing his *pings* off into the tundra while the other animals remained silent. My sonar analysis indicated that these were not single but multiple *pings* that reached into a number of directions simultaneously. The complexity of the returned signal must have been considerable, explaining the huge sonar bulge atop the creatures' bodies. Nature, as opportunistic as ever, had taken full advantage of the glacier and its acoustic capabilities.

My annoyance with the loud *pings* turned to admiration at the wonderful evolution that provided these creatures with so complex a survival mechanism. It must certainly be a clever arctic Bolt-tongue that catches any Sedge-slider unawares.

UNTH AND MUMMY-NEST FLYER

The sub-arctic biome presented me with more biological enigmas than any other region on Darwin. I came upon one such puzzle early on a spring day, while I was following a migrating herd of Unths across the flat tundra near Promunturium Weddell. The Unths, so named for the loud sighing sound that accompanies each heavy footfall, were heading for their spring calving ground to the north. The herd numbered about two hundred individuals, and their nervous energy was almost palpable. Most of the creatures were of breeding age and many displayed the distended bellies of pregnancy. It had apparently been a hard winter; the number of young was reduced and all the herd members appeared under-

PLATE XXIX. "Their stamping and wild bugling echoed in the frozen air." (Preliminary sketch)

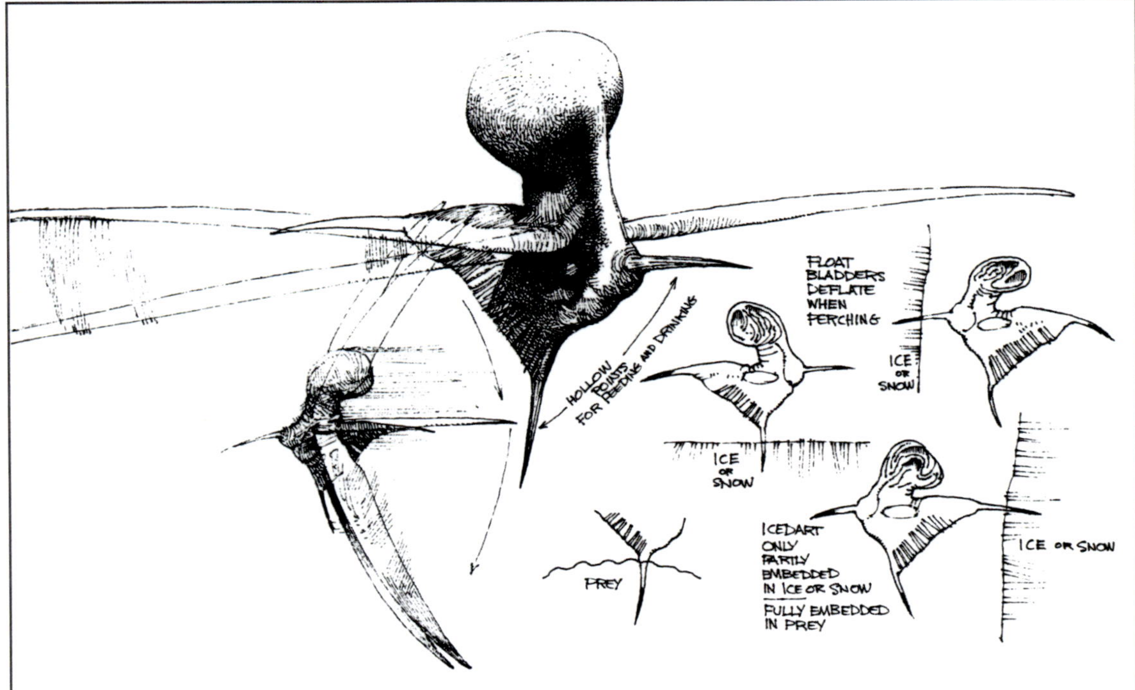

The Icedart is a lighter-than-air flyer that uses its hollow spikes to cling to the glacial ice during the fierce arctic storms. It is thought to get its nutrients from algae and microbes frozen in the ice, since it is never seen feeding on nearby tundra plants or animals.

weight. Even so, they were an impressive sight treading through the sedge.

I could not help but remember an experience I'd had with these same creatures during their fall rut the preceding year. An early snow had covered the ground and a lowering gray sky seemed to presage the hard winter to come. The bulky, six-meter-tall Unths, tails and backs filled out with their summer's stored fat reserves, clustered in pre-courtship groups. Because there is only one sex among them, the only members of the herd exempt from the ritualistic displays were the very young, the sick, and the aged. The remainder of the creatures were jabbing their tusks into the snow and earth or stamping about trumpeting. This bugling, which emanates from the eight openings on their flanks, is a deep and beautifully four-toned peal, rich with pained desire. It was easily heard for miles around.

I was hovering over the herd, sketching a couple of juveniles, when I saw two large Unths engaged in the preliminary biolight flaring of ritual combat. Standing in place, they were rotating rapidly, throwing up clods of snow and earth and *pinging* loudly. Abruptly, they would stop and face each other, tossing their heads and scratching the ground with their tusks. Sometimes mild pushing matches and tusk-clashing contests would ensue; moments later, they would begin rotating again with renewed energy. The sounds of their combat echoed in the frozen air.

This pattern would repeat itself until one of the creatures lowered its head in defeat, or charged. Whatever was the triggering element in the threat display (I certainly would not call it love), it was sufficient to create a mating pair. For copulation to occur, each partner had to withstand, and match, its potential partner's aggressive posturing. Combat is the final test of an Unth mate's compatibility and, I believe, a necessary element of the animals' sexual stimulation. Combat seems to release pheromones from both creatures that activate the urge to copulate.

I watched many threat displays, many

UNTH HERD PARTING AROUND MUMMY·NEST

of which ended in incompatibility. Sometimes, if combat ensued, the loser would be injured or too tired to engage in sex; in these cases they were left where they dropped. More often, though, the two creatures would copulate, creating offspring bred for strength and hardiness. The fall rut lasted for about three weeks during which time I recorded most individuals participating in at least three combats. Afterwards, the herd moved on to its wintering range. Calving, I knew, would occur in the middle of spring.

Spring in the circumpolar tundra is a time of reawakening, when the water, trapped for months in the spongy soil above the permafrost, begins to melt and bestow its life-giving qualities. Everywhere the low, hardy tundra plants begin to show signs of life. Gently glowing buds, in unthinkable numbers, appear upon the dark ground like a carpet of stars. The melted snow and softened ground also free the vast hibernating populations of Disk-flyers, which take wing and ascend in swirling clouds into the air. Larger fauna, too, seem more alive in their warming surroundings. The suns' rays touch the arctic like a remembered caress, charging plants and animals alike with the excitement of rebirth.

Clearly the boisterous Unth herd below me felt the excitement of seasonal rebirth; of the pleasure of their cold-stiffened hides and joints flexing more easily, and of the irresistible forces of reproduction that pushed them across the barren tundra. Filling the air with their distinctive hollow sonar, the Unths walked ten or twelve abreast toward their ancient calving fields.

Three days into my pursuit of the Unth herd, I saw the herd split to avoid an obstacle in its path. From my vantage point, one hundred meters behind the beasts, I couldn't quite make out what this obstacle was. I was not even sure if it was an animal or some inorganic formation. Then I saw that it was topped by a dim yellow biolight, which meant that the object was organic—or had once been.

The Unth's twin sets of nostrils serve different functions. The forward pair is for respiration, the rear ones are intakes for the trumpeting organs. The Unth's tongue can penetrate the ice to feed on snowbulbs without digging them up.

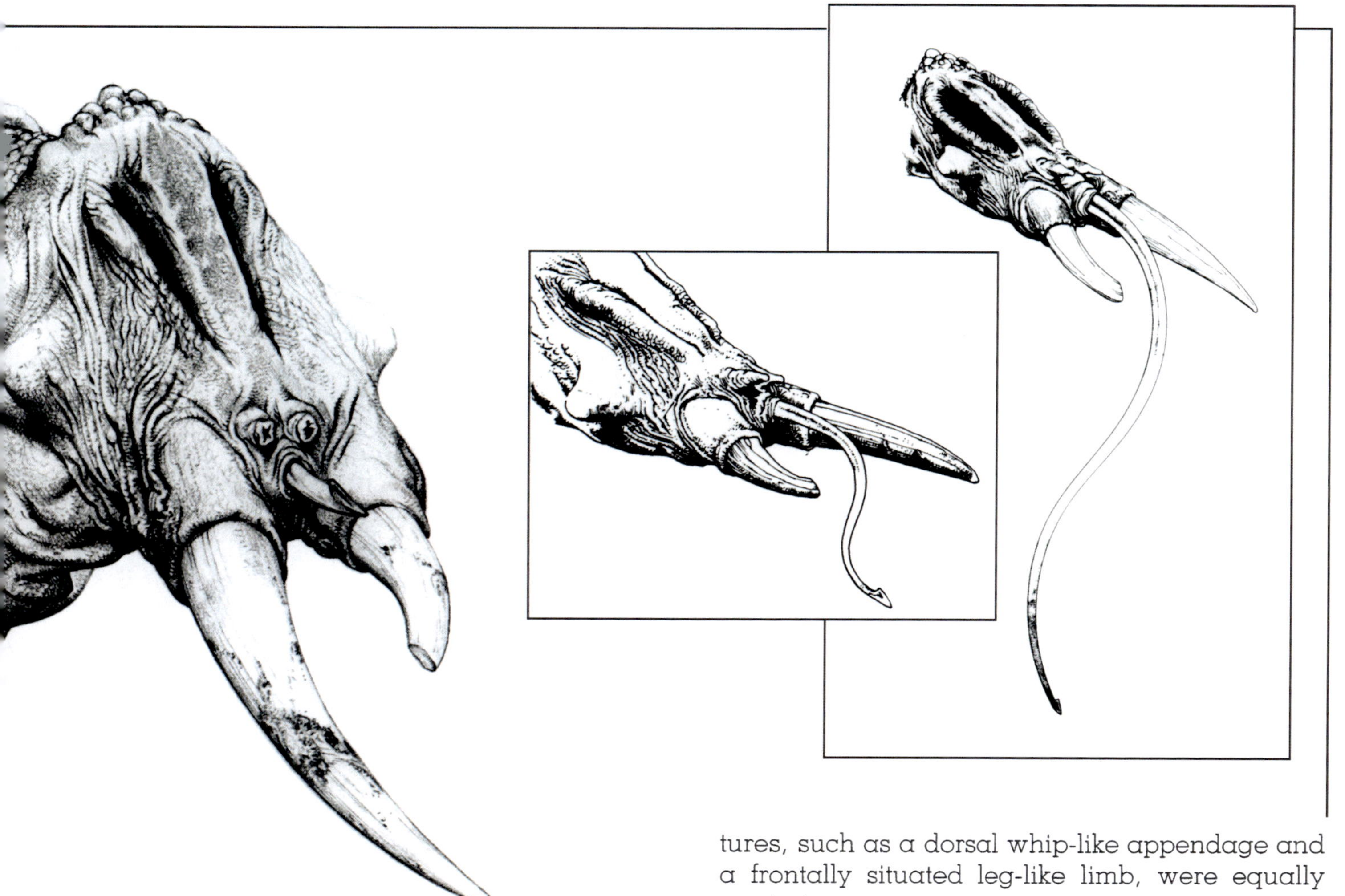

It was now a withered, flattened husk that more resembled some sun-dried vegetable than an animal. But in this case it was the merciless arctic wind, not the suns, that had brought the creature to its desiccated state.

Strange surface features became more apparent as I drew nearer: serpentine tubes twisted over and through furrowed folds which circled sphincter-like holes. Its bizarrely baroque texture shed little light on the creature's original appearance. Larger features, such as a dorsal whip-like appendage and a frontally situated leg-like limb, were equally mysterious.

I circled the three-and-one-half-meter-tall mummy until I arrived at a position directly in front of its "head." There was a dark opening just beneath the dimly glowing biolight. I shined the 'cone's narrow-beam spotlight into the hole and the emptiness seemed to confirm that this was nothing more than a mummified carcass. But why was the biolight still glowing? I was soon to find out.

I began to pick up the shrill *pinging* of a flyer as it headed rapidly toward me. In a moment I could see the small creature as it circled the mummy and me. It seemed agitated (or perhaps I was anthropomorphising) and I decided to withdraw a few meters. Within a minute of my backing away, the black flyer swooped down; with blurred wings it hovered, then landed

PLATE XXX. "With blurred wings it hovered, then landed upon the mummy's head."

upon the mummy's "head" and disappeared into the hole. I waited a full hour for the flyer to reappear, but it never did.

It had not occurred to me until then to take an IR reading of the carcass, so convincing was its moribund appearance. In spite of the biolight, the frozen husk appeared as wind-desiccated as any dead creature on the tundra. Only after I finally took my readings did I realize that this cryptobiotic mummy-nest was providing warmth and shelter to the little flyer.

My final task was to try to reason out the relationship between the nest-creature and the flyer. Difficult as this may seem, I had been presented with one small clue when the flyer had entered the husk. As it backed into the "head" cavity I noticed that its configuration seemed to line up with the rim of the opening as if the two had once been joined. This led me to speculate that the flyer and the husk were one and the same animal, separated at some point in the flyer's development. I concluded that the husk remained alive through the flyer's tending and served to protect it from the harsh climate. I have no proof to support this theory, and as this was the only individual any Expedition-member encountered, I will never be certain of the answer. I did, however, take the liberty of naming it the Mummy-nest Flyer.

I resumed my travels with the Unth herd and stayed with them for several weeks, taking notes and doing a number of pencil studies. During these weeks a worrisome rumor began to circulate amongst the Expedition members. According to the rumor, a spy had leaked the coordinates of Darwin IV to an alien hunting cartel. The rumor went on to say that some Expedition members had spotted remote hunting drones. (These are usually linked to orbiting vessels filled with "sportsmen" who sit at plush armchair controls and choreograph the kills.) I had never seen anything that aroused my suspicions, but I was sickened when I thought of the implications.

The herd below me was, of course, oblivious to these rumors. Every few days the Unths would come to a halt on finding a field that was rich in their forage, the dark-leafed snowbulb tubers. These shallow-rooted, fleshy plants which grow just beneath the top layer of soil are quite pervasive in the circumpolar region. Using their tusks, the Unths turned over acres of topsoil to get to the plants, which they sucked dry with their long feeding tubes.

Eventually, after a few weeks, the Unths reached their destination, a plain just a few kilometers from the glacier's wall. I could see no difference between this part of the tundra and any other, yet the weary Unths seemed relieved and content. Ever vigilant against arctic Bolt-tongues, Skewers and other predators, they proceeded to scoop out large cavities in the ground that I (correctly) assumed would receive their young. Into these cavities the Unths regurgitated large quantities of snowbulb pulp acquired from a nearby field. The pulp would solidify and provide an edible, cushiony nest-lining for the active infant Unths.

Soon the air was filled with the sounds of birthing. For days *pings*, groans, and sighs bounced eerily off of the nearby glacier and carried for miles into the open tundra. The breeding ground became a noisy nursery for scores of tiny, tuskless Unths. Dutiful parents went in shifts to gather food for the demanding infants. The activity and noise were ceaseless, and through it all I felt that I was witnessing behavior that had not changed for hundreds of centuries.

During my many weeks of observation of the arctic Unths I found them to be completely at ease with my presence. These were among my most enjoyable and peaceful weeks on Darwin IV. The loneliness I felt for my wife and child was assuaged, rather than increased, by the

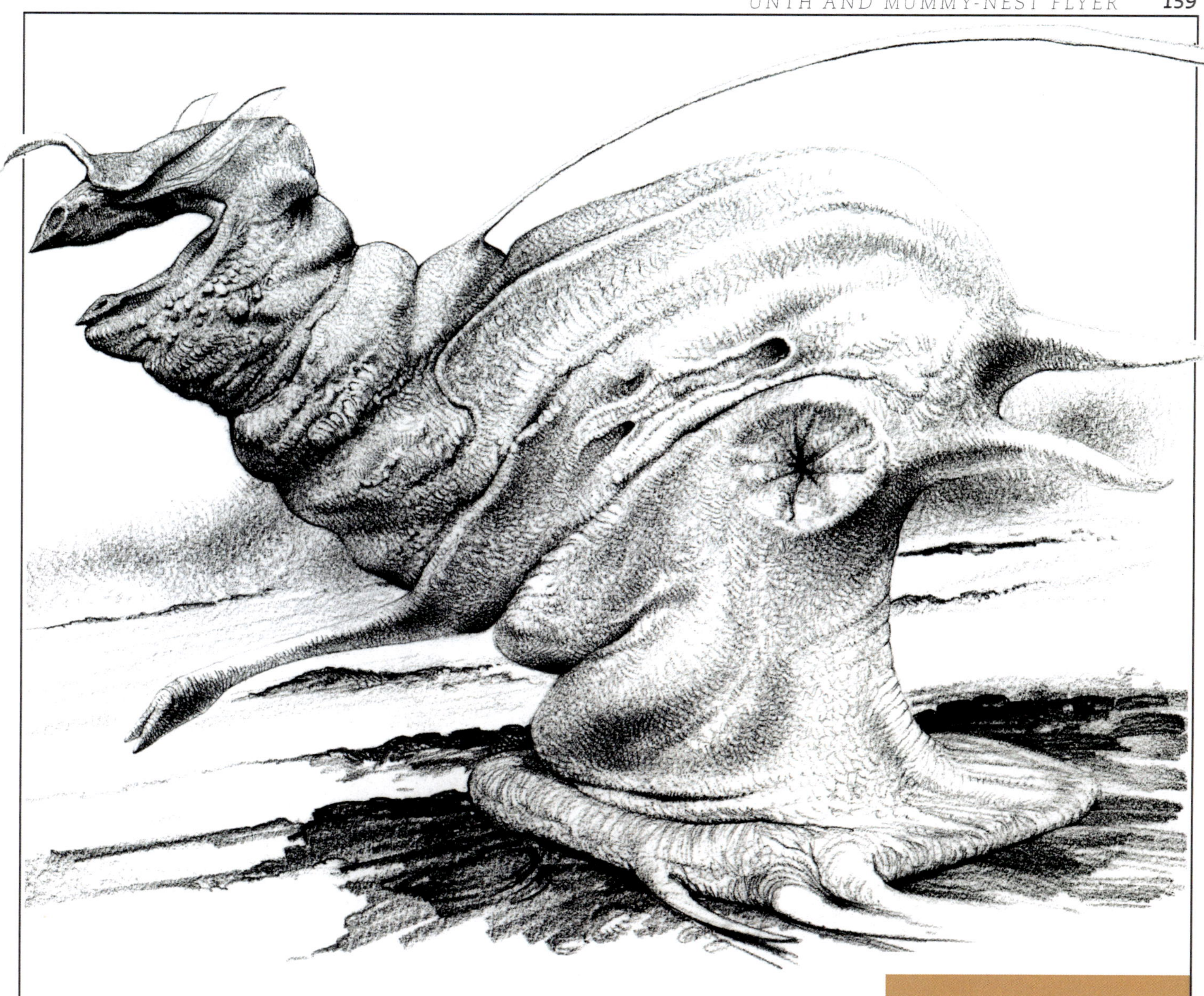

pleasure of watching the young Unths and their giant parents playing and nuzzling at the edge of the ice. It was only when I hovered too near the breeding ground that I began to sense that they were unhappy with my proximity; and rather than chance any incident that might put the young at risk, I decided to withdraw. As I pulled away I left my speakers on and I listened as the sounds of new life on the tundra faded in the distance.

This is what the Mummy-nest *might* have looked like when it was ambulatory. The "head" has not yet detached and become the separate flyer which (according to my theory) burrows in and feeds on the desiccated shell of what was once its lower torso.

PLATE XXXI. "I had a blurred impression of a dark animal speeding over the ice."

I spent quite a few months circumnavigating the great northern glacier cap that covers Darwin IV's northern pole. After the tragic loss of our two scientists, and due to the unpredictable nature of the arctic weather, I had been warned (but not ordered) not to attempt any cross-glacial explorations; I therefore contented myself with exploring the tundra-fields of the Planum Hudson.

Most of my travels took place during the months of Darwin IV's arctic twilight. The perpetual dusk made spotting animals considerably easier, as the creatures' biolights were in constant evidence. They were, however, not the only beautiful sources of light. Often, high above the massive glacier, I could see vast, crackling auroras flickering

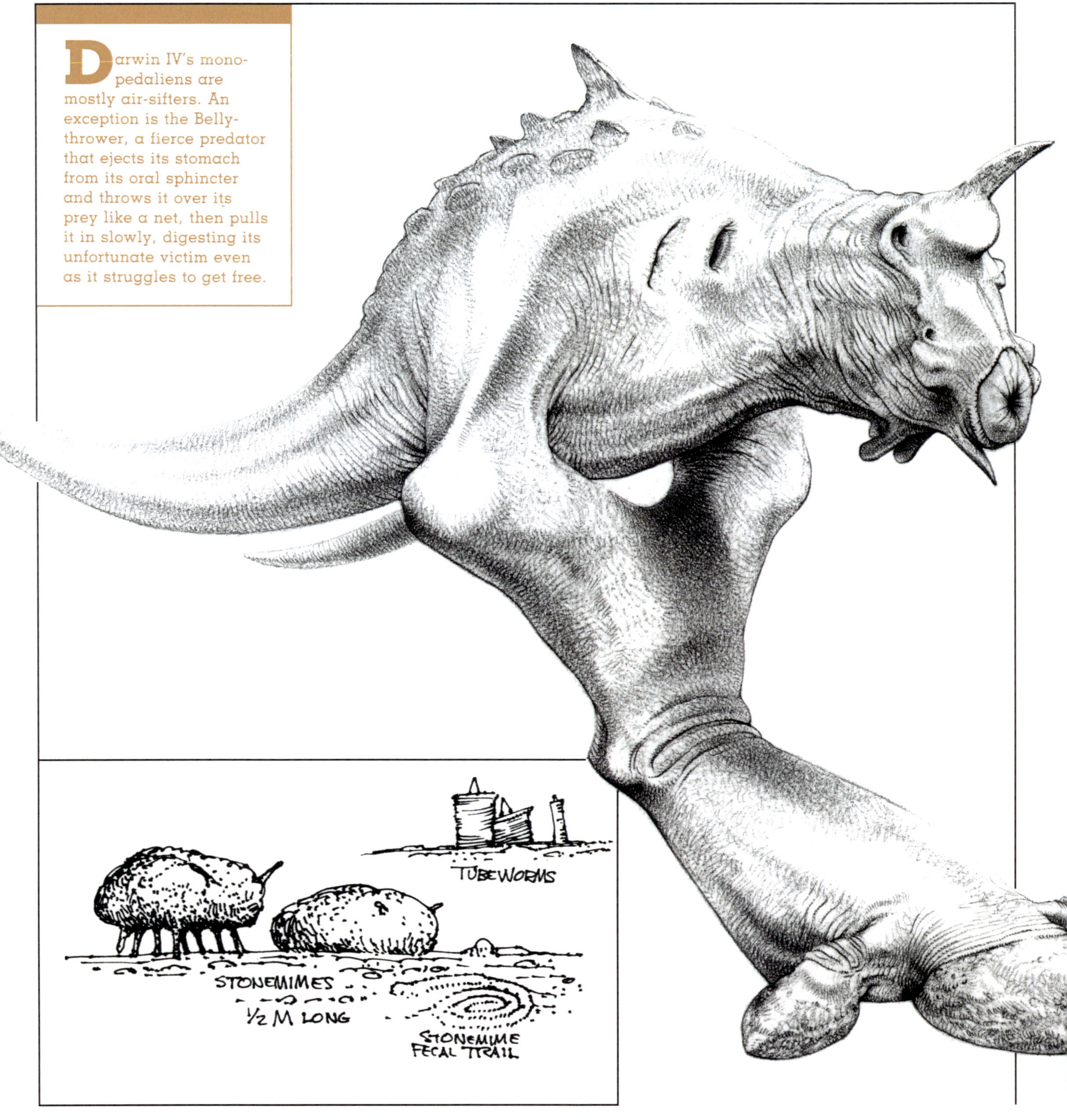

Darwin IV's mono-pedaliens are mostly air-sifters. An exception is the Belly-thrower, a fierce predator that ejects its stomach from its oral sphincter and throws it over its prey like a net, then pulls it in slowly, digesting its unfortunate victim even as it struggles to get free.

and shimmering, providing a glorious backdrop to the crags of B14 and B15. The wonderful play of light reflected upon the icy back of the glacier seemed to imbue the ice with a lambent semblance of life.

For days I floated over patches of low, blue whipweed and pointillistic beds of polardots, keeping the glacier to my left. Frequently I found areas that were crisscrossed with drag marks not unlike those of the foothill-dwelling Keeled Sliders. The scale of the tracks and the forelimb strokes were dissimilar, however, and I guessed that the two species would be as well.

Early one evening I was gazing out over the foreboding expanse of the glacier's surface when I noticed a series of tiny specks some fifty kilometers away. At this distance I could not tell if they were blocks of ice or lifeforms; I altered the 'cone's canopy to magnify the image but because of the gloom, the resolution was poor. I ate dinner, relaxed a bit and then revved up the turbo-fan. I was well aware of the dangers inherent in traveling over the glacier, but I rationalized that I was not going to be journeying very far.

I climbed to clear the one-hundred-fifty-meter edge of the glacier, the surface of which seemed to glow with an eerie, milky-white light. As in my earlier flyovers, I noticed innumerable small tunnel openings in the ice cliff. They occurred in clusters but I could see no obvious pattern to their distribution.

As I approached the thirty or so "irregularities," I began to see that, just as I had suspected, they were not features of the ice but were, instead, immobile, ice-dwelling creatures. Each was imbedded in a translucent sac which, in turn, was frozen to the glacier's surface. These sacs were roughly three meters long, smooth, rigid, and ovoid. They appeared to have been in place for some time. Though the sacs were somewhat translucent, I could not discern the shapes of the core-creatures within. Something could be seen to stir, but my scanners gave back only the weakest of signals, most of their beams bouncing off of the strange, impermeable sacs.

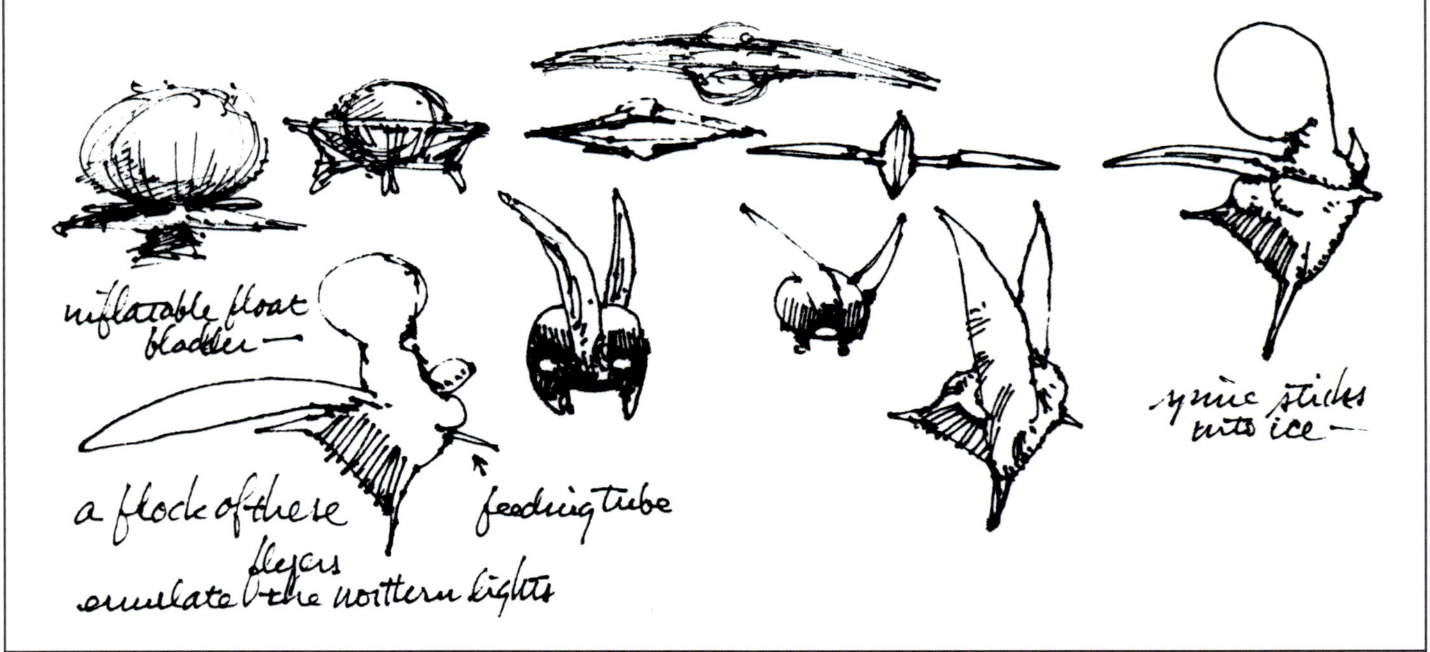

Over the next hour I made little headway with my investigations. Finally, admitting defeat, I swung my craft around and headed back out toward the tundra.

Weeks passed before I returned, out of curiosity, to the spot on the glacier where the motionless creatures had been. It was the beginning of the arctic spring and the suns were low and pallid on the horizon. Of the thirty-odd individuals I had spotted earlier, only five remained. All but one of these were free of their sacs and their transformation was remarkable.

Instead of the cryptic, featureless ovoids that had confounded me, I was greeted by four armored creatures busily ingesting their outer sacs. Each had positioned itself over the discarded and shriveled sac and unseen mouth parts sucked the membrane down until eventually nothing remained.

The fifth creature had waited, it seemed, to demonstrate the discarding process to me. As I watched, its somewhat deflated sac began to expand. Apparently inflated by the creature's exhalations, the sac grew to startling proportions before bursting, with a comically flatulent roar, in a cloud of frozen vapor. The internal pressure must have been considerable; a twenty minute rest, accompanied by much vaporous panting, was evidence of the animal's exertions.

The Icecrawlers fully revealed were almost as enigmatic as they had been in their sacs. No legs or feet or even head were visible; each animal was covered with tightly-joined yet flexible armor plates. With no features to guide me I could not even distinguish head from tail.

As the creatures finished eating, they began to move over the ice with surprising speed, each one leaving an unnaturally slick trail behind. Only their movement gave me any clue as to which end was the front. As they moved off I noticed that there were many straight trails etched into the ice, corresponding, I assumed, to the twenty-five absent Icecrawlers.

I had trouble keeping up with the two-

meter-long animals as they slid their way over the ice in very unpredictable patterns. Their speed, approaching thirty-five kilometers per hour, seemed incredible for an animal with no visible legs or propulsion system. I followed about thirty meters behind them as they zig-zagged across the surface of the glacier. I guessed that they were heading toward a patch of brownish algae-rich ice some three kilometers away. When they reached the patch, I was gratified to see them slow to a halt. I increased the magnification on my canopy glass, but to no avail. As in the case of their invisible limbs, I was now treated to invisible feeding organs as the Icecrawlers began to browse on the algae, leaving strange scalloped grooves behind them in the ice.

While I was engrossed in the grazing Icecrawlers, another creature suddenly cut into view. I had a blurrred impression of a dark animal speeding over the ice, and I quickly reset the canopy glass magnification to get a better look at it. The newcomer was a Rimerunner, an ice-dwelling monopedalien that I had heard about but never yet encountered. As it dashed across the glacier, I realized that this might be my only opportunity to observe the elusive creature. I resolved to follow it and leave the Icecrawlers to their feeding.

I pulled my 'cone back a few meters to get a better idea of where my quarry was heading, and then gunned my turbo-fan. The Rimerunner was bounding in the general direction of B14, a destination I was not about to add to my list of conquered territories. I was imprudently far over the glacier already, and because of this I allowed myself only a limited chase.

The Rimerunner is, like most of Darwin IV's monopedaliens, a ricochetal saltator, equipped with one powerful leg attached to a complex pelvis. This small species, unlike its ground-dwelling cousins, was not particularly fast, a fact I put down to the problems inherent in traveling over ice. Its dark, dorsal markings gave it a hooded and somewhat threatening appearance.

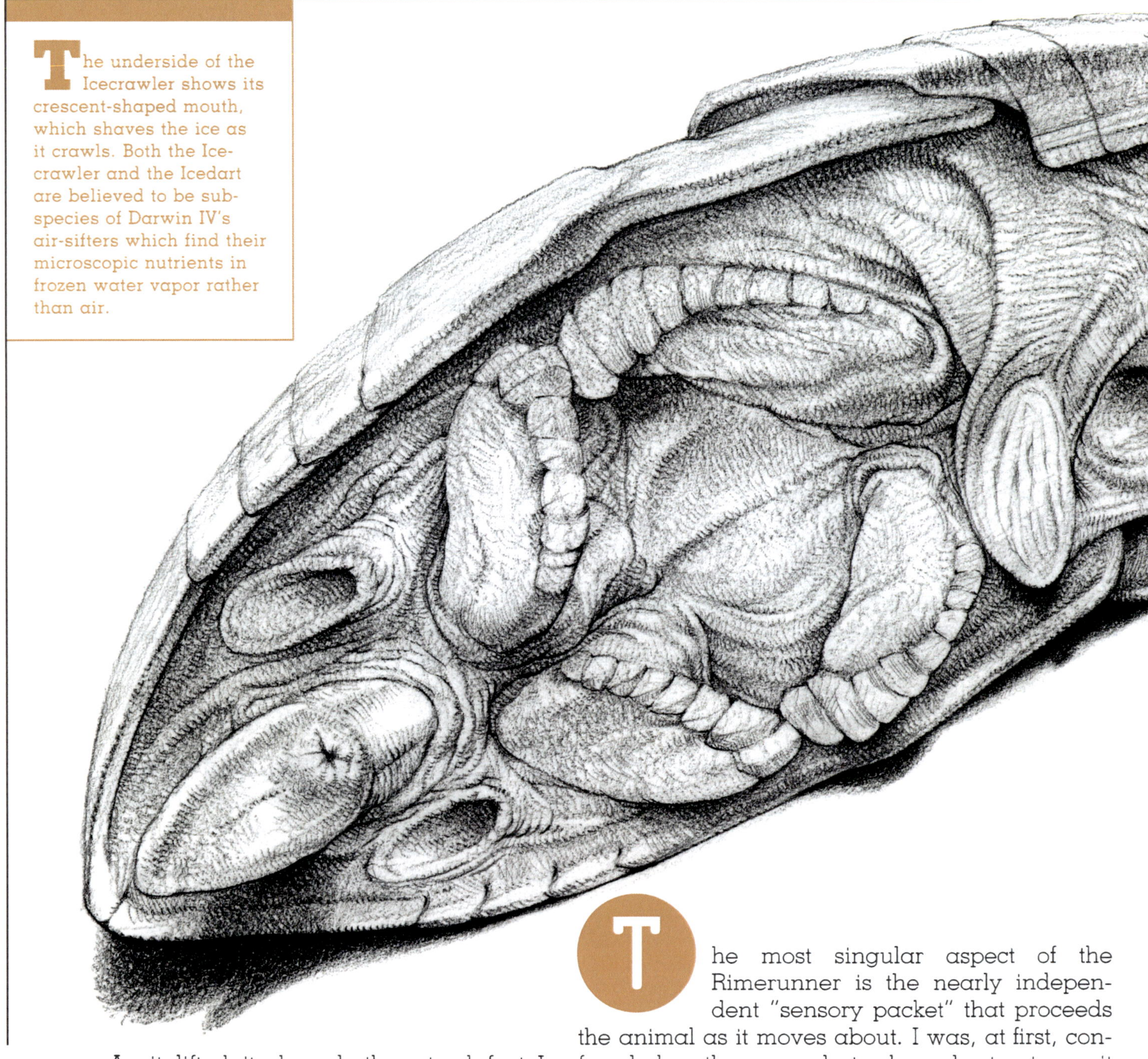

The underside of the Icecrawler shows its crescent-shaped mouth, which shaves the ice as it crawls. Both the Icecrawler and the Icedart are believed to be sub-species of Darwin IV's air-sifters which find their microscopic nutrients in frozen water vapor rather than air.

As it lifted its broad, three-toed foot I could see one adaptation that increased traction upon the ice. The padded sole of its foot was deeply channeled and grooved, and with each footfall I could see the pad expand and grip the ice. Each fold probably possesses some additional micro-structure to further enhance traction.

The most singular aspect of the Rimerunner is the nearly independent "sensory packet" that proceeds the animal as it moves about. I was, at first, confused by the parachute-shaped structure; it looked like some unfortunate prey that was in imminent danger of being caught by the Rimerunner. Indeed, the monopedalien halted only after its "face" had split vertically and the "victim" had been sucked within. But my assumption that the beast had fed could not have been

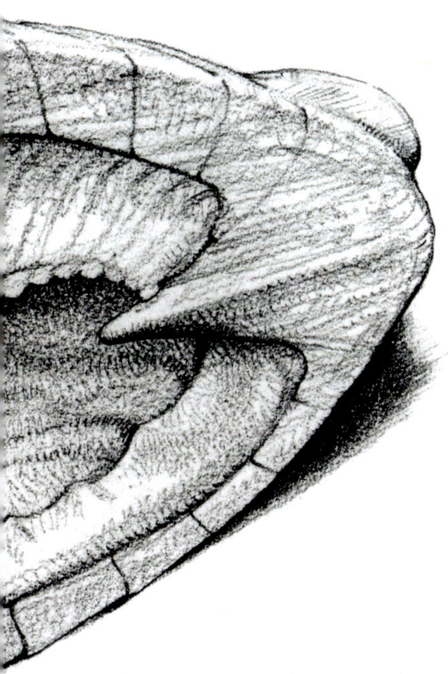

further from the truth — presently the animal ejected its "prey" and began to run again!

When I magnified and carefully studied the image, I learned that the domed, orange structure was attached to the Rimerunner by the thinnest of neural cables. I also saw numerous siphon holes on the flattened rear of the structure, each puffing continuously to keep it ahead of the trailing body. It is a marvel of physiological engineering and, even now, I am not entirely certain of its function. The Rimerunner's sonar was clearly emanating from its body, and I imagine that most of its other senses were as well. Looking closely at the structure of the floating organ, I noted a tiny, iris-like opening at the front of the organ, and I reasoned that perhaps it was a primitive light-gathering structure. Whether it was evolving or degenerating, whether it was a radical advance in Darwinian senses or an antiquated vestige that was in the process of being discarded, I had no way of knowing. I could not help but feel that it was vestigial.

As the Rimerunner, oblivious to my observations, dashed headlong over the ice, I noticed a few purple, tube-like oothecae attached to its leg, and realized that this specimen would probably be dead within a few weeks. The barb-tipped eggs belonged to an extremely aggressive variety of ectoparasitoid flyer, the appropriately named Carver-wing, and would, upon hatching, waste little time in devouring their host. Even now the eggs were sapping the Rimerunner's strength. Though I was sensible enough to understand the reality of parasitism as fitting into the scheme of nature, it saddened me to see an animal in its prime destined for such an end.

I followed the Rimerunner for an hour, breaking off my pursuit when I reached my distance limit. As I watched it run on toward the mountains I saw it stumble and fall and then rise again. Perhaps I had miscalculated how long the creature had to survive.

I returned to find my small group of Icecrawlers, but they had moved on, leaving the glacier sculpted by their scalloped feeding tracks and locomotion marks, and littered with their fecal coils.

I turned my 'cone south and left the glacier behind. The tundra stretched out below me like a velvet gray-green carpet, dotted with wind-carved boulders. The softening ground basked in the warmth of the newly-risen suns.

PLATE XXXII. *A stately flyer, the Ebony Blisterwing.*

THE AIR

SKEWER AND SYMET

I rose early one autumn day, eager to explore the golden-blue morning air above Darwin IV. I would never get used to the contrast between this pure air and the fouled ashen skies of Earth. The grasses of the Vallis Przewalski which stretched endlessly around my "parked" 'cone, were washed in the distinctive gray-greens of fall, and a light dew made the sunslit scene a glittering spectacle. While I ate breakfast I punched in the pre-flight programming for the Video/Audio Pod, or VAP, a small remote that I planned to use to track the winged denizens of Darwin's skies. Pre-flight checks went routinely and the pod's lift-off was uneventful. The voice-activated remote's camera lids snapped open at three hundred meters and,

PLATE XXXIII. *"I could almost feel the tension of the animal below as they heard the targeting pings."*

eyes glued to my monitor, I settled into my chair for a day's vicarious exploration.

Visibility was superb; the grasslands appeared in wonderful clarity as they flowed far below my speeding VAP. Eventually they gave way to the desert, which stretched away like an ochre ocean with low, rough waves of rocky hummocks. Scattered among the hills were spindly purple flex-firs with thin trunks so supple that their crowns touched the ground during windstorms. Here and there an occasional Butchertree stood twitching and snapping its arms, surrounded by its grisly leavings. Far off in the bluish haze of the horizon, a dark smear indicated a herd of migrating bipedaliens picking their way among the low hills and filling the air with their distant chorus of *pings*.

Without warning a small flight of Violet Follow-wings darted from behind the VAP and swept on ahead. I increased the pod's speed and pursued the two-meter-long flyers as they banked and turned with startling precision. I began to feel that, as far as manual guidance was concerned, I was out of my depth and ordered a computer lock-on in an effort to stay with them.

Within ten minutes we were consider-ably closer to the large bipedalien herd. It was heading toward a wide river that oxbowed sinuously across the desert. A huge cloud of dust hung over and behind the herd, lingering in the air for miles. We dove into it.

Suddenly my VAP's proximity indicator flashed as two huge flyers dove in front of my Follow-wing companions. Instantly they slowed and fell in behind their immense cousins, veering and banking as the larger flyers did. Their apparent goal was the herd and, as we vectored near, their ultra-high frequency *pings* became more rapid. I pushed the VAP ahead in an effort to get a better look at the huge flyers that had so effortlessly taken the lead. They were thick-bodied creatures, powerfully winged and equipped with long, curved lances that protruded from their heads. They exuded an aura of frightening potency.

I could almost feel the tension of the animals below as they heard the targeting *pings* and became aware of the pair and their retinue of Follow-wings. The herd members, however, wasted no time in useless panic. En masse, the entire herd started to trill in an effort to jam the hunters' sonar. The din was such that I was forced to reduce the volume on my internal speakers.

Undaunted, the two large flyers, or Skewers, as I came to call them, contracted their corrugated, leathery wings and began an awe-

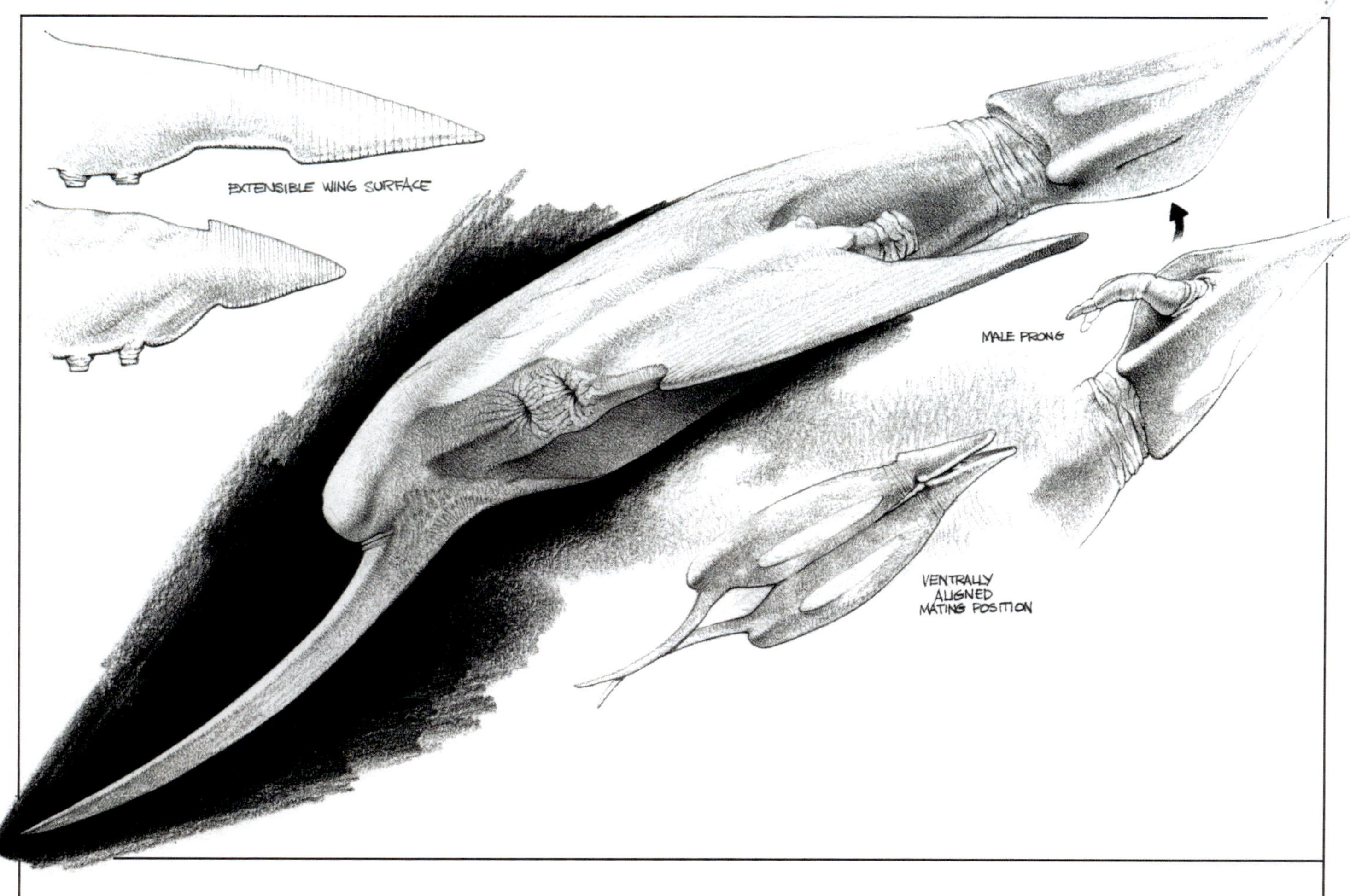

some power dive. They had targeted a pair of stragglers which had not kept up as the herd was fording the river. The herbivores were curious animals that appeared to have a head at either end of their trunk, and as the Skewers plunged toward them, they began to turn in place, rotating rapidly in a gathering cloud of dust. They stopped and I realized why nature had equipped these animals with a head and tail of almost the exact shape and size: I could barely tell which end of the beast was which. To a creature relying on sonar recognition, they presented a confusing image. The direction of their imminent flight was completely conjectural. I named them Symets for their protective symmetry.

I pulled the VAP back at the moment of attack, and I was rewarded with an all-too-clear transmission of the kill. As percentages would have it, one of the Symets leapt clear, its would-be killer veering off to regain altitude for a second pass. The other was not so fortunate, taking the full impact of the Skewer's wicked lance below the spine. The blow lifted the two-ton creature off its two kicking feet, driving it down the lance's length, while the Skewer pulled sharply up, away from the desert. The scavenging Follow-wings were in a frenzy, darting forward to nip at the impaled Symet with their vertically hinged jaws. Bits of flesh fell from the animal to be snapped up by other Follow-wings.

The soaring Skewer took absolutely no notice of the scavengers, absorbed as it was in sucking the carcass dry. A few minutes later, the Follow-wings were presented with a fluidless

The carrion-feeding module of the Scavengewing has a highly specialized digestive system capable of devouring food that is in an advanced state of decay. It is dropped with pinpoint accuracy from as high as 1500 meters. The floating module picks up the feeding module in its own mouth; thus it appears to be devouring it in turn.

husk as the Skewer let it fall. Without hesitation the scavengers peeled off and dived after their meal, making so many passes at the body that little more than bones hit the ground.

No other predator evoked the same sense of dread and respect in the Expedition members during our relatively brief stay on Darwin IV. Mating on the wing, belly to belly, the Skewer is totally at home in the air. Ranging over ninety percent of the globe, it is unparalleled in its ability to hunt and kill. Virtually no animal is safe from its attentions, including, according to an amazing

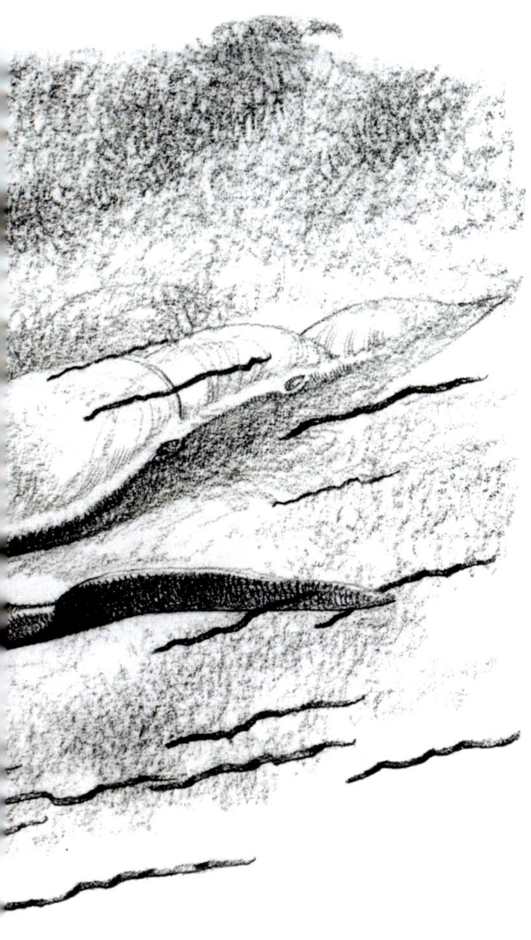

eyewitness account, the Emperor Sea Strider. Hunting in pods of up to thirty or more individuals, these predators can overcome even the largest of Darwin IV's inhabitants.

  With my VAP almost out of range, I punched in auto-return and settled back to wait. The pod would find and re-engage my hovercone on its own. My experiences had whetted my appetite for more aerial adventures, and I launched another VAP later that day.

Some weeks later I had the opportunity to study a newly-crashed Skewer that I found jammed in a cliffside crevice. I came upon it by chance while exploring a dryland canyon. The flyer's wings were shorn off from the crash, and it had been gnawed by scavengers, but, happily, the large head remained relatively intact. I found it to be of very sturdy yet light construction, with bony structures buttressing the formidable lance. The lance itself was a marvel of design, being hollow, internally braced and as strong as titanium. I also believe it was, like the best blades, quite flexible.

  Since my first encounter with Skewers, I had periodically watched them hone their lances in numerous passes on volcanic "whetting spires." But this ancient predator's lance was beyond whetting; the forward portion was broken off, a condition that had undoubtedly contributed to its demise.

  As I examined the broken lance, I discovered a battery of pointed, chitin-tipped tongues, each one capable of boring into flesh. This, then, was how the Skewer fed on the wing. Upon the impalement of prey, these tongues would snake out of a dorsal groove on the lance and penetrate the body to suck it dry. Here was a classic irony of Nature: a massive, powerful animal whose existence depended upon a fragile anatomical structure. This revelation made me respect the marvels of evolution all the more.

RUGOSE FLOATER

Icould not resist following these two heavily wrinkled floaters for about ten kilometers in the air near Mons Burton. They were lazy creatures, in no particular hurry, and they flew in wide, slow circles that afforded me an excellent view of them. I dubbed them Rugose Floaters.

They were in many ways archetypal floaters, but I was particularly intrigued by the small globules which trailed their enlarged upper and lower fins; globules which I scanned and discovered to be egg masses. These light ova-globules break down and scatter on the wind, spreading the floater's tiny progeny through the planet's middle atmosphere. When I thought about it, I surmised that the slow, circular flight path

PLATE XXXIV. "They were lazy creatures and they flew in wide, slow circles."

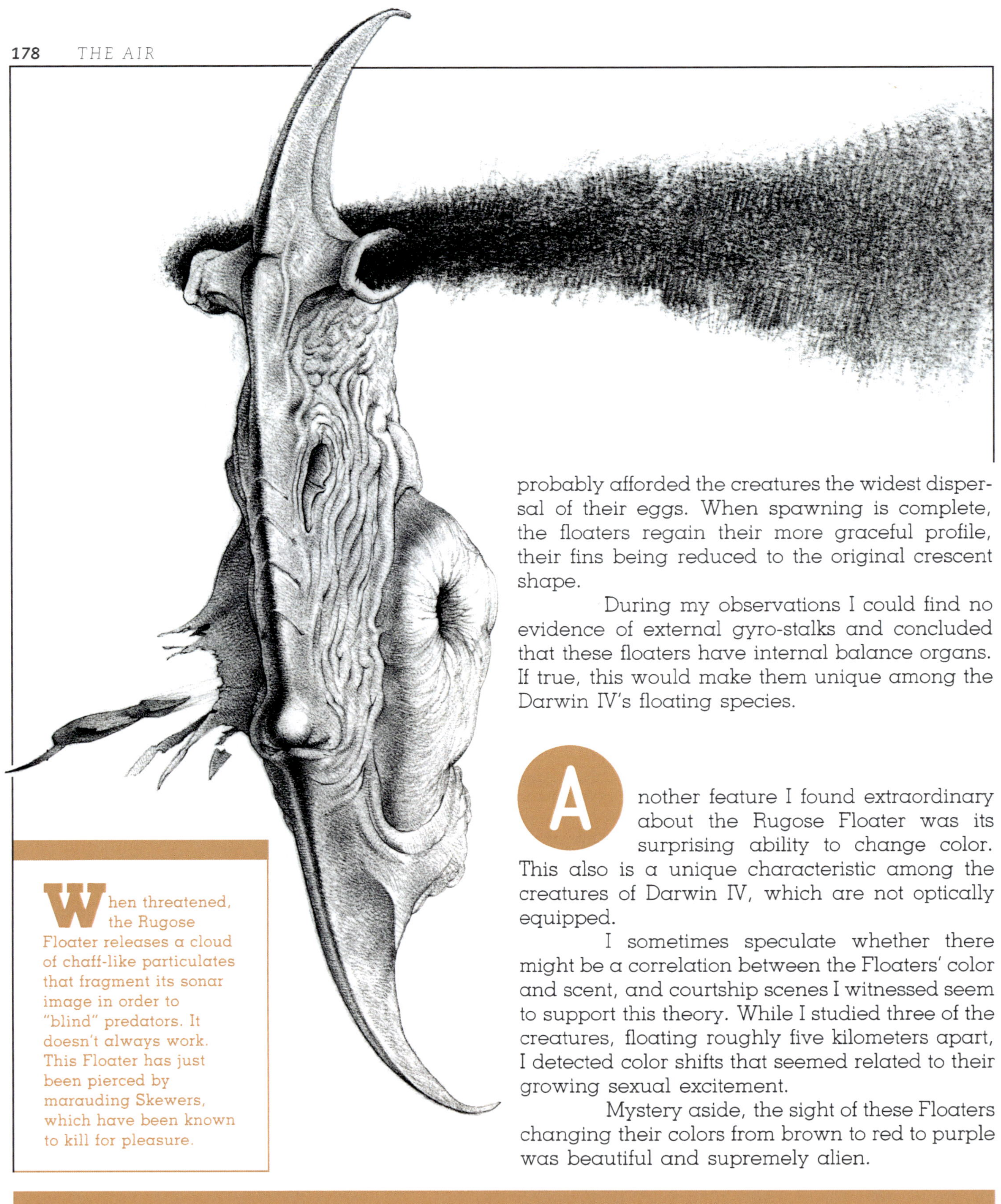

probably afforded the creatures the widest dispersal of their eggs. When spawning is complete, the floaters regain their more graceful profile, their fins being reduced to the original crescent shape.

During my observations I could find no evidence of external gyro-stalks and concluded that these floaters have internal balance organs. If true, this would make them unique among the Darwin IV's floating species.

Another feature I found extraordinary about the Rugose Floater was its surprising ability to change color. This also is a unique characteristic among the creatures of Darwin IV, which are not optically equipped.

I sometimes speculate whether there might be a correlation between the Floaters' color and scent, and courtship scenes I witnessed seem to support this theory. While I studied three of the creatures, floating roughly five kilometers apart, I detected color shifts that seemed related to their growing sexual excitement.

Mystery aside, the sight of these Floaters changing their colors from brown to red to purple was beautiful and supremely alien.

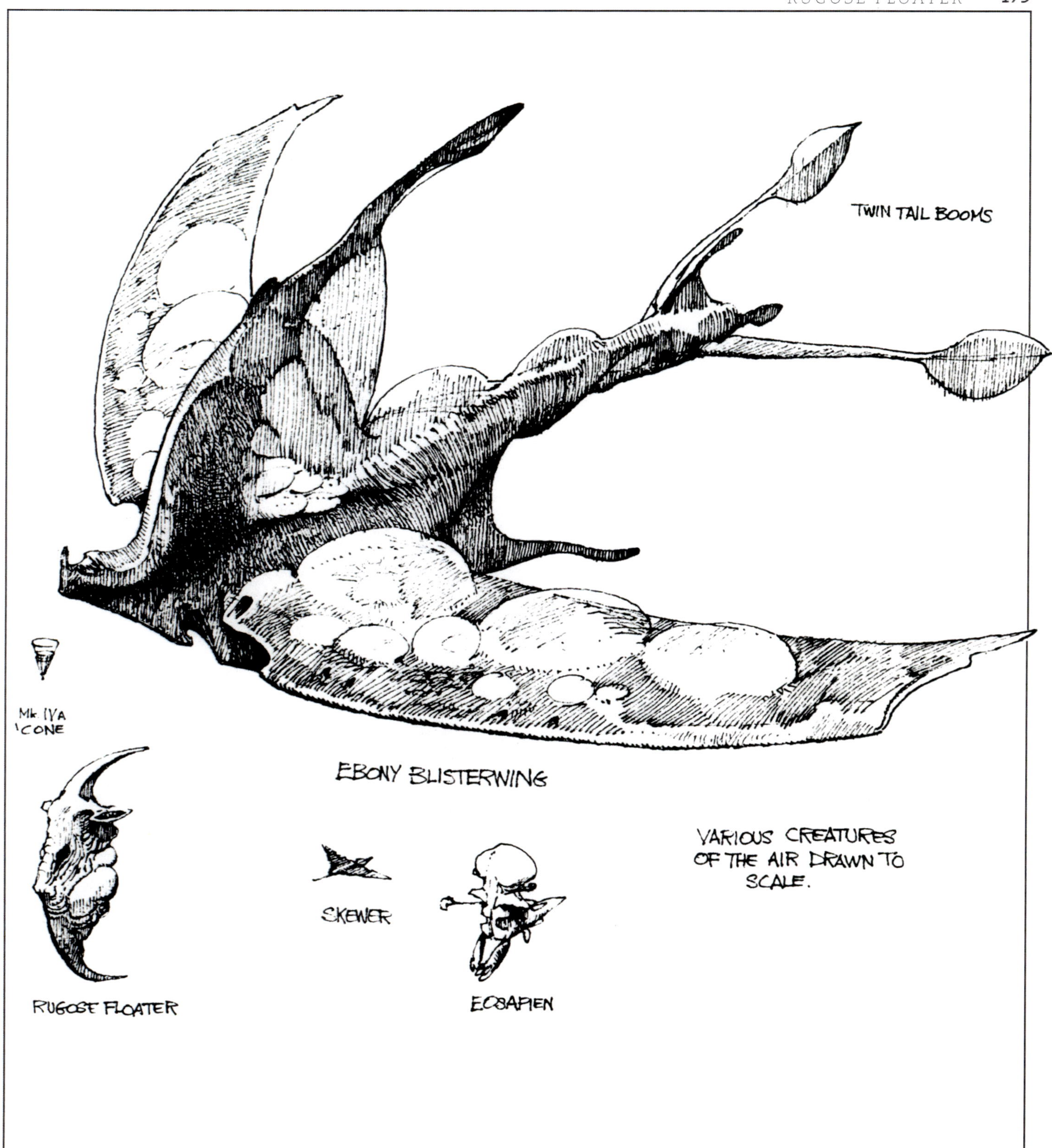

TWIN TAIL BOOMS
Mk IVA 'CONE
EBONY BLISTERWING
VARIOUS CREATURES OF THE AIR DRAWN TO SCALE.
SKEWER
ECOSAPIEN
RUGOSE FLOATER

EOSAPIEN

A fortnight before my departure from Darwin IV, I was sketching a high-altitude study of the Amoebic Sea. It was a perfect morning, golden and fresh. Fluffy clouds skimmed around me in a slow race toward the brilliant, newly-risen suns. Far below, in the purple gloom, the sunslight began to pick out the gentle crests of the gel-waves as the luminous layers under the surface began to dim. As I floated in the warming winds, I realized how much I would miss this alien place and fantasized about how I might return to continue my observations and artwork. My reveries were broken by a blinking orange light on my screen, indicating that the sonar perimeter of thirty kilometers that I had established had been broken.

PLATE XXXV. "It hung before me as if probing my 'cone with its alien senses."

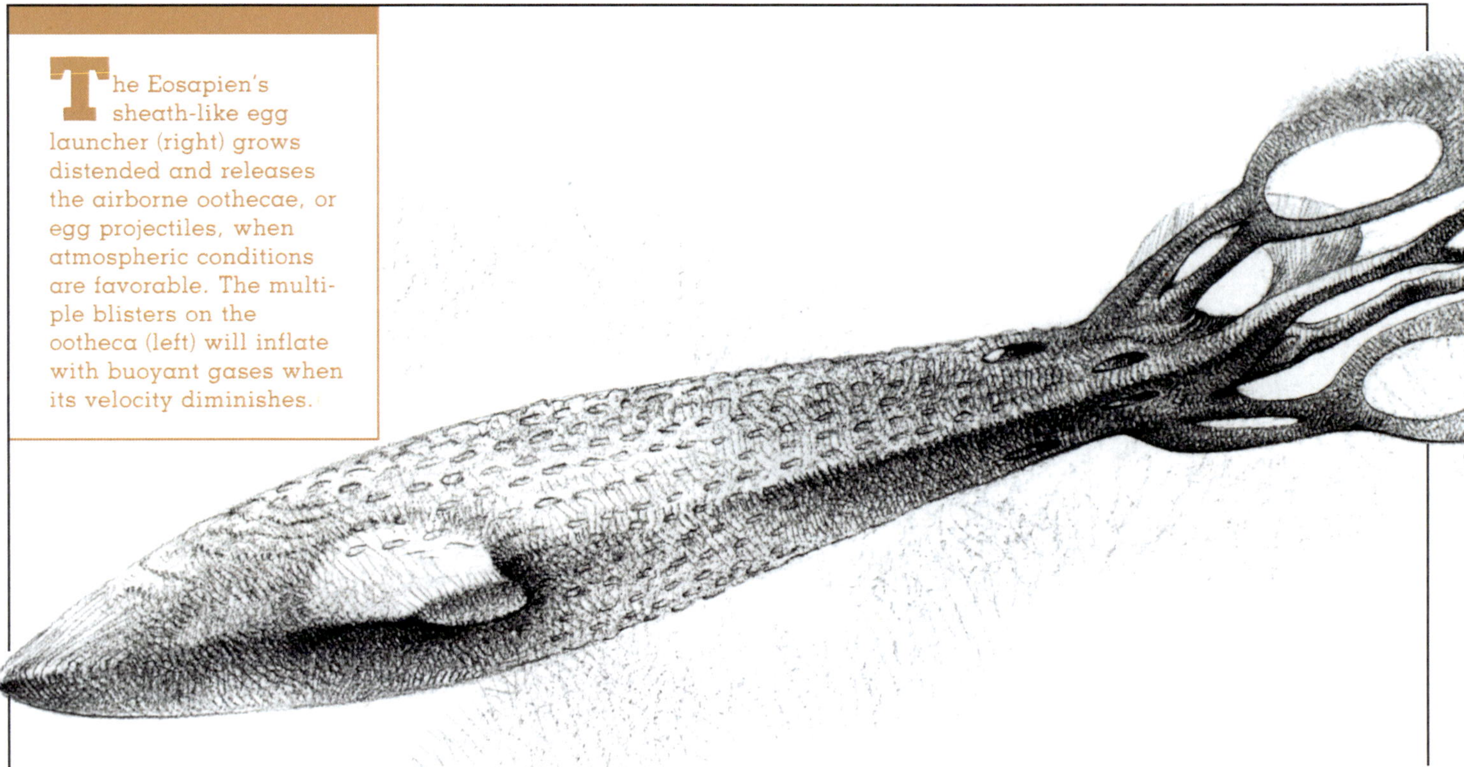

The Eosapien's sheath-like egg launcher (right) grows distended and releases the airborne oothecae, or egg projectiles, when atmospheric conditions are favorable. The multiple blisters on the ootheca (left) will inflate with buoyant gases when its velocity diminishes.

A brief analysis showed that an array of approximately fifteen two-meter-long flyers were vectoring directly toward me. My computer informed me that they had originated from one floating source roughly one hundred kilometers downrange. Even more enigmatically, this source seemed to be moving!

For an uneasy moment I wondered if I had been targeted by some unknown assailant's missiles. I flashed a querying sonar beacon in the direction of the mysterious floater, and was answered almost immediately with an identical beacon, hollow and echo-like. Shocked, I contacted the Orbitstar to determine the whereabouts of my nearest fellow explorers. Simultaneously I launched a VAP straight toward the flyers and received a partial explanation of the mystery. The probe acquired two of them sixteen kilometers downrange and flooded me with data on airspeed and direction. But the visuals were by far the most interesting data I received. The flyers were not incoming missiles, as I had irrationally feared, nor were they true flyers in the biological sense. They were, instead, some kind of organic projectiles, vaned and streamlined for subsonic flight. On their dark, chitinous surfaces I could see tiny teardrop-shaped blisters, the purpose of which I could hardly guess. Located toward the back of each projectile were four recessed holes, each complemented by an oval vane mounted on a thin stalk; these vanes would twitch fractionally to alter course.

My VAP trailed them closely. It scanned them as it flew, probing deeper with its IR sensor and sending back a thermal impression of its dart-like quarry. I discovered that though the projectile's exterior was cool, the interior indicated a single, small lifeform with a high metabolic level. The thermal image was vague, but I did get an impression of joined chitinous plates, arms and bladders, all beautifully fitted within the narrow confines of the projectile. I locked the VAP's tracker onto one of the pair and busied myself with setting my 'cone on course toward the unknown floater that had released them. Periodi-

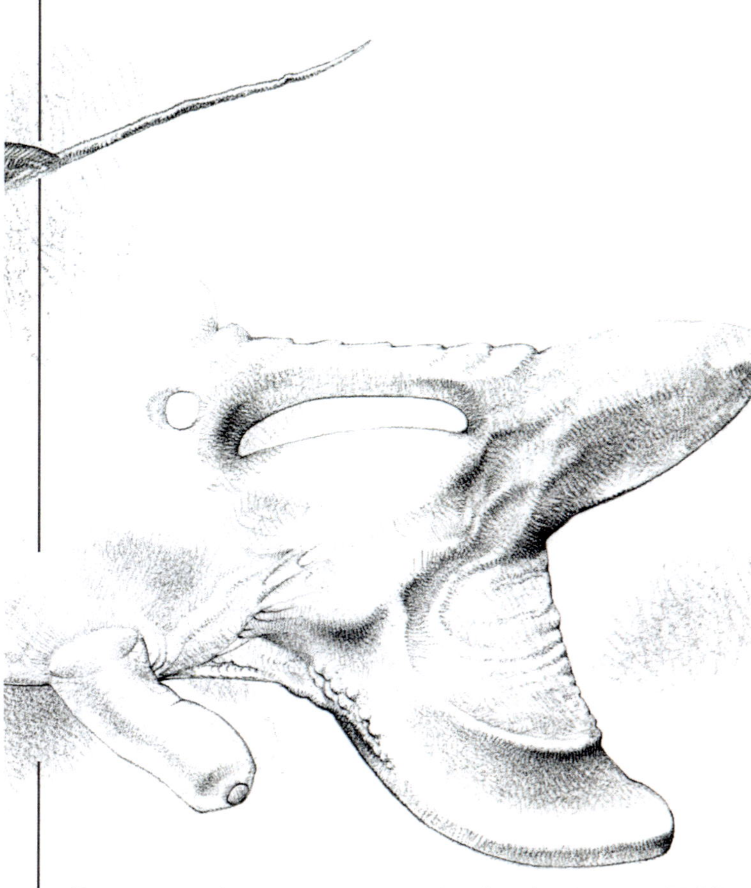

cally over the next hour I checked my VAP monitor and found that the projectile was slowing, and changing its outer conformation as it did. The tiny blisters were expanding and filling with what I presume was air. Eventually the formerly missile-shaped object was four times its original size and was drifting at the mercy of the winds.

Meanwhile, I was on a direct heading for the unidentified giant floater. It was moving at a leisurely rate through the clouds, *pinging* in a way oddly different from anything I had so far observed. There was a decided complexity to the sounds, and to the responses that were coming in. I felt as though I were overhearing a conversation.

As I approached contact, I grew more excited, eager to confront the source of both the ambiguous sounds and the strange projectiles.

I plunged into a golden, diaphanous cloud bank, pushing my 'cone as hard as I dared. The 'cone started to brake automatically as the acquisition bell began to chime. The clouds parted and my eyes widened with surprise as I stared at the huge *pinging* creature floating absolutely motionless less than a hundred meters before me. Looming a full twenty meters in height, it was a veritable study in alienness. Its cuticle-covered body was an intricate collection of ridges, folds and curves, flanged and wrinkled so as to almost defy description. Here a pair of moisture-dampened openings quivered and flared, while behind floatbladders pulsed and expanded with inrushing air. A web of glowing biolights surrounded a small pair of recessed infrared pits. Two swinging, orange sonarbooms stretched from beneath enormous, overhanging fins. Above them, a pair of gyrating balance organs oscillated in a blur of constant movement. Surmounting the forward, vertical portion of the organism's body was a great translucent bladder that seemed to be its principal organ of buoyancy. Running throughout this vast sagittal sac was a fine tracery of veins, delicately backlit by the glowing clouds behind. But most remarkable of all, two muscular arms, terminating in dextrous-looking hands,

hung from the creature's sides; in disbelief I stared at the giant club that the creature carried. It was botanic in origin, and gave the appearance of having been gnawed into shape.

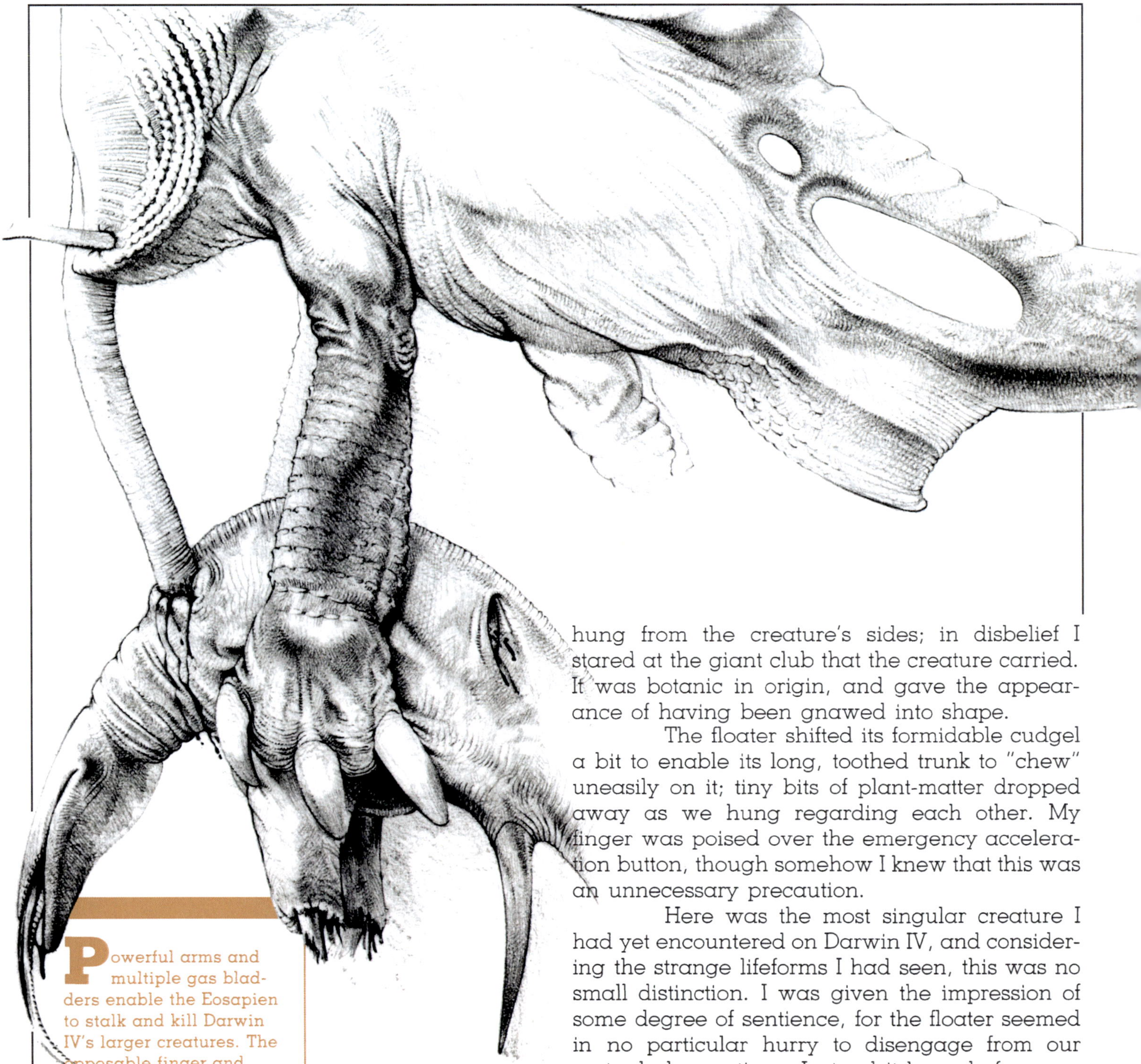

The floater shifted its formidable cudgel a bit to enable its long, toothed trunk to "chew" uneasily on it; tiny bits of plant-matter dropped away as we hung regarding each other. My finger was poised over the emergency acceleration button, though somehow I knew that this was an unnecessary precaution.

Here was the most singular creature I had yet encountered on Darwin IV, and considering the strange lifeforms I had seen, this was no small distinction. I was given the impression of some degree of sentience, for the floater seemed in no particular hurry to disengage from our mutual observations. Instead it hung before me, as if probing my 'cone with its alien senses. I named the floater an Eosapien, or Dawn Thinker, since it seemed wonderfully appropriate on that glorious morning to encounter a creature seem-

Powerful arms and multiple gas bladders enable the Eosapien to stalk and kill Darwin IV's larger creatures. The opposable finger and claw arrangement allows the limb to be used for killing, dismembering, and transporting prey.

ingly on the threshold of intelligence.

The Eosapien began to slowly circle the 'cone, its twin siphons puffing and pushing it smoothly through two revolutions. I can only guess what its conclusions might have been. My 'cone radiated a significant amount of heat, and the Eosapien may have believed it to be alive; or it may have detected my presence within the craft and come to the correct conclusion. In any event, it was clearly intrigued.

As the creature circled, I glimpsed a long tail, beneath which ran an elongated, sheathlike growth. It was from this orifice, I later learned, that the projectiles I had examined—in fact, airborne oothecae or eggs—had been launched. The suns' radiation in those rarefied levels of the atmosphere is in some way instrumental in their hatching.

Throughout the initial part of our meeting, the Eosapien had remained relatively quiet, only occasionally emitting short *pings*. With the completion of its second orbit around my capsule, however, this near-silence was broken by a loud series of pulsing signals directed out to the clouds.

Ten minutes later my sensors had picked up fifteen distant Eosapiens on a convergent course with us. They were moving quickly through the clouds, and soon I was witness to a thrilling and disturbing sight. Fifteen floating giants, all with great clubs, arrayed themselves in a tight semicircle behind my companion, which was directing a steady flow of signals into their midst. They squeaked and *pinged* attentively, shifting a club here or a sonarboom there, never drifting more than a meter out of formation. Each bore a unique pattern of biolights that seemed to distinguish one individual from another; and some wore what might have been Arrowtongue vertebrae strung on fibrous chords, hanging from their tails like trophies. They were solemn, dignified and, above all, aware.

After a few moments of silence my companion reached out a rubbery, nailed hand and stroked my 'cone's glass canopy. My heart raced in the uncertainty of the moment. Yet I stood fast, recording everything, more and more aware that I was the alien on their planet. The hand very delicately explored the surface of the 'cone and then withdrew. Its tactile inspection complete, the

PLATE XXXVI. "They ascended again, leaving the steaming carcass in the darkness."

creature slowly backed away into the floating throng. Each individual then came forward and performed the same examination, probing with the same mixture of delicacy and caution.

The air around me was filled with signals which started as irregular, staccato *pinging* and grew into a very pleasing, rich trilling. This trilling lasted a quarter of an hour as, one by one, the Eosapiens dispersed into the clouds.

I was alone again.

I had two more encounters with the Eosapiens before I left Darwin IV. The mood of these meetings was quite different from the first. That had been a large array of inquisitive individuals, and what I followed now was a low-altitude hunting party of eight. It was a day much like the one on which I had encountered the Emperor Sea Striders. Ragged, dirty-looking clouds scudded through the darkened sky as I tried my best to keep up with the adroit floaters. The Eosapiens

The primary food of the Eosapien is the Gill-head, one of Darwin IV's few ground-dwelling air-sifters.

were remarkably fast. They were in pursuit of some unseen victim on the ground far below, adjusting and readjusting their immensely powerful sonarbooms. Each floater carried the now familiar club-like implement, which I soon discovered was a huge flechette. Upon targeting their prey, the Eosapiens released their missiles with such a rapidity that I was sure a kill could only be attained by chance.

I was shocked when, following the party down to fifty meters, I saw the frightening precision of their aim. They had followed their victim, a large Symet, into a ravine where, with their missiles, they had penned it. The desperate Symet threw itself against the deeply-sunk missiles, but they did not move. Within moments the floaters were upon it, some holding the hapless beast down while others wrenched its two muscular legs from its pelvis with sickening pops. It was a terrible sight, redolent of primitiveness and savagery. The still-alive Symet was carried aloft, as were its detached legs, leaving long, calligraphic trails of black blood on the rough ground below.

That same night I followed a trio of Eosapiens on another hunt. The chase was far less frenetic, as the floaters were trailing a slow and aged Rayback. The pursuit came to its inevitable tragic conclusion as the Rayback faltered and fell. Without ceremony the floaters descended to either side of the terrified beast and, grasping its kicking legs, twisted them off. As quickly as they had dropped down, they ascended again, leaving the steaming carcass in the darkness.

These encounters left me with my last impressions of Darwin IV. They underscored the dramatic contrast between the strange beauty of the planet's life forms and their savage habits.

THE YMA STELE

DEPARTURE

It was time to leave orbit. An Yma medic was quietly running through the many preparations for hibersleep. My return trip to Earth would, he assured me, pass like the "briefest of silver dreams." A slight exaggeration, I knew.

As I hung weightless in the sleep-chamber, I peered through the clear sides of my plastic chrysalis. The dozens of pods under the glowing ceiling looked eerily like the interior of the Amoebic Sea. Within their suspended pods I could see the shapes of my fellow Expedition members, some of whom I suspected were already asleep.

My vision was becoming somewhat impaired and I remembered from my first experience with hibersleep that this was one of the early indications that I was succumbing to the alien drugs. I was naked, shaved and very cold and, to make matters worse, a roaming Yma technician came around every thirty minutes and blasted me with frozen vapor from a backpack that, to me, resembled a huge scorpion.

My sleep-pod was sealed and it slowly began to fill with a cold, gelatinous liquid. Gradually I began to notice that I could not feel the ends of my extremities. To take my mind off these unpleasant sensations, I tried to recall as much as I could about my home on Earth. The images that appeared in my mind were of a gray, tired planet filled to overflowing with gray, tired people. I thought of my wife and baby and our small home in the heart of New York's sprawl. They were waiting for me and I ached to be with them. They were my oasis of life on Earth.

My thoughts drifted back to my travels on Darwin IV. Suddenly my mind was swimming in a gentle stream of pleasant recollections. My mind began to jump from one amazing animal encounter to another. Again I followed that crazy band of Stripewings across the Amoebic Sea, and held my breath as the leviathans of Darwin IV, the Emperor Sea Striders and giant Grove-backs, plodded through my mind like creatures from some wild hallucination.

I realized that I was losing the battle against sleep. I suddenly recalled the titanium stele that the Yma had left on the plains of Darwin IV as the guardian and monitor of the planet. Its silver sides, etched with the names of the Expedition's personnel, hid a myriad of micro-systems linked to a planet-wide system of intruder alerts. The robot police-drones patrolling the Darwin system would regularly pick up and forward the accumulated data. I felt comforted knowing that Darwin would be so well protected.

As my eyelids grew heavy, many more images of Darwin IV and its fauna came to mind. What an incredible, wonderful world it was, brimming with life, unforgettable for its stark beauty. How could I exist again in my congested, chaotic world now that I had tasted the freedom of Darwin IV's rolling plains? How could I compare the strange and verdant beauty of Darwin's pocket-forests to the stripped wastelands that used to be Earth's great woodlands? What would I tell my daughter? How could I explain to her that we had squandered her world? As I drifted off into hibersleep, I realized that my tales of Darwin IV would seem as far away to her as the tales my great-grandfather had told me of Earth's extinct life. Well, I thought, at least there is a place for her to dream about . . .

Wayne Barlowe is a science fiction and fantasy author and artist who has created images for books, film, video games and galleries, and written and illustrated a number of art books, including **Expedition, Barlowe's Guide to Extraterrestrials, Barlowe's Guide to Fantasy, Barlowe's Inferno, Brushfire, The Alien Life of Wayne Barlowe,** and **An Alphabet of Dinosaurs. Expedition** aired as the Discovery Channel special, **Alien Planet.** His game concept work includes **Dante's Inferno** and **Shadow of Mordor.** His film designs can be seen in **Blade2, Galaxy Quest, Hellboy 1** and **2, Harry Potter 3** and **4, Avatar, Pacific Rim,** and **Aquaman,** and his TV work includes **Black Mirror: Bandersnatch** and Amazon Prime's **Lord of the Rings** show. He has written two novels, **God's Demon** and its sequel, **The Heart of Hell.**

www.ingramcontent.com/pod-product-compliance
Lightning Source LLC
Chambersburg PA
CBRC090957100726
47911CB00008B/175